"This way!" She hissed in the dark.

Niccolò followed without thinking. She handed him a cold black pistol. As the two German soldiers plunged through the door he pulled the trigger. There were shouts of anguish and the men fell. Lerma kept firing until the Germans were torn by bullets.

Niccolò kept clutching his pistol, saying nothing, thinking everything. He hated the loud stage guns and he hated this thing he held in his hand, this German device made to kill enemies of the Reich.

And yet . . . Just as a shot in the theater startled everyone's attention, so this Luger could be used to awaken the world. How simple it was to shoot; how simple it would be to pull the trigger again, in the theater of the world. If the target was big enough . . .

"A striking, powerful novel of suspense, mystery and courage."

—*South Bend Tribune*

FEAR ITSELF

STEFAN KANFER

BERKLEY BOOKS, NEW YORK

This Berkley book contains the complete
text of the original hardcover edition.
It has been completely reset in a typeface
designed for easy reading, and was printed
from new film.

FEAR ITSELF

A Berkley Book / published by arrangement with
G. P. Putnam's Sons

PRINTING HISTORY
G. P. Putnam's Sons edition / October 1981
Berkley edition / July 1983

ISBN: 0-425-06048-9

A BERKLEY BOOK ® TM 757,375
Berkley Books are published by The Berkley Publishing Group,
200 Madison Avenue, New York, New York 10016.
The name "BERKLEY" and the stylized "B" with design
are trademarks belonging to Berkley Publishing Corporation.
PRINTED IN THE UNITED STATES OF AMERICA

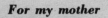

For my mother

Roosevelt was kept fully informed by, among others, long cables from A. Drexel Biddle, ambassador with the exiled governments in London and a personal friend. But given his belief that the only politically and strategically sound course was "the most effective prosecution of the war" he did not pay attention to the news about the "final solution" and he may have even considered it inopportune.

—Walter Laqueur
The Terrible Secret

FEAR ITSELF

1

Niccolò Levi: Italy, 1943

IT TOOK twenty-two minutes for Christ to become ashes. The note only threatened a fire at the theater; the Fascists did not foresee the sparks. Wind had taken them and the sacristy and church had ignited like pine cones. By the time the brigade of old men and boys filled their water buckets, the oak crucifix had fallen in red pieces and the air was torn with the laments of village women who thought that the devil had come to Larino.

Along with his fellow actors, Niccolò Levi watched from the town square, his black eyes shining with tears, the aquiline profile softened by guttering flames and tinted smoke. He was aware that the fire had been started because of him. The chiaroscuro evening was heavy with mist, but he could still make out writing freshly chalked on a stucco wall: 16/OCTOBER/43/JUDEA MORTA: Death to the Jews.

"Luck has run out," Borro said. He had the face of a grotesque: the great nose with flaring nostrils, a merry mouth and sad eyes that were always searching the crowd for widows with large breasts.

"It ran out three weeks ago." Niccolò examined the

small crowd and wondered which one of them had held the match. The troupe had been drinking at the cantina; they had heard shouts and come in time to watch the tinderbox of a stage go up with the scenery and the costumes.

"Bastards!" Lara Corella cursed between her teeth. Streaks of mascara ran down and divided her long vulpine face. "In every village is the grave of Christ."

"Pah." Borro sniffed the smoky air. It smelled of ashes, but it had smelled of ashes before the fire. Everything within miles of Naples smelled of ashes. Volcanoes. Fires. War. The Americans were down there somewhere, and the Germans were to the north. The troupe was in Larino, "between the upper and the lower jaw," as Borro had it. "Never mind," he told Niccolò. "There is always another town. Italy is made of hiding places."

"No," Niccolò protested. "I have been a burden long enough."

There was no reply from Borro or from Lara or from the others in the company who stood with him. Niccolò was not bitter; for almost two years they had kept him on, hiding him when necessary. Once, all of them had spent a week in the echoing spidery basement of a monastery, until the militia had gone. The soldiers were Italian; their hearts were not in their work. They had looked carelessly and asked stupid questions of the monks. Ten days later, the troupe was playing *Don Juan* in the sun. Still, it was not like the old days before Mussolini's war. Before the guns, the company had toured Europe. They had even played *Volpone* in London to kind reviews. When Il Duce came to Venice he refused to take any of the actors for the Army. "What they do is more important than carrying a rifle," he had told Isola, their old Swiss director. But Isola's temper had caught up with his weak heart and now he lay buried in the Protestant cemetery in Florence and the war had gone on to ruin everyone. The first thing to go was work, then bread, and then minds. As history got closer, superstition came out of the cracks of the mind like lizards into the sun. Dressed in yards of funereal black, old ladies with mustaches and warts cackled of statues that cried tears of blood, of stones that played music and cured cancer, of warplanes that fell to the ground and left no trace on earth because they had gone directly to entrances in the Inferno. "If God wills it, a broom can shoot," they said. Italians. They had no end of beliefs. The Jewish boy of Rome had grown in a forest of madonnas, crèches, saints, annunciations and crucifixes— objects of belief that moved him only the way Dante moved him, or broken statues of the Forum, as evidence of the past.

He was not much on the past. Today was what counted to radicals like the Levis. "Heaven and hell can be had in this world," his father used to boom. It was the way Socialists talked to their children, and if the words had given Niccolò no new faith, they served to erode his mother's old one. Awe for the Bible, the Torah, the rituals, vanished; he accepted the present as the only revelation. It was why Niccolò liked being an actor, with the instant gratification of performance and applause. It was why he was indifferent to political messiahs: with them everything was promises and threats; a perpetual rehearsal.

He had joined the underground because nobody promised anything except survival, which was what an Italian Jew did best. The actor used his prodigious memory: leaders trusted him with phone numbers, addresses of partisans as far away as Sicily and Lausanne; with the locations of munitions and caches of gold and jewelry. It had all seemed to work like a good play. Mussolini had toppled last month, and they had all celebrated in the streets: there would be food today instead of bread yesterday and wine tomorrow.

And then the Germans came. Niccolò was torn. As a Jew, he thought that he and Gina and their child should run north to Switzerland. There were awful rumors of what was being done to the Jews of Poland and Austria: starvation in barbed wire compounds, castor oil interrogations at midnight, torturings and beatings in cellars. Horrifying things. If true. Yet who knew what was true in these times?

In the end, with the route to Switzerland closing like the doors of the Vatican, they stayed. Gina's family could be traced back to Quattrocento Milan; they had outlasted senile

dukes and papal edicts, they had paid the tributes and
ransoms and overcome the ghetto restrictions; they would
endure these times as well. "I know my Italians," Gina
assured her husband. "We can live in the ocean; we will
drown in the lake." Meaning Switzerland. Gina, for all her
Roman fashions and her contessa friends, hated travel; she
grew homesick when they went south for a weekend. She
had run a fever in Paris and cried the whole week they were
in England. "So cold," she said. "So gray, like the skies.
The faces so pinched and melancholy." Back home she
bloomed again. In the evening, after wine, her face was
flushed and lovely and the sight of her thighs made Niccolò
look upon her as hungrily as he did in the days before they
were married. She could be like a garden in Rome, even in
winter, and they made love every night, despite the
squalling of the child or the sounds of jackboots in the
streets.

But last month, in September, when those boots sounded
through the dark, accompanied by shots and sirens, when
the bodies of partisans were taken away in bloodied fruit
carts, when the signs were put up: TEN ITALIANS WILL BE
SHOT FOR EVERY GERMAN SOLDIER, anyone connected with
the underground was told to leave Rome. Niccolò, who
knew the whereabouts of Ettore Basevi's printing press, of
four partisan leaders, of the family gold that was not
collected by the Germans, was ordered to leave.

"Go," Gina agreed. "Go on tour. We'll be all right, all of
us. In a few months you'll be playing here in Rome. Out in
the open. With all of us in the front row—bravo, Niccolò."

Bravo, Niccolò. He felt the last of the flames on his skin
and sensed that they were the flames of a conflagration
wider and more lethal than anything this little town could
provide.

"I want to go home," he told the others.

"After the tour," Borro insisted.

"No. Now."

They tried to dissuade him, to sit down for a while at the
trattoria, but he was not in a mood to listen. All he had with
him was a makeup bag, they objected. It was all he needed,

he said; there were clothes back in Rome. He had enough for the railroad ticket. Sooner or later, even on this crazy night, there would be a train.

They walked through the mist in small groups toward the railroad tracks at the far end of town. Lara Corella drew up to Niccolò and the others dropped back.

"Nicco." She took his arm and pushed her breast against him, "Nicco, don't go."

"I have to. My family—"

"Your family. Always your family."

"Yes. Always my family."

"The girls called you Fidelio, you know that?"

"No."

"They did. We all tried. You never responded. We thought maybe you were impotent."

Niccolò smiled. "If only," he said.

"Your wife gives you everything?"

"Everything."

Lara shrugged; Niccolò could feel it, even though he could scarcely see her face. "You're a good man, Nicco," she said. "Maybe too good for this world."

They were nearly at the station. A few passengers waited on the platform, looking down the tracks. Niccolò could see steam coming from their mouths. The air was growing colder. Two soldiers walked restlessly without talking.

"Stop," Borro said. The clown face without makeup was still a clown face, but the eyes were large and wet. He ran up to Niccolò. "They might be looking for you; they might just be going back to Rome to join their outfit."

"And if they're looking for me?"

"Then you stay with us. We'll get you back home some other way."

"No. I must take this train. They need me at home. I feel it."

Niccolò's eyes were too bright and he was unable to stand still. The others stayed with him while Borro went to the platform. They could see the fat man with the soldiers, making pleasantries, forcing his hard bass laugh. The soldiers laughed back and he offered them some wine from his little goatskin, but they said no, and he withdrew, still laughing.

"They're harmless," he assured Niccolò. "Just finishing up a leave. Still, it would be safer if you ride in a cart with farmers."

Niccolò tapped his makeup kit. "I have this," he said. "I can be an old man if I have to. Or a priest. Or a paisano with a mustache. Don't worry about me, Borro."

The train came groaning in. Some old women, a priest, then a soldier, obviously drunk, got off. Niccolò embraced his friends and got into a second-class compartment. He opened the window wide and forced a smile, looking down at the men and women with whom he had shared so much. They looked like a postcard: the comedian who got out of breath even from talking about women; the sisters, who were the women he talked about, good actresses both of them, but crazily jealous of each other; the cadaverous, perpetual villain; the juvenile lead, a homosexual who was probably older than Niccolò, maybe even thirty; the old man who was younger than he appeared. I will never see any of them again, he thought. Unless the war ends well. Then we could be together. In Rome, perhaps, or right here. Perhaps. Maybe. If.

The train gave a quick lurch and nearly knocked him down. He waved violently. The wet wind rose out of the north and brought the chill of death with it. The metal wheels rolled on in the dark and the faces of the actors became memory.

Sleep was impossible. Normally a trip like this would take only a few hours, but what was normal anymore? Rome itself had been bombed and the roadbeds of all the trains, the trains that Mussolini was so proud of, now seemed as worn and demoralized as Italy itself.

Great drops hit the windows and scattered the light from farmhouses and villages. The wind made the doors rattle, and the locomotive screeched on steep grades. The cars lurched at stops and whenever people got off they complained about the unseasonal chill and the broken seats.

There was talk of the Germans occupying Rome. Niccolò tried to pick up broken pieces of conversation in the corridors. The four old men who shared his compartment went on sleeping. One of them snored so loudly that he periodically woke himself up, glared angrily at Niccolò as if he were responsible, then went back to sleep. At Altura there was a harsh knock. The compartment door slid open and a small bald man got on, nodded vigorously to Niccolò and sat opposite him.

The new passenger was silent for a long while, but every time Niccolò stole a look, the man was examining him closely.

"I know you," he said at last. "You were in a movie I saw last year: *The Windmill*."

"Yes?" Niccolò replied cautiously.

"You were the wine seller."

"Yes."

"A fine picture. I cried."

"It was a comedy."

"Ah well, my fault. I have no sense of humor."

The train shrieked at something and picked up speed.

"Talking of humor," the man said, "I heard today a story. Mussolini goes to a gypsy fortune teller. 'Tell me, gypsy,' he says, 'I want to know on what day I will die.'

"The gypsy looks in her crystal ball. 'You will die on a Jewish holiday,' she says.

"'But what Jewish holiday?'

"'Duce,' she says, 'any day you die will be a Jewish holiday.'"

Niccolò could not even force a smile.

The man shrugged broadly. "I told you I had no sense of humor. Still, I suppose there is nothing funny about being a Jew, eh? Come, come, I know your name. Niccolò Levi. I saw you also in *Six Characters*. At the Alhambra."

"What do you want?" Niccolò looked at the other passengers. They were all asleep.

"Nothing, my friend. Nothing."

• • •

Niccolò felt abashed. The man seemed hurt. He had offered
a little conversation, that was all. Probably he was an
innocent theatergoer, perhaps a little stagestruck.

"Have you been in Rome recently?" Niccolò began
tentatively.

"Only two days ago."

"Is everything . . . quiet?"

"Yes. Nothing to fear. The gold was paid; you knew
about that?"

Yes, I knew about that, Niccolò thought. I was there
when it was extracted from the ghetto. Obersturmbann-
führer Herbert Keppler had given the order on September
27, a Monday: fifty kilograms of gold for the lives of 200
Jews. Otherwise the Jews would "be taken and deported to
Germany, where they will be sent to the Russian frontier or
otherwise rendered innocuous."

And the gold had been paid. Every gram. The Jews had
come to the synagogue with rings and coins and jewelry.
And thank God, not only the Jews. I remember Signora
Vivanti gave her ring, a chain, then another ring. A boy,
unfamiliar with Jewish customs, ignorant of whether to take
his hat off or to keep it on, opened his cigar box and shook
out coins. Romolo Balzani, the singer, removed his thick
gold ring and sang:

> *Credi che chi cia' l'oro*
> *sia un signore*
> *L'oro pe' me nun conta*
> *conta er core*

> For you, maybe it's gold
> in big amounts;
> For me, it's the heart
> that counts

But it was the gold that counted for the Germans. Keppler
had taken it away. Old lady De Porto warned everyone,
"The gold will not be enough. The Germans want blood."
But Gina had assured Niccolò, "Now it will be quiet. Go on

the tour." Obediently, he had gone south. He would be there still, if not for the fire. And the premonition. If it could be called a premonition. A better name would be fear, the same he had felt every night he had been away.

The talkative man consulted his watch by the lights of a factory. "We have only an hour. Then Rome. A strange hour to be traveling. Soldiers' hours. Old men's hours. You are neither an old man nor a soldier."

"Nor you."

"True. I have urgent family business in Rome."

"I, too. My wife is ill."

"I pray nothing serious."

"I won't know until I get there." Niccolò started to ask what the family business was, and stopped himself. The traveler might be just a businessman, the kind you met on trains before the war, lonely, willing to talk about anything, curious but harmless. Or he could be a Fascist, an informer, even a Nazi, a Jew-hater. These days you couldn't tell. Anything was possible in 1943.

Niccolò decided to shut out the man by taking a nap. By Fiesole, the nap took him. He dreamed briefly of fire and gold. Noise woke him; soldiers were going down the corridor, rapping on doors. The old men stirred and fumbled in their jackets. The bald man searched his billfold abstractedly. Niccolò breathed deeply, rising to full consciousness, preparing for a role. He found his wallet. The knock was peremptory; the lieutenant cleared his throat before demanding "Papers."

He examined the offerings, the far ones first, then those closest to the door. Niccolò peeked at the credentials of the bald man. Aldo Rovigo. Salesman.

The officer looked at Niccolò's papers, then at Niccolò, then at the name: Jan Isola, Director of Theater. The lights illuminated the carriage from outside: they had entered Rome station. The officer nodded and closed the door. Niccolò breathed easier.

"A near thing." Rovigo smiled. "Come, we'll get out early, before the others."

Niccolò followed him. They walked to the end of the car

and when the train pulled to a stop they were the first off.
The platform echoed with their footsteps; hardly anyone
was moving at this hour. At the end of the platform there
was a weary old ticket-taker, and beyond him three men in
dark raincoats, talking and smoking. A boy was opening a
stand to sell coffee and papers. The saturated air smelled of
rain and bituminous coal and the fatigue of a great
discouraged city. It was almost dawn, but through the glass
panels of the station roof the sky was black with rainclouds.
There were no colors in it and even a young soldier looked
as gray as his uniform. Middle-aged men seemed ancient,
and old men resembled corpses. Niccolò and his companion
handed in their tickets and began to walk toward the door.

"Wait," Rovigo said. They were only a few yards from
the trio in black. All three men looked alike; overweight,
but hard and featureless:

"Arrest him," Rovigo said. "He is using the papers of a
dead man. His name is Niccolò Levi. He is a Jew."

"Oh God, oh God," Niccolò said, or thought he said.
One of the men started for him and Niccolò swung the
wooden makeup kit hard at the wide flat face and split it
open. Blood spilled from the teeth and Niccolò seemed to
move faster than the noise. He ran out into the wet and
wind. Drops fell with such force it seemed to be raining
upward. Water coursed over the cobblestones and leaped
the curb; a primal storm, a Roman rain. The street was
eerie: a few trams and one bus. There were no cars. In
Niccolò's absence it had become a different Rome, sullen,
afflicted with the unnatural silence that attends funeral
parlors and hospital waiting rooms. It was the town of
Niccolò's birth and childhood and he knew how to hide in it.
He ran down the Via Caravaggio; footsteps sounded a long
way off, but they were swallowed by the rain. A church
stood at the base of the street, a little stone affair where he
had once watched a wedding so that he could duplicate the
priest's movements onstage. Everyone had been amused at
the time; the Padre—Menna, was that his name?—had
come backstage to tell him that he should have been a
Catholic. "We'll get you yet," he said, and smiled.

Well, now they had him. Niccolò wrenched the church door open and ran inside. It closed silently behind him. The place was empty. He looked at the stained glass windows depicting scenes of agony and turned away. There was a little closet in the back with two vestments in it. The steps outside grew fainter as he changed clothes. He opened the makeup kit and took out a white stick and went over his eyebrows and his hair. He put the collar on, and the black hat. There was an umbrella in the corner of the closet. He took that, too.

As Niccolò approached the door, he heard the voice of a beadle from the other end of the church. "Father," it said. The speaker was very bent and old. Niccolò hoped that he was also hard of hearing and half blind. "Is there to be a funeral today after all?"

"Yes, yes," Niccolò used a lot of hand gestures. "Prepare—everything."

"Yes, father."

Niccolò opened the umbrella and ventured outside. He did not dare take any public transportation; it would bring him too close to people and they would observe the makeup. He began to walk north. His legs felt strained; it had been a long day and a longer night. He was hungry; but he could not stop now. If they were so anxious to arrest a Jew on a train, what might they do to Jews in their homes, to a woman and child?

He pushed on. People began to appear; stores opened and there was the intoxicating aroma of coffee and rolls. German trucks were everywhere; German soldiers were in the cafés and on the squares. A priest came from the opposite direction; Niccolò pretended to be absorbed in thought and absently crossed the street. Noises started, but still Rome sounded abnormal. He heard a vegetable seller explain it to his customer: "I had to bring these in on my back; the Germans have forbidden private vehicles."

His frock felt confining; no wonder you never saw a priest run, Niccolò thought. If they find me now, all I can do is surrender. I should have taken a gun when the partisans offered me one that time in Lagorno and I thought, of what use would a pistol be except to kill? I was not a killer then. Only a target.

He tried to think of a prayer, but he knew so few. Nothing to cover this occasion. His family was truly irreligious, his father probably the only Jew in Rome who had ever drunk himself to death. A weaver, a radical, and a scandal. He had died when Niccolò was fourteen, a boy who was good as a mimic and nothing else. He had become the class comedian, then a student clown at the Commedia, then a part-time actor until Isola had discovered him, twelve years ago. Then had come the small parts and the featured roles—just in time for Il Duce's entrance with its sudden declaration: "The Jews do not belong to the Italian race . . ."

After that, even the air had tasted bitter. Formigini, the Jewish publisher, leaped to his death from the Ghirlandina tower in Modena. At Vercelli, Colonel Segre called his troops before him, and, astride his horse, shot himself to death. Enrico Fermi and his Jewish wife left for the United States. But Niccolò and Gina stayed; they had money, they could buy their way out of anything. Besides, they were assured, it was well known that actors are children, and the Nazis did not bother with children.

Niccolò saw the face of his own child on the infants that he passed. The mothers nodded to him or curtsied. He let a benign, uncommitted smile stay on his face; he reached in his bag and pulled out a pair of rimless glasses; they helped him look a little more confused and softened the lines of fear. He hurried his steps. When noises sounded in an alley he pretended not to hear as he made his way to the Via Piemonte off the Via Veneto.

Niccolò could make out his house now, through the spattered glasses. He wiped them and looked down the street. There were two brown trucks outside and German soldiers huddled under the awning across the street. Activity was visible inside the bakery; steam came from the roof of the trattoria. But the street was devoid of movement. He had the city child's instinct, an awareness of imminent malice. He felt it more acutely as he approached the house. The soldiers were talking in guttural syllables. Niccolò could hear little of it and understood nothing except the word *Judenaktion*. Jewish something, probably action, like the Italian *azione*. It was a harsh word, but everything in German had a metallic sound, like a rachet. The insignia on the soldiers' uniforms showed a double lightning bolt: SS.

The men looked at him. He could see the frightened face of someone, probably Falcone, the owner, in the steamy window of the trattoria. It pulled back. Niccolò had no idea whether Falcone had identified him in the priest's uniform or not. The soldiers seemed satisfied that the black cassock was legitimate. Niccolò walked to the door and knocked. It would not do to open it with a key; the whole show would be given away. The rain let up. He knew these sudden ferocious shifts of weather. Many was the night he and Gina had been awakened by the sound of rain stopping. The black door opened. Margherita, the servant, was in a white uniform. Her eyes were red and swollen and she crossed herself when she saw Niccolò.

"Good morning, my child, good morning. God bless you." He grabbed the doorknob behind him and shut himself in with her, away from the eyes of the soldiers.

Margherita screamed, "Mother of God, it's the Monsignor and the Signor, my God, two men in one cloak, the work of the devil!" He put his hand over her mouth and she bit down and he withdrew it. "The work of the devil!" she screamed again. He put his hand against her neck. She began choking.

"It's me! For God's sake, it's me! Only me!" He had not meant to shout; the men were just outside. He thought he heard them at the door.

The girl was racked with sobs. She pointed upstairs wordlessly. Niccolò bolted up the steps two at a time; she was behind him, tripping loudly and whimpering. There was no one in the parlor or the bedrooms. Chairs were knocked over and drawers were pulled open. Pools of water stained the carpet: people had come in violently out of the violent rain.

Niccolò turned to the servant. "They cut the telephone," she babbled hysterically. "They spilled the flowers." He saw that the cord had been severed; he had not noticed the daisies on the floor. He was too busy looking for the child.

"They took them. The signora, the baby." Margherita began to cry again. Niccolò grabbed her by her scarecrow shoulders. Boots made a flat, hollow sound at the door and reverberated up the stairs.

"Who took them? Where did they take them?"

"The Germans, signore. They have occupied Rome. They have taken away the Jews."

"But we gave them gold!"

As his last words tumbled out, the door cried in its hinges and banged open. Niccolò looked down the staircase. A young blond soldier stood with a rifle held in both hands. He held it more as a shield than a weapon. At his side an officer stood, shouting: "Come down!"

He shouted something else in German. Niccolò acted on pure instinct. With a sound that was not quite a cry and not yet a word, he ran down the stairs, directly at the Germans. He could see the astonishment in their faces. They were used to fear or resentment. They did not expect a priest to run at them like a madman, making the halls shake with his voice. The soldier could not bring himself to use the rifle for a moment, and the officer, instead of concentrating on the target, turned his fury on the boy, yelling at him to fire. Niccolò ran past them, a mass of rain-soaked cloth, and hurtled outside.

He looked neither left nor right; he ran with only one purpose: escape. The partisans were at the apartment near the Osteria dell'Orso or perhaps in the restaurant downstairs. He could not run there and betray them. The Chief Rabbi, Israel Zolli, was in hiding at the home of Amadeo Pierantoni; it was too far away; and besides, Niccolò felt uneasy about him; the old man was a bad mixture of the pious and the confused; the stuff of saints, maybe, not of resistance fighters. Niccolò ran north, toward the profusion of alleys and past more soldiers across the street. They gave him perfunctory, curious looks until the officer followed, shouting. Niccolò moved toward the Piazza Navona. He knew every twisted alley; somewhere in that stone maze he might lose himself. The steps grew louder and there were more of them. He heard a shot and a ricochet. God almighty, he thought, my family, my family. From some deep region of memory he dug out pictures of Gina walking near the Tiber with the sun in her eyes, squinting and laughing. A bullet scattered some stone near him. They were close now, he knew. If he could just have ten minutes, he might find another disguise, a mustache, a pillow for a fat waist, hair dye, a fake scar; there were so many ways to change. Suppose they were to capture him? Could he stand up under torture? He wondered about pain again, and then he no longer had to imagine it. A bullet cracked through his back, somewhere near the heart. It was as if some of last night's fire had extended itself to Rome, through the streets and into his flesh. He heard sounds issuing from his throat and wondered how long he could keep silent about the names and places of hidden Jews and partisans.

If the Germans found out who he was, what would they do to Gina and the baby? Feverishly he prayed for them; for the Jews; for Italy. The fire burned in his skin. His mouth fell open and his legs gave way. The stones were wet and cool on his burning face. As the steps clattered nearer he felt blood spreading like a sound, outward from the mouth of the wound. He prayed that it was fatal.

2

Carl Berlin: New York, 1943

"YOU AND ME, buddy, you and me," Carl Berlin said to the hornet. It kept banging its head on the glass until a window was opened. The insect took its angry buzz out over Central Park. The air of New York and the air of the room were the same temperature. Ellen squinted in the morning sun.

"You want someone to let you out?" she asked Carl.

"Sometimes."

"Wish you were in the war?"

"Sometimes."

"Very loquacious this morning."

"I have a lot on my mind."

"Really? There was only one thing on it last night."

Carl ceded her the last word. He was through with argument. If they parted, they parted. If not Ellen Howard, then someone else. When he was recruited, the Old Man had inquired about women. "You were divorced four years ago. We understand you have no serious romantic liaison."

Carl had been amused at the Romantic Liaison: the Office of Strategic Services had to have their euphemisms, even when it came to fucking.

"I have no steady girl," Carl had told him.

"Just as well. A marriage provides the best cover: job, regular hours, a home life. But if problems arise, a single man . . ."

"Is more expendable."

"Well, this *is* war, Berlin."

Carl had accepted a drink after all. He listened at first with civility and then with intensity. He was astonished at how much the Old Man knew, sitting there in the Harvard Club like any gray, overfed bank manager with a lined face made of old memos, class of '09. The Old Man knew that Carl's name was really Baline, changed at Ellis Island; that his limp came from a case of polio contracted in Germany before the war; that the Balines had once been bootleggers; that they had strong ties to the Jewish councils in Europe. That after the murder of the father and the uncle, the family liquor-importing business was used to send money and sometimes weapons overseas.

"We could have stopped it at any time," the Old Man informed him.

"Then why didn't you?"

"We thought you might be useful. And we still have a few humanitarian goals. But only one of them is important. Winning the war. If we thought you were hindering us, we would eat you for breakfast, I assure you."

For the first time, Carl sensed the armature of this phlegmatic executive, a man so confident of power that he needed none of the trappings: the executive manner, the big office, the title.

"We know," he had persisted, "that you have a certain amount of sangfroid, operating under the noses of foreign governments. A requisite. There is a splinter of ice in the heart of every agent I have. If it melts, he's useless to me and to himself. Often he dies."

Often. Say 80 percent? Interesting odds, Carl thought at the time. Yet he was glad to take them. A chance for vengeance for his father, an opportunity to go overseas. He had not been there since 1936. Much was promised: even with his bad leg he had endured an abbreviated ranger training course, and once he and five others had gone on a parachute drop over some remote dunes in Georgia. His leg, heavily protected by cotton batting, had held up. And for what? To hobble around in New York, monitoring the activities of a few clanking Nazi agents in Yorkville. He felt as embittered and useless as an admiral stationed in the Painted Desert.

The Butcher was the last good case, and that was finished. The young were getting the action now, as they always did in wartime. It was awful to be overage and lame in this war; Jews were dying in Europe, and Carl knew where they were dying, and so did Washington, and nothing was being done.

A few humanitarian goals. But only one of them is important. Winning the war. Only that. It was enough to make you crazy; no wonder the rabbis were talking to themselves on the street, no wonder there were hysterical meetings at Madison Square Garden and confusion in the synagogues. Rabbi Wise apologizing for Roosevelt; Ben Hecht hating him. Where does a Jew stand today, especially a Jew too old to fight in uniform? Whoever thought thirty-nine would be too old for anything except center field for the Yankees? He turned to look at Ellen again and the phone rang. She answered it and then handed the receiver to Carl. The message was terse. Come down to the morgue immediately. There were no details.

Carl started putting on his clothes hurriedly. Ellen looked at him. "Something's wrong, isn't it?"

"Yes."

"Something between us?"

"No."

"Carl, Carl, stop with the monosyllables. Talk to me. Don't just stare at me with those cold gray eyes. I can't stand it when you do that. It's not sexy at all."

"It wasn't supposed to be sexy."

"The man on the phone said he was from your office. Is it something about business?"

"Yes."

"Yes. No. Yes. No. Why can't you talk to me?"

He came over and sat on the edge of the bed. Now that he was clothed she seemed even more naked.

"Somebody died, that's all," he said. "Nobody I know. Just someone connected with the business."

Ellen nodded. "Is there anything I can do?"

"Nothing."

"When will you be back? Or should I put it, *will* you be back?"

"Not for a while."

"William comes home tomorrow."

Carl shrugged. Those were the breaks, his shoulders said; you carry on with married women, you had to expect roadblocks.

"Don't you ever get jealous?" Ellen lay back and let her long auburn hair flow over the pillow and the sheet.

"I can't afford to."

"I can. I'm rich."

"You have nothing to be jealous of," he said, because she wanted to hear it. He started to get up. She pulled him back by the arm.

"Yes, I do. I'm jealous of your job, whatever it is. I'm jealous of your life, whatever it is. I'm jealous of your privacy."

"I have to go."

"Not yet," she said. She reached inside his trousers. Her hand felt cool and very certain of itself. She moved closer to him and her hair brushed his hand as she moved her head closer to his lap. "This morning," she told him, "if you meet any interesting women you won't have much to contribute."

Carl looked down at the pool of hair. "I find it very difficult to argue with you when you take that position," he said.

The policemen turned away and filed quickly out of the morgue room.

They knew what they were doing when they recruited me, Carl thought. If I can look at that and keep my breakfast below my throat I am the right man in the right job.

"Cover it up," he told the attendant.

"I never seen anything like that," the black man said. "Never."

"Yes, you have. The Butcher's been at it all winter."

"I wasn't here all winter. I just got discharged." He tapped his leg. "I got lucky in Midway."

The attendant also walked with a limp. Wounded in action. Maybe what he tapped was wood. A lucky man, even so. At least he got to see what an enemy soldier looked like. Here in New York it was all bloodless chess; I spot your intelligence agent, you spot mine. I break your code, you break mine. Sabotage, occasionally, but no real battles.

Except for the Butcher. Go explain that. Captain Rosen was waiting for him in the corridor.

Carl said, "Jesus. They ought to have a bar in every morgue."

The captain only asked, "You sure it's the Butcher?"

"You saw the report. Nobody else kills like that. He had her hanging up by her ankles. Cigar burns all along the calves and thighs, applied over a few hours. Mouth gagged so the neighbors didn't hear anything. Acid burns on the vaginal canal. Breasts swollen and covered with animal stings. Bees, probably. Skin lacerated with marks from a looped cord. Death was by strangulation, just like the others. She had probably been raped while she was still living, but who can tell?"

The captain looked away. He put his head in his hands and said, "So it isn't Werner."

"No."

"We have the wrong man in jail."

"Correct."

"What do you want from me?"

"To keep him there."

"Berlin, you going to tell me what this is about?"

"I can't, Captain."

"You want me to sit on this but you can't help me."

"I can tell you this much: we think the Butcher is working for the Germans. The other three women he killed were people we employed. One of them was a German who went over to us. But this one, Anna Caras, was a nobody."

"A waitress in Schrafft's is all." The captain consulted his papers. "Relatives in Kansas. Lord, wait till they see the body."

"They don't have to see the body."

"I don't care who you are." The captain colored deep red. "We don't do things like that in New York. I don't lose bodies and I don't do cremations—I don't give a shit where your orders come from."

Berlin betrayed no hint of emotion. "You don't have to do anything at all, Captain. Just get the best embalmer in town and dress the body and get the bones in the face straightened out and the flesh colored right. We'll pay for it. The relatives won't want to see the Butcher's work, and we don't want it talked about. That's all."

Captain Rosen said nothing.

"We want the Butcher, Captain."

"You're one cold bastard, you know that?" The heavy policeman shook his head and walked out. At the door, he said over his shoulder, "What gets me is you're a Jew."

Carl paused for a minute, thinking, and then took another exit. He walked for a while in the spring air and tried to rid himself of the morgue stench. He lit a cigarette but it tasted of formaldehyde and he threw it down and stepped on it. He breathed deeply; the air was oppressive and made him cough. All in the head, he thought, it's all in the head. What I smell is dread.

He hailed a cab and went to his office in the Chrysler Building. The gold lettering on the door said ALSACE IMPORTING. There was nothing in the place but an old rolltop desk and a teletype machine, a typewriter, two telephones and a few chairs, and a metal cot. The ashtrays were stolen from the Latin Quarter. Every now and then someone came in and typed and made the place look busy. Once he had even found part of a ham and rye sandwich in the bottom of the wastebasket. Carl was sure that no one had eaten the other half. Very likely it was left in some other false office to give the impression of life. The Old Man thought of everything.

He sent the message in code: *The Butcher is still at large. We screwed up. What we need is ten men on this job, not one, especially not this one.*

He went to the cot and lay down and smoked again. He napped briefly and dreamed of a red room with no doors and a noise that kept striking him and knocking him down. He awoke to the noise: it was the rattling and banging of the teletype.

Let us push on, it read. The standard reply, Carl noted. *We expect the Butcher to be apprehended and that you will apprehend him. Watch maintained on Gower. Need confirmation from you soonest. Uncoded report on Mark 5 follows.*

He rose and went through the mail, pushed through the slot while he had slept.

It was all junk, sent there to keep the place looking official: cards for discount subscriptions to *Collier's* and *Look*, a plea from the March of Dimes, an offer for sensational new recipes for meatless Tuesdays, a chance to learn how to rhumba the Arthur Murray way, complete with a foot chart you could put on the floor and follow. Stuffing for tomorrow's *Times* was delivered; the magazine section had a picture of Field Marshal Montgomery and General Mark Clark; "On the Road to Rome," it said. That served to increase Carl's depression. The Allies were at the Volturno River, only ninety miles from the Eternal City. About the closest he would get to Italy was Mulberry Street.

There was a knock; Carl looked out the peephole and saw the little bent figure of Sussman. He opened the door.

"I'm beck from Chicago," the old man said.

"You know better than to come here," Carl told him.

"I telephoned but no answer." Sussman pronounced the *w* in answer.

"I'll meet you in the cafeteria in twenty minutes," Carl closed the door.

He got out the little file of names and pictures of known or suspected collaborators: old Nazis from Yorkville Bund meetings, a couple of Mussolini Mafiosi, the freelance goons who occasionally did jobs with ice picks. None of them seemed likely candidates for the role of the Butcher. Carl was looking for a psychopath, somebody who probably hated women in general and his mother in particular, perhaps worked for the Germans and might have no criminal record.

He kept examining the files until the names blurred. Then he put everything away and went downstairs. Carl walked to a cafeteria on Forty-fifth Street. The Automat was a province of the old; white-haired men and women sat at scattered tables haranguing each other or enveloped in their own hard silence. A few old ladies gave each other porcelain smiles. The only young people were a group of deaf mutes arguing furiously with their fingers and their noiseless lips. Carl found Sussman on line in front of the sandwich windows.

"Did you know a *schwartze* discovered peanut butter?" Sussman asked.

"*Invented* peanut butter."

"Not only colored but a slave. If I was a slave I wouldn't invent anything. Except a way to escape."

"Maybe that was his way to escape."

They paused before a zinc counter. Sussman put a nickel in a slot. Milk poured from a silver metal dolphin into a tumbler. "Watch," said the old man. "It knows exactly how much." The milk came within a micrometer of the rim, paused and stopped. "America," Sussman declared proudly. They worked their way to a table.

"There's a lot to what you say," Sussman conceded.

"About what?"

"George Washington."

"Carver."

"That's the guy. On the one hand he resents his master. On the other hand he has to do *some*thing with his mind. On the other hand—"

On the one hand, on the other hand. Carl turned away. It was the trouble with these old emigrés. Every one of them had the mind of a Talmudic scholar and the hands of an octopus. They weighed every decision: in the meantime their brothers were being marched to gas chambers.

When they were seated, Sussman said, "I'm sorry I called on you like that. I know it's not allowed. On the other hand—"

"Just tell me what you want."

"What do I want? What does everybody want? The truth. In Chicago I heard terrible things. There is a place . . ." Sussman rummaged in his pockets and found a wrinkled piece of lined paper. "Himmel."

"Himmeldorf."

"They kill us there, right in the camp. Also at other places. We hear they use chemicals."

"Who is we?"

"You know, Marks, Lassman, the usual." Sussman sipped his milk noisily. "Well . . . it's true?"

"We have no eyewitnesses. From the intelligence reports, yes, it's true."

"My God!" Sussman held his cheeks with his hands. "You and I, we got to do something."

"Sussman." Carl grabbed the old man's narrow wrist. "We're trying."

"Not enough. How can I go back and tell them we're sitting on our hands, that the President don't care, the Congress."

"They care, Sussman. It just takes time."

"Meantime, we're dying over there. Some help you are."

"Goddamn it!" Carl began. Diners at other tables looked at him. He lowered his voice. "Listen, you wizened old *momzer,* can't you understand? I couldn't keep giving your organization money unless I joined the OSS. They could cut us off whenever they feel like it. I give you what information I know, I give you cash as soon as it comes in from my company. Sussman, all I really want is to go to Europe and rescue Jews myself. But they won't let me go."

"Yes," the old man commiserated. "I onderstend. I'm sorry. I'm upset is all. You're our greatest friend, since Isaac died. I miss Isaac."

"I miss him too."

"He was a very sentimental man, your father."

Yeah, well that's why he's dead, Carl wanted to say. Walking into a trap, trying to help the Jews of Warsaw escape. Shot on the street by a Polish cop, before the war began. A mistake, the government report said. Regrets. The old bootlegger hadn't carried a gun since Prohibition or he would have taken some of the Fascists with him. He was tough, Old Isaac Baline. But grown soft inside from too much time in America.

Carl took out his checkbook. "Here," he said. He wrote a check for $25,000. "Give it to Lassman. He'll know what to do with the money. And say that I'll do whatever is humanly possible. Only it takes time."

"On the one hand, everything takes time. On the other hand, Jews are perishing . . ."

"I know," said Carl. The roll he held in his hand was squeezed down to a cigar-shaped mass. Crumbs fell between his fingers. "I have to go."

"You'll call?"

"Sooner or later."

"With God's help, sooner. *Kinnehorah.*"

Kinnehorah. The Evil Eye. This is the way they shield themselves, Carl knew. Probably in Poland they were mumbling "Kinnehorah" as they marched with their hands high into the barbed wire compounds. The evil was too big for Polish hicks to recognize. They were looking for Satan dressed as a dybbuk or an imp, something they could put in a box and bury.

When Carl got back to his office the machine was chattering about Mark 5, the German code, broken two months ago. The Germans were still broadcasting in it, and every now and then there was a message Stateside, undoubtedly broadcast from a submarine. From 1942 on they were sent to a Mr. Glenn Case of Tudor City, arrested in June. A big mistake, Washington came to realize. The Germans stopped broadcasting, the agents became frightened and the whole network was quiet for three months. Then a new code

began. It had taken two weeks to crack, and two more
weeks to locate Martin Gower, a Yorkville merchant, a
vestryman of St. Luke's Lutheran Church of Forest Hills,
and the new head of German Intelligence in New York. Carl
had seen Gower's cables. Plans to take over a radio station
should there be an invasion. An idiot scheme, Carl thought,
and typical of krauts to believe that yelling lies into a
microphone would alter anybody's mind. Except in Germany, of course. There it had worked fine. Then Gower
mentioned explosions in the Brooklyn navy yards and that
was not so absurd. And then there was something a little
closer to home, a late and unsettling bulletin: the Germans
were searching for someone they referred to as *Vier*: four in
English.

Number One was the President; and the head of OSS, Bill
Donovan, was Two. Three was the Old Man, and Vier was
Carl himself, the man who had shot a Nazi named Werner.
Carl had been examining a cargo of boxes in a Canal Street
warehouse when Werner surprised him; there had been no
time to aim low. Certain that Werner was the Butcher, Carl
had immediately dialed the police and sent in an anonymous
tip. The man had lived. A pity, Carl concluded later; I
should have let him bleed to death. For Werner had
somehow sent a description to the German underground and
they had fingered the American agent they now called
Number Four. *Vier.* Pronounced "fear."

Carl thought about the Germans and their possible plans
to rid themselves of Number Four. The picture of himself as
target was not altogether depressing. On the one hand,
Sussman would say, Carl would have to watch himself. On
the other hand, there was a warm feeling engendered by the
notion of Nazis afraid of a Jew.

But not warm enough to melt the splinter of ice.

3

FDR: Washington, 1943

"I SUPPOSE there's no way to put them off," he said. His secretary shook her head. Roosevelt adjusted the heavy braces around his legs, combed his hair and arranged his smile. At his signal, Anita Kelly admitted the five visitors.

The first was Rabbi Stephen Wise, the long, humane face carefully hiding its sorrows.

He was a different kind of Jew. FDR liked to see him around the White House, a white Jew, like Governor Herbert Lehman; a man you could not only appear with in public, but in private. Someone who could share a drink and a laugh. A good man, but under the influence of men not so good.

Powerful men, rich men, Jews with money. Men who controlled blocs. The President resented them, and resented even more the smile that he had to assume for them: the large head thrown back, the hand extended. Rabbi Wise introduced Roosevelt to his colleagues. Three of them were well-barbered men in their sixties with noses that filled the expected measurements. Their intelligent, uncultured visages might have been associated with pushcarts on the

Lower East Side or with overfurnished corner offices in some Hollywood studio. Avid faces, hungry faces, ghetto faces. The men's silent respect, their little bows were, Roosevelt felt, merely charades. The fourth man was another matter. He was small and the bones and muscles of his face were apparent under the pale stretched skin. He might have been forty or sixty: it was impossible to tell. He was introduced as Jakov Wolf, and his soft, almost inaudible voice made every pronouncement, even those on the weather, seem like cabala.

Rabbi Wise spoke first; he made references to the war and asked, as he always did, about the President's health. Roosevelt tried not to drum his fingers on the desk; there was a ritual to these meetings and he had to let it play itself out.

"I'm well, Steve," he said. "Well as the war permits."

"The headlines are not all bad." The rabbi had the *Times* in his hand.

Roosevelt tried to listen quickly: he knew what the headlines said. He bent forward with an attitude of close attention and extreme courtesy; after all, he was listening to the Jewish vote. Even so, after Wise had rambled on for a few minutes, Roosevelt looked at his watch and the rabbi quickly came to the point.

"I know what your hours are like. We are grateful even for these few minutes."

One of Wise's colleagues leaned forward in his chair. His hands were manicured, Roosevelt noticed, probably for this occasion. "Permit me," he said with a trace of a Russian intonation. "We have no right. Yet, if we cannot come to you, whom can we come to?"

"Rabbi Wise," said another, "says that you and you alone understand our—what shall I call it? Problem is too weak a word."

"Catastrophe," said the third.

"Even this is too weak. Nothing anyone says can convey properly what is happening. No one except someone who has been there can report. And this is why, this is why—"

Rabbi Wise took over. "We have invited Mr. Jakov Wolf

to come here to speak—as we can never speak—about what he has seen and heard, and which, I pray, we will never see and hear."

Roosevelt looked at the little man. Wolf had obviously rehearsed his speech. He spoke in chopped, fragmented sentences, as if he had memorized the words phonetically.

"Mr. President it is an honor I am grateful for this opportunity. Right now men and women are being taken away and killed just because of their religious beliefs.

"Uncountable people have been packed into cattle cars—children, old persons. They are taken to camps in Poland, the Germans have ways of killing, we think gas is being used, we don't know, someone must speak out."

There was silence. Roosevelt made sure Wolf had stopped before he began. "Surely Rabbi Wise has told you—"

"This must stop, this is crime against humanity not just Jews but also others. Catholics gypsies partisans."

Silence followed. Now Wolf was truly finished. He sighed loudly.

"Gentlemen," said the President. He paused: the statement would be quoted, he knew that. It would be off the record, but repeated in thousands of synagogues and clubhouses and boardrooms. Why couldn't these Jews be like Steve Wise here? Left to himself, Rabbi Wise would be an understanding colleague, a friend of the administration, a man you could take to any home, any country. Roosevelt inserted a new cigarette in the long holder, lit it, took two puffs and watched the blue smoke. "Mr. Wolf, Rabbi Wise." He lowered his glasses and tilted his head downward. He had all of their attention now.

"Do you know what they called me during the last campaign? Rabbi Wise will bear me out: they called me Franklin Rosenfeld. My enemies gave me a Jewish name. Because they thought I was too sympathetic to the Jewish cause. Well, gentlemen, I own up to it. I am sympathetic, and I regard their label as a compliment."

Smiles of relief showed on the listeners' faces.

"What you tell me is all too tragically so. The Jews need relief from their torment, and they need a place to go to."

"I knew you would understand. I told them." Rabbi Wise shut his eyes in a thankful attitude. The others exchanged warm glances. Roosevelt continued.

"This administration works night and day to that end."

The rabbi rose, and the others immediately got to their feet. There was an awkward pause. Do they shake hands with the President? Have they been dismissed? Will someone come to the door? But Roosevelt went on speaking.

"Be assured that your co-religionists are to be rescued. We believe that the way to achieve their liberation is, in our words, Rescue Through Victory. Only by vanquishing the Axis can we assure true freedom."

"But in the meantime—" Wolf protested.

"We will save those who might be saved and end these crimes. The mills of the gods grind slowly. But they grind exceedingly small."

"Yes," Wolf agreed. "But if the mills grind too slowly there will be no Jews left."

The President's face darkened. Clearly, Wolf had stepped over the line of deference. But the man went on: "Permit me, Mr. President." His voice cracked. "Every insect is fond of life."

It was the opening the President needed. He lowered his voice. "By conquering Germany we will liberate your people."

"And when they're liberated," Wolf persisted, "where will they go? In Palestine, we—"

"The stability of the Middle East," Roosevelt told him, "is part of our policy. You must think of Zion as the United States."

A marine officer with a great many ribbons on his chest suddenly stood at the door.

"Mr. President," Wise began hurriedly. The others filed out, exchanging confused whispers. Roosevelt could see a group of men in dark suits in the corridor. Their faces were furrowed with worry, and one of them asked Wolf, "So how did it go?"

He could barely hear Wolf's reply. "How *should* it go?"

The Jews, Roosevelt thought, always answering a question with a question.

"Boss"—Rabbi Wise used the name the President liked to hear in private—"thank you, and heaven help you."

"Heaven help us all, Steve," said the President and shook his hand.

When the rabbi left, Roosevelt unlocked his braces and sat down. His head ached a little and he washed down two aspirins with some cold water. He rang for Anita. She entered carrying her steno pad.

"You look tired," she said. "How did the meeting proceed?"

The President looked at her and shook his head. "How *should* it proceed?" he answered.

4

Niccolò Levi: Rome, 1943

*Corsi al palude, e le cannucce e il brago
m'implar si ch'io caddi, a li vid' io
delle me vane farse in terra lago*

I ran to the marshes, and the reeds and the mire
entangled me so, that I fell; and there I saw
a pool growing on the ground from my veins

Dante. He recognized it. It was coming from his own
mind, mingled with sounds from outside his skull.

The measured clamor of jackboots echoed below. German soldiers were moving in the streets.

"A bunch of geese." A woman was watching the soldiers
through a blue muslin curtain.

"He's awake," someone else said.

Niccolò opened his eyes. There were three people in the
room. The woman at the window had a heavy, worried face
and an old body. Her bosom seemed to have fallen of its
own weight. But her eyes were peculiarly youthful and
shone with fierce intelligence. Niccolò did not recognize

her, or the man he assumed was her husband, a gnarled little figure who held her large waist with one hand and gripped a rifle with the other. The third person was familiar: Borro. But that was impossible! How did he get here? I left the troupe in Larino. Then the long train ride, the run through a soaking Rome. The pursuit by the soldiers, the bullet in the back. . . . Niccolò tried to gesture, but bolts of pain made him lie back on the pillows.

The man with the rifle came to the pallet where Niccolò writhed. "My name is Leo. This is my wife, Anna. Borro you know."

The clown laughed his stagey cackle. "You were a long time in the dark, Niccolò," he said. "Three days?"

"Four." Anna pushed something around on the stove.

Borro came to the edge of the bed and sat in a hard wooden chair. It creaked with his weight. "Naples has been evacuated. The Americans are occupying it. Little food, hardly any water, no salt, no soap. No money. Nothing. Our company has disbanded. I came back. I heard about your family. A terrible thing, a tragedy within a tragedy. Other families also were taken. The partisans contacted me. I came here as quickly as I could. For twenty-four hours the doctor and I have been watching."

"You are the doctor?" Niccolò looked at the gnarled man.

Laughter greeted the question.

"I take lives, I don't save them." The gnarled man shifted his rifle. "The doctor is away. He has more important patients than you."

"Gina, little Nardo . . ." Niccolò cried. He sat up and pain radiated from his shoulder.

"The Germans have them. Them and a thousand other Roman Jews. They took them north somewhere. Southwest Poland."

"We have to get there. The baby—"

"The Americans will get there soon enough, Niccolò." Leo had a small, tight voice. "Our job is to get rid of the Germans."

Niccolò sank back on the pillows. He had no idea where

he was; someplace close to the shooting, he guessed. His rescuers would not have been able to move a body around the street. Maybe they were right above the restaurant. He had a memory of the La Scala sign just before he fell. It was not where the partisans usually met. Still, things had changed so rapidly that fall. The Germans would uncover one place and everyone would move overnight. The partisans had saved him, Niccolò realized. They were his only hope. Yet they moved so slowly. He would have to rescue his family by himself. He knew of the existence of some family gold, still secreted in the house. He would purchase his way north.

Niccolò had visions of himself with a machine gun, like—who was it in the movies?—the American actor Edward G. Robinson. He too was a Jew. Also Paul Muni, Scarface. In his mental film Niccolò had a rifle in his hand, and the Germans were against a wall, fifty of them, with their arms raised, and Gina and the child were behind him, protected by his body. He heard music, opera, *La Bohème*, cascades of melody. He was in the scene and yet watching it and he knew he was hallucinating with fever, and dreamed on. It was not until the next morning that he was fully awake and able to rise.

He was ashamed of himself. Others were on their feet, moving in and out. There was a sense of movement, of partisans coming and going. Slowly he washed at the sink and dried himself with a piece of old red flannel. He could not raise his left arm, partly because of the pain but also because of the bandages. He managed to put on his shorts and trousers but the shirt was impossible. He was still struggling with it when Leo came in. With him was a serious, lean shadow of a man whose cheekbones protruded. He needed a shave.

"This is Professor Caro," Leo said. "He will examine you. You have questions, ask him." Leo exited with an air of annoyance. He had better things to do than change the dressing of fallen actors, he implied; outside, Rome was fighting for her life.

The Professor told Niccolò to sit while he unwrapped the

dressing. There was more pain from the adhesive ripping out the hairs on his shoulder and chest than from the wound. All through the examination the Professor said nothing. He puffed on a dead cigarette and hummed something under his breath. When he was finished he sat down.

Niccolò could no longer keep still. He had a rush of demands: "When will I be well? How can I get new papers? What is going on outside? Exactly where did they take the Roman Jews?"

The Professor held up his hand for silence. "Too many questions, actor."

"But my wife, my baby—"

"You are not the only one whose family was taken." The Professor's eyes shone and he turned away and, at last, lit the cigarette.

"Let me tell you." He lowered his voice. "Everything that can be done will be done. You will be expected to help."

"Of course. Anything." But Niccolò did not speak to him about the gold.

The Professor fingered the blanket absently. "The partisans have changed locations. Two of the leaders, Maricelli and Giordano, were killed two days ago. Things are not good. The Germans are capable of murdering many before the end. Already they have announced that ten civilians will be shot for every German soldier we kill. So we have to be careful. As for when you can get up, who knows?"

Niccolò knew. After the Professor left he tried to walk around the room and move normally. At first he felt sharp reminders of the wound when he reached out with his left hand. But his legs were strong and his head was clearing. He had no temperature that afternoon or that night. The next day he got dressed and did some stretching exercises. The third day he ventured outside with Borro. They had worked for an hour on Niccolò's hair and his face, using the makeup brush lightly to whiten the hair and create artificial wrinkles. Niccolò had played old men before, but the injury added new conviction to his role. Neither the German soldiers nor the Roman civilians gave him more than a perfunctory look as he walked slowly toward the Tiber.

"I must find out," he said to Borro when they were alone. The day was warm and sunlight bounced on the pines and geraniums. The red blossoms hurt Niccolò's eyes when he looked at them through the flat lenses of his glasses.

"We have a network," Borro assured him. "Angels can do no more."

"We *must* do more." Niccolò gestured with his hands and aggravated his wound.

"You hurt yourself. We'll go back."

"No. I'm all right. The real pain comes from doing nothing." Niccolò fought back tears and the two men walked on in silence until they came to a little bakery with German and Italian signs. An SS trooper was leaving as they entered. The proprietor was little and bent with arthritis. He had gray fringes of unbarbered hair and a dingy, corrupt air, a man whose hopes had died young. He regarded Borro warily.

"Yes?"

"We want two loaves of black bread like the Venetians bake it."

"We can give no more than one."

"We will take no less than two."

The old man put out his hand; the code had been accepted. Borro introduced Niccolò and they talked briefly about the roundup. The baker knew all about Niccolò. He, too, counseled patience. But he gave the actor a folded paper with a name on it.

"Open it later," he said. "See him and ask for the same thing: bread like the Venetians bake it."

Borro had something more to say to the baker. Niccolò went outside and unfolded the message. It read: Contessa Stella DaPonte, 11 Via Re. It was near Trajan's Forum, a place of polished stone and history. A rich locale; it would be surrounded by Germans.

He watched Borro through the glass door, gesturing broadly, always the clown. He would be a big target, Niccolò thought. He wadded the address into a little paper ball and swallowed it. When Borro came out, Niccolò started talking about audiences and how much harder they laughed in times of war.

"Gallows humor," Borro theorized. "Better peace and empty seats."

"Tell me that next spring when the war is over."

"You think next spring? I think two springs, or three, Niccolò. These are stubborn troops, the Germans. What did the baker give you?"

Niccolò did not say. "Borro"—he took hold of the fat man's arm—"I have to believe that the war cannot last in Italy."

"I know." Borro's eyes were like marbles. "I'm sorry. I exaggerate always. Soon the Germans will go. Before we know it Americans will be in Rome." He paused. "You mind if I criticize?"

"No."

"You walk too fast. You move with too much life for an old man. Bend over more and don't move your hands with quick thrusts. Also, balance is difficult for old people."

They worked their way home slowly. Occasionally Borro stopped to correct a movement or to adjust Niccolò's makeup. It used up time and conversation; there were no more questions about the Contessa's address. A blessing, Niccolò felt. If the Germans chased me again, possibly I could escape. The fat man, never.

Getting away from Borro presented a difficulty. Niccolò solved it by complaining about fatigue when they got back.

"My legs hurt even more than my shoulder," he complained. "Let me lie down. Afterwards we'll talk." Borro helped him up the stairs in back, so that they did not have to go through La Scala in case any German soldiers were at the bar. Niccolò lay down and closed his eyes. He did not have to feign sleep. He awoke alone, to conversation and clattering of plates in the restaurant below.

Niccolò came down the stairs cautiously and peered through a crack in the back door of La Scala. The place was filled with soldiers. At a table in the front a group of Nazi officers were laughing.

Leo obsequiously fussed over them and opened a bottle of wine with great ceremony. Borro was at a back table, alone. From time to time he looked up, as if he expected some sound from upstairs. Niccolò pulled away and started off.

He worked hard on his bent stature and old man's shuffle as he made his way to the DaPonte address. Once there, he paused and considered. There were no names on any of the bells, and no concierge in sight. He was about to call out when he heard a voice behind him.

"Can I help you, signor?" A narrow, nervous woman looked at him with a hostile expression. She was dressed in gray muslin and she held a broom as if she could turn it, at any moment, into a rifle.

"I'm looking for the Contessa DaPonte."

"I am Stella DaPonte."

"I was sent by the baker."

The information did not seem to impress her.

Niccolò tried again: "I want two loaves of Venetian bread."

"I can give no more than one."

"I will take no less than two."

"Follow me." She opened the copper door and led him down a cool marble corridor to a room with rugs on the wall and oil paintings of martyrs.

"Your name?" The Contessa sat down. Niccolò remained standing until she indicated a vast upholstered seat for him. He sank in it; such chairs were usually the property of museums or rented for certain dramas from an antique store on the Via Veneto.

"I am Niccolò Levi," he said.

"The actor."

"Yes."

"Do you know me?"

"By reputation only, Contessa."

She reached under the cushion of her chair and drew out an artist's sketchbook. From across the room Niccolò could see that it was covered with entries, names of some sort and information following the names. He imagined that he was one of them.

"I not only know who you are." She kept her eyes on the page. "I know what happened to your family." Before Niccolò could reply she went on: "They and about a thousand other Jews were rounded up and taken—"

"To Poland."

"Yes. To a concentration camp."

"Contessa, I must go to them."

"Impossible."

"Then they must get out."

"With God's help. And ours." She looked hard at him. "With the partisans there is some hope. Without us, you have none."

He agreed, but he did not tell her about the gold either. Instead, he listened to instructions. The Germans were everywhere, she said, and nowhere. You could never tell about the night raids, or whether they intended to preserve Rome or to destroy it, whether they were truly losing in the south or merely falling back for a counteroffensive. The partisans could no longer wait for the Germans to make their move. The Fascist militia were seizing people and torturing them. Every week bodies of patriots were found in the Ardreatine Caves with their brains shot away. The only thing to do was to aid the American troops with intelligence and weapons and to confound the Germans. To this end they would blow up railroad tracks, find German arsenals and explode them. The Contessa added, without changing her matter-of-fact tone, "We must, of course, kill them. Together where possible, singly if necessary."

"But the reprisals—"

"We will worry about reprisals when the time comes. There are instances when one German is worth any number of Italians. How many would have been willing to die if only Hitler could have been assassinated in 1939?"

Pain suddenly made Niccolò's eyelids heavy. He shuddered feverishly. This skinny aristocrat with the veiny arms wanted to use him? Very well. And he would use her.

"What is it that you want me to do?" he asked.

"What you do best. Stage work."

"I can no longer appear in public, Contessa. Even in makeup I might be identified."

"In the theater, yes. That's where they look for you. In the streets is another matter."

"You want me to appear as old men, priests, that sort of thing?" She wanted him to be a courier, he guessed. He welcomed the choice. With luck he could get through the lines, go north. Maybe even as far as Poland. . . .

"I need you here," the Contessa said. "In this room. You have clothing?"

"Only what they gave me."

"And devices for makeup, disguises, mustaches, facial paint, the sort of things you are using now?"

"I have a kit in a place over La Scala. After that runs out—" He showed her his palms.

"Don't give me empty gestures. What you need we will get." She pressed a buzzer on the floor. A weary old servant came and the Contessa got up and whispered some directions.

"Pietro will get your things. You will move in upstairs with the Professor and Lerma. Does anyone know you came here?"

"Only the man at the bakery," he said.

She nodded, satisfied. "Come, I'll show you where you will live."

Niccolò followed her, past carpeted stairs and places where for centuries candles had lighted the way for cardinals.

There were several rooms on the top floor, formerly servants' quarters, outfitted with minimal plumbing and naked light bulbs. The doors had been removed and the rooms were joined. The window of the farthest room gave out onto the roof of another house, and Niccolò could see that it was used as an entrance and perhaps as an escape route. The Contessa assigned him a bed and showed him where the Professor slept, and Lerma, whoever he was. When she finished, she said, "You must still be tired. Lie down. If you have any questions, the Professor will answer.

Under no circumstances are you to come downstairs. Police and German officers come here frequently. I give parties. If you need anything, pull a bell. Pietro will come."

With that she was gone. Niccolò sat on the edge of the bed and tried to force the tears back in their ducts. He remembered that Giacometti, the sculptor, said that one year he had reduced all of his work to a few essential objects, and these were concentrated even further so that at the end of twelve months the artist could have put his entire output into a matchbox. But the matchbox would have been so heavy that no one could lift it. It was the way Niccolò's brain felt now: uncrowded, holding only a few major concerns, but those concerns so powerful that they pulled like the earth itself.

He lay down and closed his eyes and slept fitfully and then could sleep no more. He looked on the little shelf of books for something to occupy the time while he waited. He fingered an Almanach de Gotha and two books on Marxism; there was your Italian aristocrat, he thought, hedging bets at all times. Next to the New Testament was a book called *Diseases of the Soul*. Niccolò recognized the author: J. L. Caro: the Professor. It was published in 1929 on cheap paper. The dedication read: "To Rachel, Michael, and Jacob. Next year in Jerusalem." So, what can you tell from such an inscription? Niccolò pondered. First, that the Professor is a Jew. His affiliation on the title page was the University of Padua, although he spoke with a Neapolitan intonation. A wife, two children in 1929. So the children must be twelve, thirteen by now. Michael probably already bar-mitzvahed. A rose was pressed in the book, and there were spidery notations in the margins. A feeling like prudery overcame him when he tried to make out the words; Niccolò felt like a spy. Well, but that is what I am, he argued. Or will be.

He was holding the book in his hand when the Professor came to the doorway and said, "A souvenir from the days when I used to think."

Niccolò put it down.

The Professor regarded him carefully. "Lie down. You

look pale. You should not have been up so much today. You are still recovering from a very serious injury."

Niccolò obeyed. A great fatigue newly overcame him.

"I, too, am tired." The Professor kicked off his shoes and stretched out on his own cot. His long feet stuck out over the edge. He took a book from his pocket and read. After a while he asked Niccolò softly, "You are asleep?"

"No."

"The Contessa told you what you will be doing?"

"About the makeup? A little, yes."

"You want to do more."

Niccolò hesitated. He felt the way he did when his father asked him why he had not gone to school on a certain day. Invariably he lied; it was the love of deception that first made him an actor.

"I will do what they ask me as long as my family has a chance to be saved."

"Mmmm." The Professor looked at him, considering. "Rest," he said. "Tomorrow if Lerma gets back we will put you to work."

"Lerma," Niccolò repeated.

"Our roommate. You don't know Lerma?"

"No."

"Family destroyed by the Germans. Wants only vengeance. Marvelously inventive with explosives, invaluable to the underground, but driven half mad, I believe."

"Why is it I never heard of him?" Niccolò wondered.

"Perhaps," the Professor said, "because Lerma is only a pseudonym. Her real name is Linda Ermanelli."

DOCUMENT TOP SECRET CLASSIFIED

THE JEWS FROM THE GERMAN ZONE OF OCCUPATION WERE
DEPORTED TO THE EASTERN TERRITORIES AND "SONO
STATI ELIMINATI MEDIANTE L'IMPIEGO DI GAS TOSSICO NEL
TRENO IN CUI ERANO RINCHIUSI." (ARE ELIMINATED BY
THE USE OF TOXIC GAS IN THE TRAIN IN WHICH THEY ARE
LOCKED.)

(SIGNED) "VISTO DAL DUCE"—SEEN BY MUSSOLINI: 4
JUNE 1942.

5

Carl Berlin: New York, 1944

HE TURNED the volume down and stuck some more pins into the Mercator projection of Europe. Last week's information had confirmed the worst. The State Department knew it; the cables mentioned the Morgenthau File of atrocities, originally titled "Report to the Secretary on the Acquiescencc of this Government in the Murder of the Jews," and then watered down to "Personal Report to the President." So. Roosevelt knew about the death camps. As did Secretary of War Henry L. Stimson, and Secretary of State Edward Stettinius, and God knows who else. Germany: Dachau, outside of Munich; Buchenwald, near Weimar; Ravensbrück, in Mecklenburg. Torture, imprisonment, death. Poland: Auschwitz, Treblinka, Maidenek, Himmeldorf, Birkenau, Chelmno. Yugoslavia: Benjicea and Tilpovske Supo. Czechoslovakia: Theresïenstadt.

How many victims per pin? No one knew. The coded bulletins could only guess. Besides, that was the business of the State Department. They thought about such things in Washington. Maybe the Old Man gave it some of his time. Maybe. But on this level, in the sub-basement of the war, there were other things to worry about. Like chasing a maniac called "the Butcher." I feel like Dick Tracy pursuing Flat Top, Carl thought. Except that even Tracy has a commission in the Navy. Sabu is a tail gunner, for Chrissake. There it is in the *Daily News* in black and white. Color on Sundays.

In the middle of a newscast Ellen phoned. "All clear," she announced. Lovers have adopted the language of the air raids, Carl noted. Next they would be barking orders like a master sergeant: "Clothes off; in the sack; shlong at attention; doubletime screwing, hup, two, three, four; parade rest; at ease, privates; company dismissed."

Still, he wanted to see her and he was glad the major was out of town in Washington, getting briefed or debriefed or whatever people in the Quartermaster Corps did. Probably order K-ra . . . Let me have nine million cans of processed hog jowls to go, dried eggs on the side.

On the way to Ellen's, Carl stopped at his office. He had meant to stay only a few minutes, open the nonmail, go through the files that had chattered in overnight. But at the bottom of a long sheet of drab entries were two arresting items. One asked for a "list of any potential assassins/ anarchists/known saboteurs with records, who should be held in preventive detention on upcoming week." Apparently to dispel rumors of his ill health, President Roosevelt had decided to ride through New York in an open car.

Carl went over his files again. He teletyped the listings on his cards, all of them surnames of his little Yorkville group. Grantz, Hassen, Murer, Rathenau, Gower. It would have been pleasant to list the Butcher, but the fact was that the Butcher, whoever he was, was not a marksman and, so far as Carl knew, had nothing against presidents. Women were his meat. Carl looked at the list and wondered whether the police would actually take any of them in, and whether anyone would indeed try to gun down the President. Impossible, it was once thought. Then, eleven years ago in Miami, a bricklayer named Joe Zangara had aimed a pistol at FDR and missed him and shot a bystander named Anton Cernak, who happened to be the mayor of Chicago. Carl remembered the story well; he remembered his father at the dinner table:

"I heard Zangara. An Italian name! I started to breathe for the first time since the flash on the radio. Thank God it wasn't a Jew." A classic reaction of these immigrants, and, secretly, all Jews. There were still times when Carl felt it: he knew that certain incidents of arson were referred to by the police as "Jewish fires." Like his father, whenever he heard a story of gangsters, of someone cheating big on his income tax, of war profiteers, of child molesters, he always looked at the name to see if it was Jewish, and he too breathed easier when it was not. Well, he mused, the one thing he needn't worry about was a Jewish assassin. Roosevelt was still a god to the Jews.

The second item rankled. Ruth Silver was now in Italy, working her way from Naples up the boot, translating, coordinating intelligence and sending it back.

Again he would be getting messages from her, the combatant, the adventurer, the soldier. While he, the clerk, would sit out the war. He slammed his fist into the side of the cabinet, loudly denting the metal. Abruptly, he was drained of any desire to see Ellen. He walked aimlessly at first, then deliberately uptown to Yorkville. Calling on Martin Gower would accomplish nothing, he knew. It might even cause some short circuits. It was indiscreet. Carl was aware that the Old Man would disapprove mightily. You never walked in on the enemy unexpectedly unless you wanted to jar him into an error. It was in Clausewitz, it was in the OSS Manual, it was probably in McGuffey's Reader. Carl knew that he was only going into the shop to keep himself from going stir crazy. And, perhaps, to be self-destructive; war could do that to noncombatants as well as to infantrymen.

The door banged against a little bell as Carl entered. Gower appeared to be alone.

"Something?" he began. He had a generous professional smile.

"I'd like to look at toys."

"Toys. Mr. Berlin, shall we stop this childishness?" He went around to the door and turned the lock. He reversed the cardboard sign to read CLOSED from the outside, then pulled down the shades across the dusty windows.

"Please." He pulled up a metal bridge chair for Carl. "We should talk, you and I."

Carl wondered whether he could rush and hold him if someone broke out from the back with a gun. Gower read Carl's face. "I am a harmless old citizen, unarmed." He seated himself. "Please. We will talk, yes?"

Carl sat down.

"You like a shnapps?"

"Too early."

"Yes. Good. The first discipline is self-discipline."

"Spoken like a true German."

"Come now, Mr. Berlin. You are German yourself."

"No longer. You saw to that."

There was a line of distaste around the old man's mouth. "That was not my doing. I hate the style of National Socialism. Dreadful stuff."

"But it's the only wheel in town?"

"It's the only Germany there is. You want to destroy it. I want to preserve it. Not for Hitler. I don't care about him and his gang. They can drown in the Rhine for all I care. Perhaps they will. But if Germany loses, if it agrees to the unconditional surrender your President wants, the country I loved—and that *you* loved once—the country of Beethoven and Goethe and Kant and Schubert is finished. You know that."

"I know it," said Carl. "I look forward to it."

A chorus of cuckoo clocks sounded stupidly in the background. "I don't believe you," Gower said. "Surely the high Germany is worth saving?"

"The high Germany, the old Germany, isn't worth the price of a new one." Carl knew none of this was getting through; he talked on only as an escape valve for the months of silence and frustration. "A handful of artists for millions of innocents killed and tortured. Maybe millions more to go before we all stop. It's not worth it. The world would be better if Germany had never been born."

"Ah, but it *was* born. And then another Germany was born. So, in fact you have two countries: the elevated one of Schubert and the low one of the Third Reich. Schizophrenia." He did something with his mouth to indicate distaste, but a trivial kind, the sort one might feel after biting into a bad pear.

The old man shifted in his chair. "Well, Mr. Berlin. You didn't come here to discuss national character. Tell me what you want."

Carl thought he might take Gower by surprise, but there was no change of expression when he answered abruptly: "I want the Butcher."

The old man said, "Ah. Who does not? We all want him."

The Butcher . . . Far from here there were men with death's-heads on their caps, and long black boots, shouting words to living corpses, ordering children into flames. True Butchers, in a real abattoir of Europe. While the civilized men palavered about some psychopath.

"A footnote in a book."

"I beg your pardon, Mr. Berlin?"

"You and I are the fine print at the bottom of the page. Tell me who the Butcher is or I'll kill you."

Carl rose. Gower cautiously got to his feet. This was all very risky, Carl knew; a long shot. He could not kill Gower, and the man did not look as if he would frighten easily. The Germans would pick someone unshakable for the job. Still, an effort had to be made. They were afraid of Vier. He reached out.

"Take your hands from my neck," Gower protested. "This accomplishes nothing."

Carl unsheathed a four-inch knife from his coat and held it at Gower's throat. The legend SOLINGEN STEEL, MADE IN GERMANY caught the light. "Tell me," he demanded. Gower said nothing, but he was very pale and his mouth trembled. Carl drew the knife across the skin swiftly and drew blood. "Speak," he said.

Gower closed his eyes. "He has only worked for us a few times. No one has seen him kill."

Carl widened the cut a little.

"No! Stop! Stop!" Gower whimpered. "Conrad Berger," he said. His eyes rolled. "110 Flatbush Avenue Extension, near Hoyt Street. In Brooklyn." He grew pale and slumped against his attacker. Carl could feel the mass of unprotesting weight. He let go and Gower collapsed at his feet.

Carl was to recall the look on his victim's face, the fear of a Nazi for a Jew, and the complete control that he had felt of the man and the moment. He abandoned the German, unconscious and sprawled on the gleaming floor, unlocked the door and walked away without a backward glance. The bell chirped behind him.

He called Ellen from the corner candy store. He would be late, he told her. Business. Her reply was not indulgent. He telephoned the precinct. When Captain Rosen picked up the phone, Carl said, simply, "I've got him."

"Got who?"

"The Butcher is who."

"With you?"

"No, not tied up in a bundle." Carl started to give him the address, then interrupted himself: "Pick me up and I'll tell you." He gave his location.

"That's me in the squad car in three minutes."

It was six minutes, but the noisy arrival made the wait worthwhile. The green and white Ford screamed down Third Avenue dramatically. It screeched to a stop, even though the driver had spotted Carl a block away.

The car went through lights all the way to the Brooklyn Bridge. The wind across the water was high and it blew the car across a lane; there was some trouble with traffic on the other side. When the trucks made way for the patrol car the driver found Flatbush Avenue on his map and proceeded past rows of private homes and two-family houses until he came to 110: a lot with a fence around it. The car halted and Carl and Rosen emerged and looked around.

"Wrong number?" Rosen asked, and as his mouth formed the question Carl knew that it was no mistake. He looked past the fence at the graves in the Sephardic cemetery where Jews had been buried for over a hundred years, and he saw the shadow of the synagogue falling over the crowd of stones with their eroded Hebrew testimonies. One commemorated the life of Conrad Berger, 1851–1919.

The captain stared at Carl, bewildered. But Carl knew what had happened. He had been the butt of a little prank, the sort Herr Hitler might have enjoyed. Gower had been well chosen for his job. Even under the threat of death, with a knife on the skin of his throat, he had furnished a false address. No, worse than that—a false *Jewish* address. Carl knew that when they returned to Yorkville the shopkeeper would be long gone, his house abandoned, his shop shut "For the Duration," and that now the Butcher and all the others would be at large. It was a sly performance, done in the spirit of the Nazis who liked to stage their biggest roundups of Jews on Rosh Hashanah or Yom Kippur, another in an unending series of German jokes.

6

Niccolò Levi: Rome, 1943

MOST OF THE mornings were spent deciding who should be disguised as what. Partisans entered and Niccolò gave them lessons in how to walk, told them what kind of intonation or vocal characteristics to use, and helped them with their makeup. The partisans varied as much as any amateur performers. A few were truly gifted at mimicry and alteration; they came out as new men and women. The rest were a collection of jittery no-talents who always managed to bungle their instructions. Whether they completed their assignments, Niccolò never knew. Few of them returned for another disguise, and none of them gossiped.

Twice he had asked for an assistant, although what he really wanted was company, someone to stay with him to keep his repetitive nightmares at bay. Borro was his first choice.

"Unreliable," the Professor said.

"But for months he was with me, hiding me, carrying messages."

"Conditions were different."

"How different? At any time he could have been killed."

"It was before Italy surrendered. Before we were occupied by the Nazis."

"But Borro is an actor. He can look more innocent than the Pope."

"A bad example. The Pope has blood on his hands. Besides, Borro is fat."

"You can't hold a man's weight against him."

"Look around you. Everyone is losing weight. There is little food. Yet he finds more than enough. From where?"

"You don't know Borro. I can vouch—"

"The answer is no. We'll hear no more about it."

Something in the Professor's voice did not brook contradiction. Niccolò forgot about Borro. His mind kept circling like a dog over the same incidents: why couldn't he have returned a day earlier and saved his family? Why hadn't they fled to Switzerland? Why were his wife and child singled out for capture when so many had escaped, hidden, it was said, by monks and priests and private families? And why were those churchmen so indulgent when the Pope himself refused to speak out? His roommates were of no help. The Professor was too remote, and Lerma—

She came in when he was thinking about her, a nervous, staring woman. Thirty-five perhaps. Her hand shook all the time; she could scarcely light a cigarette for the tremors. Lerma always seemed driven to prove herself to herself. Twice she had taken children to Switzerland. She had returned through Nazi lines dressed as a nun, a farmer, and, once, as a German soldier. Even here, in the room, she was never the same woman two days running. If she was euphoric on Monday, she was inconsolable on Tuesday, with crying jags and long periods of silence. Then on Wednesday she would offer long diatribes, exhortations to anyone who would listen, about the necessity of running salt into the soil of Germany when it was defeated, as inevitably it must be, by the Americans.

"Where's the Professor?" she demanded. She sat down, out of breath. "I ran all the way to find him."

"He left an hour ago." Niccolò regarded her warily,

trying to guess which woman she would be today. "Out for the afternoon, I think. Something about going for clocks."

"Ah. Timing devices. For the bombs. So. You and me alone." She smiled at him. "The first time."

The Professor said Lerma was a bit of a coquette, but Niccolò saw no trace of it until now. He looked away and sat down on the bed and opened the Professor's book of myths.

"You don't say much." She sat at the foot of his bed. "You prefer to read than to talk?"

"Yes."

"Good. Go ahead. I won't bother you." She looked at the spine of his book.

"Thank you, Lerma."

"It's good to read about gods. Gets your mind off the war."

"Yes."

"Also you can learn things. A good book. I read it." Niccolò turned a page ostentatiously.

"For example," she continued, "Mithra, the god of the Persians. He also demanded that his followers have the Sabbath on Sunday. Also made the highest holiday December 25. Also had baptism and communion. Why then should Christianity have caught on in Rome? Because it is true? But then, why should Fascism have caught on? Because it is true? Incredible problems."

"I suppose—" Niccolò began.

"You go ahead and read. I have work to do. Work. That's the antidote to sorrow. You must not think today. Thinking is bad. Except about revenge, about expunging these Germans. About—"

Niccolò put his hand over his eyes. He wished he were an Indian god with two more hands to plug up his ears and another set of hands to put over Lerma's mouth.

"I'm sorry," she said suddenly. "I talk only to shut out the roaring in my own brain. You have your own roaring?"

"Yes."

"You never talk about it."

Niccolò took a long breath and let half of it out. When he

had brought his voice under control he confessed, "I . . . I find it difficult . . . I could never talk about sad things, even as a child." But now, once he began, he could not stop. "When I played in tragedies all I had to do is think about loss—loss of my father, a friend in school dead of a fever. Even sometimes the death of a cat I had. I named it Caesar, but the children called it Jew."

"Let's talk of something else then," Lerma said. "Come. We'll play a game of casino."

She got out the cards. Niccolò had never liked the game: the Good Ten, the Good Two, building fives. Still, it passed the time. They sat on the edge of the bed like children and played in silence. Niccolò became self-conscious and his hands began to tremble when he felt her eyes on him.

"Look at you. Shaking. Like me." Lerma held out her own hand. "I must be a kind of witch, a gorgon. In one hour I will walk from this room, go outside and kill a man with these fingers."

Niccolò felt a revulsion spreading across his skin like a shadow.

"Could you kill a man?" she demanded.

"Once I thought not. Now I'm not certain."

"You could. Believe me, you could. Once I was a convent girl, white gloves. Everything. I even thought once I had a vision of the Virgin. Now, all because of the Germans, my faith is gone."

"What is lost can be found again."

The thought seemed to start something in Lerma's mind. They played out the hand. She gathered up the cards.

"When do they say you will be able to go out?" she asked.

"When the shoulder is completely healed. And when the Germans have stopped looking for me."

"They will never stop. You must understand that."

"I am not afraid."

"Maybe not. But you don't—"

"Don't what?"

Lerma slammed the cards down on the bed. "You don't *burn*. I see it in your big eyes. You think, if I'm quiet, if I'm decent, if I show the partisans how to act, to dress, to play the parts, then maybe God will be good and bring me back my family. You don't raise a fist to heaven. You don't hate."

He looked into a taut, shiny face that might have been pretty once but was ravaged long ago, by the war, by wounds that had nothing to do with Germans, he guessed. With the Church, maybe. Or a crazy family. Or perhaps she was just trying to talk herself into murder.

"Give me your hands," she said. She held out long, thin fingers like inverted rakes. "I can give you strength."

Strength for what? Niccolò wondered. To kill? To heal? In some indefinable way the woman seemed to radiate a power that was neither sexual nor intellectual, a feeling of rage looking for outlets, of intelligence short-circuited.

She kissed him. He felt nothing, no lust, no revulsion; nothing.

He thought only of Gina and the child. Lerma smiled in the odd way she had and took the cards up again and began dealing out hands. They finished the game in silence.

"Lerma, listen," Niccolò said finally. It was as if he overheard someone else talking, as if the words were thread coming off a spool. "Tell me what to do. My wife, my baby, everything . . . gone. I have to do something. I can't sit here any longer giving dumb instructions to dumber partisans."

"I know," she said with great melancholy. "I know. My own family was taken. My husband is already dead, shot in the streets and taken to the cemetery in a wheelbarrow like dirt. I look at you and think, how lucky. At least his wife is alive."

"I don't even know that. I believe it, but I don't know."

"Maybe it's better not to know."

"No. I have to find out. At night I dream I'm with them. I even see myself rescuing them. Like in the cinema."

"Maybe the best way to rescue them is to stay here. Doing what we're doing."

"How can killing Germans here help my people there? No, I have to go north, somehow."

"Niccolò. No one can escape from those camps. Barbed

wire, electric fences. Guards. This we know. It's like the labyrinth of the Minotaur. Lots of ways in, no way out."

"But still in the labyrinth there was a way out. For Theseus."

"Yes, well, you're not a god, and Himmeldorf is not a myth."

Niccolò did not hear her. He was thinking about how the Minotaur died.

He was still thinking about it when the Professor came in, chuffing urgently, out of breath from the stairs.

"A change of plans. We have to leave now." He turned to Niccolò. "Your arm is better?" He turned to help Lerma with her coat.

"Yes. Better. Please. Look at me."

Lerma and the Professor turned around.

"Let me come with you."

"Impossible. You'll be recognized."

"Why is it I can send everybody else out and not go myself? My arm is almost healed. Look." He picked up a chair. Niccolò had practiced lifting it. Pain shot from his shoulder to his spine, but he forced a grin.

"It's not your arm." The Professor rummaged through a drawer until he found a pair of glasses. "It's your face, your manner."

"God damn it!" Niccolò came over to him and grabbed the Professor's arm with his good hand. "I can change. You know I can change. I can look like an old nun if I want to. A Chinaman. A red Indian."

Something glinted under the Professor's stiff face. "Easy, you think. Just put on a beard and walk into German quarters?"

"No, not easy."

"You'll do what I say? No going off on your own?"

"Yes."

"Your arm feels well?"

"Yes."

"Liar."

"All right—not well, but satisfactory. I can use it."

The Professor walked around him. He opened a footlocker and drew out a suit of khaki. "Get into these. This afternoon for one hour you are a soldier. On medical leave. With crutches."

He gave Niccolò a small pistol. It fitted snugly inside the gray tunic. "You know how to use one of these?"

This time, Niccolò thought, I had better tell the truth. "I never fired a gun except onstage. With blanks."

"It works the same way," the Professor said. "Only, if you point it at somebody he doesn't get up and take a bow at the end."

Niccolò finished dressing in the bathroom. The mirror gave back the reflection of a young lieutenant with a hollow, wounded face.

Out on the street, no one seemed to notice him. Lerma's hair was whitened; she and the Professor seemed the parents of a fine young man who had been grievously wounded, probably in Sicily. One heard of terrible losses in the south. The citizens of occupied Rome gave them no special attention. They had more immediate concerns: the Germans, for instance; and eating. The faces on the street were all pinched and furtive. The meat stores had scraps. There were rumors of dogs and cats slaughtered for the table. The vegetable shops sold only hard, knobby roots and bad lettuce and underripe tomatoes. The few street children had an enervated appearance and their games lacked vigor. They barely had energy to argue. No beggars could be seen anywhere; they were either indoors or dead.

When the trio came near the Hotel Excelsior they paused. Only a handful of people were on the street, moving slowly. To Niccolò they looked like sinners in the *Purgatorio*. Color seemed drained from the place; he saw it all in black and white. One of the walkers was Borro, who was out of place, a figure from someone else's dream. Niccolò did not know whether to greet him or if Borro was part of the Professor's scenario. He said nothing. The Professor whispered a set of instructions to Niccolò: where to deposit the papers he was shortly to receive. He would take half, the Professor the other half; that way, if either were captured, the other might still deliver to the partisans the intelligence they needed:

locations of German arsenals and food supplies. The
Professor stayed back with Niccolò and let Lerma go ahead.
She approached the entrance just as a soldier emerged,
carrying a leather case. He started toward the Via del 23
Marzo. Lerma hailed him. She asked the German corporal
for something and gave him an unprovocative social smile.
He leaned forward; he had trouble understanding the
question. Then he nodded and looked down the street,
pointing. The shot was barely audible, a mere snap. The
soldier fell down like a column of water and lay spread
across the sidewalk. Lerma picked up the briefcase and
walked briskly to the Professor, handed it to him, turned and
walked on without a backward glance. The Professor took
the letters in the packet and walked to Niccolò and gave him
a handful. "Go," was all he said. The actor put the papers
in his tunic and limped on.

He made his way awkwardly but with great determination
to the trattoria off the Piazza San Cosimato, near the empty
vegetable stands. An overturned red box was chalked with
the Partisans' code mark. Niccolò put in the papers, then
limped on to the trattoria in the square. The Professor and
Lerma were already there. She sat with her head in her
hands. "So young," she kept saying. "Younger than
Niccolò, far younger. A boy."

The Professor let her cry.

"We are only liberators of Rome," he said. "We do what
we must."

Niccolò thought: Yes, and what must we do? Kill boys?
How will this free my wife and son? He thought of the
Minotaur and the maze and was silent.

He was still thinking of them when the German officers
slammed the front door open and shouted something. The
few people standing near the door washed back and the
officer pointed to the table where Niccolò and Lerma and
the Professor were sitting.

"All of you! Up!" He spoke Italian with a schoolboy
accent.

They obeyed. Two enlisted men ran to them and patted
their pockets. They found Niccolò's pistol and took it.

Lerma had got rid of her weapon and the Professor was unarmed.

"You will come with me," the officer ordered.

"On what charge?" the Professor demanded.

"On the unprovoked and cowardly attack on Reichskorporal Kurt Essen less than one hour ago outside the Hotel Excelsior."

The three walked out wordlessly, before the Germans. Two rifles were trained on them; there was no escape. Borro, Niccolò thought. It had to be Borro. The fat man had betrayed them all. He looked at his fellow conspirators. Lerma had begun to cry again. The Professor tried to walk with dignity, but his posture betrayed a sense of failure and wretchedness, the corners of the mouth turned down and the eyelids heavy.

"The soldiers are talking about a death camp," he whispered to Niccolò. "Poland."

"Silence!" said one of the soldiers.

Crowds on the street watched them pass by. Nothing was said. Flocks of pigeons beat their wings against the dead air and filled the afternoon with little thunders. Soiled feathers drifted down and settled and swirled up again. Marched toward German headquarters, on the street where the murder had occurred, Niccolò felt a strange exhilaration. It took him the rest of the journey to define it. It was only as the door to the commandant's office opened that he understood. Poland. Why have I not seen that this was the entrance? I didn't need the others. I could have done it myself.

His heart lifted and he swung into the room on his crutches with an exhilarated air. This was the beginning of the Minotaur's maze. Niccolò Levi would enter it and find his family. And he would escape. After all, he had made other characters rise from the page. Now he would play Theseus for a while.

7

Carl Berlin: New York, 1944

IN THE MILITARY, he grumbled, disgrace at least had style: epaulets ripped off, drumrolls, the reading of orders to an assembled troop. Drama worthy of Errol Flynn and C. Aubrey Smith. But this: silence and the inane staccato of machines. No command decision, no reprimand beyond the Old Man's shaking of his head and the official removal of Carl from pursuit of the Butcher. Quinn was doing it now. A fat FBI man who used a gold toothpick and said "Between you and I." And worshipped the Director. He even looked like J. Edgar Hoover—or a pit bull terrier, which amounted to the same thing. Leaving Carl with the dreck of intelligence work: processing messages from overseas, decoding troop movements and positions of field agents, then relaying the information. Approximately as exciting as watching a chess match through wax paper.

Months of this had given Carl the eerie feeling of dislocation, as if he were machinery. There was nothing he did that a high school math brain could not do, provided he knew the code. Intelligence was boy's work anyway, he decided. Spying through keyholes and windows, steaming open a stranger's mail, sending words in a made-up language. It was right out of a radio serial: send a boxtop and get a Captain Midnight Decoder Ring.

How much better to walk through a fiery land or fly over it with unambiguous bullets. To face the Germans on their stolen earth. The war would mean something then, and vengeance would have a solid feel to it. Not like this gaseous business of counterintelligence. And yet, Carl knew that the information gathered *was* valuable, that it did have to be processed and sent out. And that, above all, he had been wrong. Hubris had done him in. A mortal sin for monks, Carl acknowledged, and for the careless.

So all those weeks he had attended to the paperwork, loathing it and doing it well, hoping that headquarters would relent, but without any belief that the Old Man was even checking on him. Messages came in all the time, at any hour. When he went off duty after twelve or fourteen hours, one of Quinn's assistants, a furtive, spaniel-faced bureaucrat named Maslin, entered, tending the machines, gathering papers for the next day's decoding. Maslin always left some indefinable odor, a mixture of hair oil, cabbage, and inadequacy. Usually he was early, but tonight Maslin had called in hoarsely complaining of the grippe. He would be tardy; did Carl mind?

"No," Carl retorted, "I have no plans. I'll stay till you arrive." Then he called Ellen and told her that he had the grippe. The excuse germ, he thought, a lot of it going around.

In fact, he was grateful to miss the Howards' cocktail party where, with his luck, he would be caught in the corner with her husband, chatting with grim bonhomie about the Dodgers.

At two A.M. he was doubly glad that Maslin had called in sick. Agents were not supposed to transmit personal messages, but headquarters blinked if the messages were brief and did not come from critical areas. This was from Piombino Harbor, in Tuscany, now safely in Allied hands.

He who believes in luck has it, they say here, she began. *We are safe and the losses are decreasing. No one will know how much the Italians have endured, and still they sing, and still they laugh. If you could hear them. Ah, but you will, you will. Soon enough. I move on soon. I am sorry for not writing. Time does not permit. Happy birthday in case you don't hear more.*

The rest was a list of casualties and the relative strength of the Gothic Line in the north of Italy.

When he read her message Carl realized two things: Ruth Silver had never been out of his thoughts, and that he would be forty next month. Depression assailed him in waves. He was neither soldier nor civilian: welcome in no camp, unknown, a failure in his chosen profession, or in the profession that had chosen him.

He continued his work mechanically. Casualty reports and relocation of divisions, movements of the British XIII Corps near Siena. Departure of the French Expeditionary Corps to take part in Operation Anvil in the south of France. The expected retreat of the German Tenth Army from the Albert Line. It all poured through him and emerged altered, like breathed air. He had transmitted the last of his work to Washington when Maslin came in, wheezing.

"Jesus," he said, hanging up his soaking coat on a nail, "I *hate* diseases." Maslin blew his nose into a soiled linen handkerchief and inspected the contents. He looked up at Carl.

"You don't like me much, do you?"

"I don't think about you much."

"But when you do, you don't."

Carl thought it over. "I guess that says it."

"OK. I don't like you so very well."

"We're all right, then. For the duration." Carl put on his coat and prepared to leave.

"Gawd. The duration." Maslin put his hand to his chest. "You know what they call this place at HQ? Siberia."

When this failed to draw a rise, Maslin added, "And you know what they call you?"

"Captain Marvel?" Carl offered.

"The forgotten man. You must really have bitched things up. I mean, you must really—"

"You'll find everything in order," Carl broke in. "Enjoy your grippe. And don't blow your nose on any of the code sheets. That's how I became the forgotten man. Blowing my nose on the code sheets."

Maslin sat and shuffled through some papers and began to clean his fingernails with a matchbook. The machine resumed. Carl went to the window and gauged the speed of the wind. The rain had let up a bit, and he hated umbrellas. He would not get a cab at this hour, in this weather, not in Manhattan. The hell with it. He would walk home hatless and kill Maslin's germs with two double scotches and a hot bath and then sleep until noon.

Maslin looked up cheerfully. "For you." He clipped a piece of message paper and handed it to Carl. "The Old Man wants to see you."

"Tomorrow?"

"Now, it says."

"Now? At two in the morning?"

"The Old Man doesn't sleep. Don't you know that by now? He's part owl."

"That's the part I like," Carl said. "It's the human portion I can't stand."

He clicked the door behind him, went downstairs and got wet. He was still wet fourteen blocks and forty-five minutes later when a secretary came out and ushered him into the inner office.

The Old Man was using the small one tonight, the room without a fireplace or books. He looked drawn and pale; for the first time Carl thought of him in lower case—as an old man. The surroundings were strictly workplace, metal desk and chair, black phone, window overlooking a wall. The chewing-out room. Surprisingly, he offered Carl his hand and motioned him to a chair. "I haven't much time," he said. "That's why I brought you here at this ungodly hour."

"It's all right," Carl returned. "I didn't have anything else—"

The Old Man showed his palm impatiently. "We have a problem," he continued. "Italy is going well. We took the bastards. We really did. We've lost men, as you know, a lot of men. But we should break the back of this thing in a few months. Maybe. A lot depends on intelligence. More than I suspected. Cigar?''

Carl refused, partly because he disliked whatever brand of spinach they were using for tobacco in panatellas, partly because, given the tone of the moment, he thought it might explode. The Old Man kept on: "Cooped up, waiting for things to happen; you can't be very happy."

"No," Carl admitted. "As a matter of fact, I hear they call me—"

"We have not forgotten you. We've just had other things—bigger ones—on our minds." The Old Man examined a wall map of France and Italy. "If matters are looking up overseas, they may be looking down over here. We have reason to believe German Intelligence may be planning something fresh. Some dramatic acts of sabotage, maybe worse. We don't know. The cables we've decoded are very euphemistic." He blew some smoke across the desk. Carl was sorry now that he had not accepted the offer. This was pre-war stock.

The Old Man admired the smoke himself. "Trouble is, they've gone underground. Like worms. We've got to draw them out. Keep them on the run. I'd like to get the Butcher, of course. But who we really want now is Gower. Ironic. We could have had him for the asking."

There was nothing accusatory in the Old Man's voice, only a chill. The air in the room suddenly seemed to be drained of oxygen.

"Never mind, no matter." The Old Man dismissed it all by cutting a swath through the blue haze with his hand. "We'll get them."

Carl began: "I have a suggestion—" It was as far as he got. Ideas from the audience were not being entertained.

"We've intercepted two cables," came the reply. "Sent from the mid-Atlantic to Christ knows where. Their newest term is something or someone called *Ziege*. In German—"

"Goat," Carl offered.

"Affirmative. Any significance?"

Carl thought back through the years of files. There were

no references to goats, no special Nazi rituals with them, no agent called Ziege."

"Could be it's an operation, not a man."

"So we assume. All the more reason to wedge Herr Gower from his hiding place."

The Old Man rummaged through his desk drawer, searching for a paper clip. He bound several pieces of paper and returned them to an out box. "The other is a standard mention of One. Apparently they've decided he's dying. Could be just wishful thinking, but as it turns out they're right."

"I didn't know."

The news made Carl uncomfortable. He knew the President was sick, but like the rest of the electorate he expected Roosevelt to go on forever, along with Churchill and Stalin and Chiang Kai-shek and Joe Louis and the Yankees.

"No one knows how long he's got left. But the cable suggests something vague about 'beating nature.' Could be a reference to European weather or some plan for a counterstrike in France. It might be about Roosevelt. We don't know. But we mean to find out."

The long hand on the school clock jumped twice before Carl asked, "What do you want me to do?"

The Old Man handed him a paper. There was a small photograph attached to the upper right-hand corner. Under it was a name.

"That is Frederick Rathenau. Not unfamiliar to you?"

"I know the name, that's all."

"Lives in the Village. Leroy Street. A bookbinder. No record of any kind. Second-generation American. We have no proof of his complicity; we only know that he traveled to Germany several times in the thirties."

The years of the visits were recorded: 1936 for the Olympics. Then in 1937 and twice in 1939. The Old Man fussed with some papers before returning to his subject. "We also know that he was a customer of Martin Gower. Sales receipts and so on. But he has received no mail, no calls from anyone. Still, we're certain from our interceptions of the German code, that he's in touch with his chief. The Germans call him Fritzl. We don't know where they contact him. We don't know how. All we know is his name keeps coming up."

"And you want me to find out," Carl volunteered.

"Not at all," the Old Man said, rising. "We want you to confront him. In public. Where people can see you."

"I'll never get anything out of him that way. They don't scare that easily."

"We don't want you to scare him, Carl." It was the first time the Old Man had addressed him by his first name since the early days of 1942. "We want you to kill him."

Carl tried to understand the mind that had conceived this. "Why?" he asked. "Once he's dead—" And abruptly he saw it all. "You want me to be the target," he said. "You want Gower to come after me."

"It's the only way we can get him out."

"And afterwards? If I'm still alive . . . Will you send me to Europe?"

"Of course," came the warm promise. Carl could see by his eyes that survival was not on the Old Man's program.

8

FDR: Washington, 1944

HIS WIFE TREASURED the story. It was typical of Eleanor, who cried at Andy Hardy movies. Anything moved her. The Girl Scouts, folk songs, sharecroppers, Negro spirituals. Refugee plaints: Overheard aboard the *St. Louis,* full of German exiles seeking a homeland:

Child: Permission to pass through?
Guard: Are you a Jew?
Child: Yes.
Guard: Jews not admitted.
Child: Oh, please let me in. I'm only a very little Jew.

Christ, if Eleanor would just let up once in a while. Maybe she *was* letting up. Maybe he was just suffering from fatigue. Noises seemed louder these days, and some mornings the braces seemed to weigh more than he did.

He was almost always tired now; the notion of reelection, something no one dared to talk about a year ago, was something that he could read on everyone's face. What was it Sherlock Holmes was fond of saying? When you have eliminated the impossible, whatever remains, no matter how improbable, must be the truth. There was no one else the party could accept as long as the President wanted another term. And, given all this: the certain defeat of the Axis, the need for continuity, the chance to preside in a postwar world, there was nothing else to do. But the campaign, Lord, the campaign. . . . All those trips, those speeches and conferences and pledges. Jim Farley out on the hustings, whispering the names of local delegates: "That's Howard Graham, machinists' union. Wife's name Myra, two kids, one at State, controls half of downtown Cleveland."

"Hello, Mr. President."

"Why, hello Howard, how's Myra and the boys?" A great open smile from the Chief.

"He remembered us, honey."

Repeated five thousand times across the country on legs that were failing, on a racked body. No one, not even the doctors, could know how tired he was. He needed a change. A rest. A pool where he could become, at least for an hour, weightless. Until then he had to be two men, the Chief and the Candidate, the man who would have to appeal once again to the special interests. The labor unions. The local machine Democrats. The farmers, the Irish, the Jews. The Jews . . .

Would they never let him alone?

Rabbi Wise, Judge Sam Rosenman. And, worst of all, Henry Morgenthau. A fine man, a great public servant. And a relentless pain, constantly pushing for rescue of his people in Europe. As if the President were not fully aware of the plight of refugees. Or of those in concentration camps. He knew what the Germans were doing. They were systematically wiping out Jews. But they were also killing Russians, Frenchmen, Belgians, and, damn it, Americans. U.S. troops were dying in Italy every day. How would Morgenthau like to sign letters to gold star mothers as part of his breakfast?

And now they wanted the President to issue orders to bomb the concentration camps. The Jews themselves were squabbling constantly: some Zionists wanted Jerusalem; some wanted Madagascar. Some Jews knew that the war had to be ended by military means, others wanted to trade money for people, as if you could buy every refugee with dollars. Where did they think those dollars would go? Into bullets to be used against American boys. Various Jewish committees sniped at each other in print. Ben Hecht was putting crazy ads in the paper about the Rumanian offer to sell Jews. How Hecht found out was anybody's guess. Today Hecht was being criticized by his fellow Hebrews as a "sensation monger, a liar." The Jews, the Jews. As if no one else suffered.

And now this memo from Morgenthau: "The matter of rescuing the Jews from extermination is a trust too great to remain in the hands of men who are indifferent, callous and perhaps even hostile." Meaning the State Department.

Well, the State Department was hardly a repository of the brilliant. Hacks, many of them. Timeservers. Polonius times 200. Nevertheless, the President could not entertain attacks on his right flank. Fortunately, he could show Secretary Morgenthau General McCloy's communiqué. No, he would not show it, Roosevelt would read it to him. It was not yet official, and it was marked *President: Eyes Only.* He waited for the long, sad face of the Secretary, and when Morgenthau tried to begin his familiar "Could we speak for a moment about the terror in Eastern Europe?" (translation: Why don't we bomb Auschwitz?), FDR leaned back in his swivel chair and said, "Let me read you this, if I can find it." He pretended to search among his effects for a paper and put on a pair of reading glasses. "John McCloy, Assistant Secretary of War: 'After a study it became apparent that such an operation—'" Roosevelt peered over his spectacles: "He means the bombing you are asking about—'such an operation could be executed only by diversion of considerable air support essential to the success of our forces now engaged in decisive operations elsewhere—'"

"But, Mr. President—" Morgenthau tried to interrupt.

Roosevelt thundered over the objection, "'and would in any case be of such doubtful efficacy that it would not warrant the use of our resources. There has been considerable opinion to the effect that such an effort, even if practicable, might provoke more vindictive action by the Germans.'"

Roosevelt leaned back. He let the words hang in the air. Morgenthau looked impressed. Naturally, he would have to say something. Roosevelt wondered what.

The Secretary shook his head. "Mr. President," he began, "knowing what we know about those camps, about the gas chambers and the inhumanity, the systematic slaughter, what more vindictive action could there be?"

Silence.

FDR pressed the button for Anita. The meeting was over.

DOCUMENT FOR THE PRESIDENT EYES ONLY
FOREIGN AND DOMESTIC PRESS

THE JEWISH POPULATION IN POLAND IS DOOMED TO ANNIHILATION IN ACCORDANCE WITH THE MAXIM "SLAUGHTER ALL THE JEWS REGARDLESS OF HOW THE WAR WILL END." THIS YEAR VERITABLE MASSACRES OF TENS OF THOUSANDS OF JEWS HAVE BEEN CARRIED OUT IN LUBLIN, WILNO, LWOW, STANISLAWOW, RZESZOW.

RECORDING, GENERAL WLADYSLAW SIKORSKI, BBC
9 JUNE 1942

MORE THAN 700,000 POLISH JEWS HAVE BEEN SLAUGH-TERED BY THE GERMANS IN THE GREATEST MASSACRES IN THE WORLD'S HISTORY . . . THE MOST GRUESOME DE-TAILS OF MASS KILLINGS EVEN TO THE USE OF POISON GAS. . . .

LONDON DAILY TELEGRAPH
25 AND 30 JUNE, 1942
REPRINTED NEW YORK TIMES
30 JUNE AND 2 JULY 1942

9

Niccolò Levi: Poland, 1944

As a child Niccolò would sometimes watch a classmate take a beetle and enclose it in his hands, letting it crawl around in a dark and airless world until it stopped struggling. "How would you feel if you were a bug and someone did that to you?" he used to ask. Today he knew.

In the sealed freight car, inhaling the mephitic air, the Roman prisoners were as trapped as insects in a fist. Their train traversed scarred lands. Niccolò could make out the rumblings of war, but they were always diminished by the screams of the other prisoners. For the first few days children's voices pierced the perpetual night, then the screams of women and, finally, men. The air grew worse; for two days there was neither food nor water. When the doors finally creaked open, it was so that an officer could demand "the dead and the other garbage." Niccolò knew that they were headed toward Poland. He forced himself to think only of that, of going north to the place where Gina was. Still, he could not look away from the weeping mothers carrying the corpses of their young or the human stench of fear and death. Once the car was sealed again he

had no idea of time or place. He sensed only that this
journey was some kind of test which the strong alone would
survive, and that the survivors would be put to work as
slave laborers. The German commandant had promised his
captives "a living death."

When they arrived at their destination more were dead;
but neither the Professor nor Lerma had succumbed. They
and twenty-four others climbed down, aching and weak,
obeying without thinking. Soldiers yelled orders in German;
the Professor understood and explained everything to the
other prisoners. Men at desks wrote down names and
occupations without comment. The women were separated
immediately from the men. Lerma scarcely looked back as
she was marched off, but she carried her head high. The
men were marched deeper into the labor camp, past barbed
and electrified wire fences, past the sign that said ARBEIT
MACHT FREI—Work Makes Free—past low brick buildings
and places where prisoners broke stones and loaded flatcars
with dirt. Before a narrow wooden building Niccolò noticed
a freight platform. Above it was something he had seen only
in pictures of medieval Rome: a gibbet with three nooses
swaying slightly in a mild breeze. He turned away and
looked at the ground and made himself go back to Rome.
He thought of the Via Rasella.

He was eight years old and he was walking there with no
particular purpose, studying a page of Hebrew. Near the
Tittoni Palace a gang of boys began to taunt him. They saw
the lettering and began calling him the killer of Jesus and
Jewface. He kept his head down and recited the prayer he
was studying. One of the boys knocked his cap from his
head and when Niccolò turned to see who had done it,
another hit him in the face, and a third and fourth tripped
him. The gang pummeled him on the ground and made his
nose bleed, but before they could do any real harm a baker
came out from his shop wielding a broom and yelling
imprecations. The boys scattered, and the man shouted after
them, his face almost as red as the bloodstains on Niccolò's
shirt front. He helped the child up and went inside muttering
about youth and noise. Niccolò bent over and gathered up

his papers. On the page he was studying were large black splotches: one of his attackers had spilled ink over the Hebrew. And over those stains were blood drops. It was impossible to read the prayer anymore; circumstances had covered it.

Now, in the concentration camp the Germans were amused to call Himmeldorf, the Village of Heaven, history had accomplished the same swift ruin. The residue of Jewish belief, of recited prayers and incantations, was covered with dirt and blood.

For the first few weeks he was shocked by the inhumanity, the perpetual filth and the shortness of rations, the watery soup, the cries in the night. Then as the weather grew colder, he was shocked by his own capacity to adjust. Every morning was the same: gray Polish dawn, gray faces, gray uniforms. Always the identical command, "Come on you human shits, you Yid dogs. Out! Line up here!" As his shoulder healed, he grew more numb. Insults, indignities, meant nothing. He concentrated solely on the chance to see Gina and little Nardo, to take them away. He looked at his surroundings with the mindlessness of an animal in a cage. No regret, no anger. Only a doggedness, a will to stay alive, a far-off dream of escape. He was lucky, he knew. He and the Professor and Lerma could have been shot in retribution. Why they were not he never learned. Maybe Borro made a deal after the betrayal. Maybe the Germans thought that laborers for the Reich were more valuable than dead Italians. It was impossible to read the Fascisti mind.

Soldiers and guard dogs appeared everywhere. The guards liked to call people dogs, but the real dogs were fed meat that was denied to prisoners. Men in uniform maintained a look of revulsion, as if to be near an inmate was to suffer risk of infection. It was easy to see why. Dirt was on every skin; water was available only a few times a day from open rusty pipes. There was no soap. Shaving was done with rusty blades once a week. It was like pulling the hairs out instead of cutting them. Niccolò and the Professor and five others were assigned jobs as stokers. Niccolò imagined that the furnace pipe went into officers' barracks;

perhaps in some way the heat drove turbines that operated the lights. Certainly nothing went to the cabins where the prisoners lived. Niccolò shivered all the time. At night the threadbare blankets were all that intervened between the growing coldness of the camp and the chill of the soul. Yet the body remained intact. Niccolò actually gained in strength, and the Professor refused to succumb to the frosts. Because they seemed such able bodies, one morning they were marched to a whitewashed cement building in a new area. Talking was forbidden. One of the soldiers commanded them to enter the building and clean it out. "An infirmary," he said. "Old people. Prisoners. Dead of typhus. Remove them and load them on the truck."

Niccolò and the Professor opened a heavy white door and entered. The inside of the building had nozzles on the walls and some holes in the ceiling. There were no beds, no sheets, no medical equipment, nothing. Only the corpses, all of them nude, all of them emaciated old men. Through the open door a corporal shouted his orders: "Remove all rings and bring them out!" There were twenty-eight men on the floor and each was searched by Niccolò and the Professor. Briefly, Niccolò considered taking a wedding band to bribe a guard, but he thought better of it; a Jew taking a ring of a Jew—the old man was bearded and circumcised—it would not do in the eyes of God. Even in Niccolò's own eyes. He tossed the gold circle into a box that the corporal held out at the door. The box was quickly filled. The prisoners loaded the dead on a truck and then a man in a white tunic, a doctor with a stethoscope around his neck and silver forceps in his pocket, bent over the bodies. The sides of the truck were raised and Niccolò could only see outlines as the doctor quickly did something, a gesture that he repeated on corpse after corpse. In a few minutes he climbed down with a small bag in his hand. He emptied it noisily into the corporal's box. Niccolò was almost twenty yards away, but his focus had always been sharp and the shape and the clatter was unmistakable. The doctor had removed gold teeth and inlays from the dead.

In the days before they returned to the white building

Niccolò tried to forget, or to misunderstand what he had seen. To dwell on it was to make it an obsession within an obsession; it was bad enough to be prisoner in the same camp with Gina and the child and not to know where they were, or even if they were alive. Yet they must be alive, he told himself; I would know it if their hearts stopped beating. Mine would, too.

He focused on thoughts of them, on finding them and running away. Every new face became a possible source of information; he asked all of them about the Roman Jews. He learned nothing until the day of the tattooing. Prisoners were lined up in order to have numbers imprinted on their arms. As he walked toward the specialist with the needle, Niccolò saw a new kapo, a helper of the Germans who spoke a few words of Italian. Yes, he said, he knew of Roman Jews who had arrived some time ago. Yes, they were here in Himmeldorf. He pointed to the interior, past structures and quarters of German troops. "In there, no doubt. Farther than the eye can see, beyond what the heart can hope." There was great fatigue in his voice. He had seen too much; he had been here a lifetime: five months.

"There must be a way I can get to see them," Niccolò insisted. The man shook his head. "You have to bribe." He moved away, frightened at the notion of anyone suborning the Germans. "And we have nothing to bargain with. They have taken everything."

But they had not, Niccolò decided. There was still the gold hidden in Rome. In the early evening he whispered to a sallow guard who understood Italian, "Permission to speak to you, Corporal Keller."

"Speak."

"I have money."

Keller smiled and showed good white teeth. "Yes, and I have wings."

"No, really. I do. In Rome."

"Fat lot of good that does you here, Jew."

"I can get it to you."

"How?"

"Let me escape."

Keller laughed. He kept laughing. Even when he hit Niccolò in the head he laughed. The Professor tried to aid his friend and Keller hit him in the neck with his rifle butt. Watching the men on the ground, their faces contorted, struggling for consciousness, he still laughed. Keller looked down and said to Niccolò, "What were you before this?"

"An actor," Niccolò grunted.

"You should have been a gambler. Taking a chance like this and still alive. A lucky man." He commanded two soldiers to take Niccolò and lead him to a wooden workbench. While the new prisoners watched, Niccolò was thrust over the bench and his trousers pulled down sharply.

"Eins! Zwe! Drei! Vier!" Keller called off the blows as he flailed away with a rubber truncheon. After the first three Niccolò felt nothing. He seemed to remove himself from his body. Something in his mind hurt, something in his head screamed, the world that he saw when he opened his eyes was red, and there were shouts of agony in his ears, but the voice was not his. At the fifteenth blow Keller demanded, "Is the money helping?" He laughed. But the fact is, Niccolò reflected, the gold *is* helping. It is something to think of, to anesthetize the brain.

Niccolò was surprised to find himself unable to rise after the punishment. Keller moved away, laughing again. Niccolò leaned on the Professor and then the pain came in ceaseless waves. Blood stained his pants. Twice he nearly collapsed, but both times the Professor came near and let Niccolò lean against him. At mealtime, Niccolò washed himself in rusty water and prayed that there would be no infection; he had no idea what would happen if he got sick. He did not even know whether the camp had an infirmary.

That night he ran a fever and the dogs barked in German. They were not nearly as cruel as the dreams that followed toward morning. Nightmares, no matter how violent, could be alleviated by his open eyes. Good dreams had no such cure. In his sleep he saw Gina in a white dress, holding the baby's tiny hand. She had to bend over to reach the crib and her breasts looked like the two young roes of Solomon's Song. The room leaped with sunlight; there was no ceiling.

Someone was playing on a harpsichord: his mother. Impossible. She had always been tone-deaf. She liked to say that she only knew two composers: one of them was Rossini and the other wasn't. Niccolò laughed. The baby laughed. His mother and the harpsichord laughed. He awoke to cold dawn and angry commands and distant barking. A new group had arrived.

These were Greek Jews, adolescents, bewildered, chattering to themselves, unwilling or unable to talk to the other prisoners. The guards yelled at them but the boys comprehended nothing. The guns were another matter. Those they understood. The boys were marched away in the cold, before the sun was halfway to its zenith. Niccolò might have forgotten them, but three days later, reassigned to the white building, again removing bodies, he suddenly knew in his bones what was happening here. There could no longer be any doubt. When he was young there was a great deal of speculation about what language would be spoken in heaven: Hebrew? Italian? Some celestial communication never heard on earth? But there could be no doubt about the language of hell. *Tedesco*: German.

For there on the cement floor, again between the blue crystals, in positions that testified to a last hysterical protest against the death sentence, were the same boys. The doctor would be disappointed today; poor Greeks could not afford gold teeth.

Thereafter life divided for Niccolò. Only parts of him seemed to work. How he survived the cold, how any of them lived through the wind and the barked commands, he could not understand. He merely rose like a golem and obeyed.

Part of him he felt was already dead. The other part was alive; it writhed with energies and lived in the future, like an architect or a child. The "cleanup duty" came more frequently now, and Niccolò knew now that they would kill all the Jews if someone did not stop them.

Afternoon. The wind bitter, the thermometer plunging. Possibly a Sunday because he heard one of the soldiers talking about *die Kirche*. Church. Niccolò was on line for delousing when he saw her. The long, starved face had altered, but there was no mistaking the eyes: it was Lerma.

She was walking alongside the small knot of bent men. Niccolò lost some words in the wind, but he heard her say something about Romans.

"Gina is in Cell Block E." That was all, but it was enough. He felt a resurgence; his blood seemed to thicken; color came to his face. Gina was alive; the child was certain to be with her.

"Tell me where is Cell Block E," he pleaded.

"To the north. But guarded always. Worse than here. You have to know what you're doing."

"I will devise a plan."

"You will do nothing. Let me think for you."

Guards moved closer, but the cold was too much for them. They walked away.

"I can persuade one of the Germans," she went on, talking without moving her lips. "The best of a bad sort."

Persuade him how? Niccolò wanted to ask, but he said nothing. He could guess what Lerma had to do.

The Professor shivered. "Sometimes I think I will never be warm again."

"You want to generate heat?" Lerma looked around. A guard crunched by on some pebbles. The steps grew distant. "Anger. That will make you forget the ice and the wind. Rage."

"I have hated Germans all my life," the Professor replied. "Their myths. The windbag Hegel. Wagner: dwarfs and women with staghorns. Their language. Still I feel no warmer."

"You hate old," Lerma hissed. "I hate new. I hate Americans. I hate English."

"Why?" Niccolò was astonished. "These are our friends. They can rescue us. In Naples—"

"In Naples. Yes. In Rome perhaps. But by the time they get here—" she made a short, empty gesture.

"You can't ask for miracles, Lerma," the Professor insisted.

"I don't ask for miracles. I ask for bombs. For a single

plane. For a sign. Anything. See out there? Railroad tracks. Leading to the country. Every day the locomotive comes bearing sealed boxcars with people. Not just Jews. Children. Gypsies. Old partisans. Enemies of the Reich. And every day, in these chambers, people are crowded in to die in the poison gas. Yes, yes, that's how they die. Inhaling death. And still the Americans send not a single bomber, not a single bomb. Not even to destroy the railroad tracks."

"How do you know all this?" Niccolò rubbed his blistered hands together for warmth.

"I listen. I talk. The soldiers tell me. They themselves are astonished that the Allies do nothing. Rescue through victory, Roosevelt says on the radio. We will all be dead by then. Some victory."

"If you know German soldiers so well," the Professor began, "perhaps you can convince them—"

"I don't like your tone, Professor, in this place you do what you can to live."

"I said nothing."

"Your face said it. Don't condemn so quickly. *'Erst kommt das Fressen, dann kommt die Moral.'* You understand?"

"Yes." The Professor looked away. "I understand."

Niccolò knew his Brecht better than they did. First food, then ethics. "Lerma," he said, "I will do anything to get to Cell Block E."

"Very well." There was a sudden gentleness about her that seemed artificial and strained. "The trucks come in every morning at eight-thirty. Doubtless you have seen them."

"We didn't know the time; no one has a watch."

"The cleanup detail begins shortly after that. The bodies are put into the truck. It drives to a crematorium."

The Professor turned away.

"What did you think they did with the corpses? Give them a hero's funeral? They burn them. That's why this place stinks even out here. Why there are no birds, not even sparrows. In the summer there will be no butterflies. Only dead air. Niccolò, are you strong enough?"

"Yes," he assured her.

"You will put yourself on the truck tomorrow and we will cover you with the dead. The truck will drive to the chimneys. You will get off then. Ahead of you will be a white structure with small windows. That is Cell Block E."

They were silent for a moment. Niccolò sensed that Lerma knew more, far more than she was saying. But he was afraid to ask more than one question: "How will we get back, Gina and the baby and I?"

She would not look at him. "There is one German, a corporal who can help. His name is Helmut. He has a red mustache. I can try to get in touch with him. But I promise nothing."

"I understand."

"Now," Lerma insisted, "I have things to discuss with the Professor."

Whatever those things were, Niccolò had no curiosity about them. His animal existence resumed its human dimension. He could foresee the next day and the next night.

He slept decently and when they put him to work digging up stones to put in the commandant's rock garden he felt no fatigue. The wretched bread and watery soup stayed in him: he could feel his body using it. The corpse detail began. He and the Professor carried the body of a fat man. When they dumped it on the truck, Niccolò got under it. The rest of the prisoners seemed to know what was going on; they covered Niccolò with dead bodies and never said a word. Niccolò lay with the cadavers and listened to his heart.

Lerma lived on loathing, he reflected, as bears made it through the winter on stored-up fat. He could not allow himself to hate. He would have to live on hope if he and his family were to make it to daylight and—where? Switzerland, probably. Or Italy. Yes, Italy. Home. A nation full of hideouts. There were many ways to get there. Trains, cars, even farmers' horse-drawn wagons. There were hundreds of methods. Thousands.

The truck slowed down and shuddered to a stop. He heard German commands. The gate of the truck came down with a heavy metallic clank. Orders were given in Polish. A detail began to unload its cargo. Niccolò worked his way off the truck, sliding down with a corpse. No one paid him the slightest attention.

When all the bodies were put on a wooden platform with small rubber wheels, he dared to peer forward and saw a soldier with a red close-cropped mustache.

The work detail pushed the flatcar of bodies closer to the building with the stark gray chimneys. Without appearing to veer from his course, Niccolò managed to work closer to Helmut.

"I am Niccolò Levi," was all he whispered. The soldier said nothing. Then, without turning his head, Helmut instructed, "Straight ahead. The door is open."

Niccolò never looked back. He walked directly to Cell Block E and pushed against the door. It was heavy and a spring resisted his effort, but the bolt was undone. He entered a dark hallway and only then realized how bright it had been outside. There was only one light bulb, and all around him everything was brown or devoid of color. All he saw was shapes. Heavy, warm air nearly choked him. At least there was heat in this place. Coal. He could smell the fumes.

A voice said something in Polish. He could make out a form in the hallway, and then a face. The woman was dressed in a gray smock. She resembled one of the corpses he had handled, except that her angry eyes were alive, witnesses that would not turn away.

She tried to block him; for Niccolò it was like pushing against coils of wire and bone, but she gave way. He burst into the little room. Two old women looked up at him with hollow stares. Their faces testified to the mixed terror and pain they felt; yet they could not have known that this was the husband. Unless there was something in the scream or in the expression of the woman on the bed.

He looked at her face. It was scarred and puffed; only one eye functioned. The sheet covering her had dried blood on it.

"Gina," he said.

She made no reply. Something in her stiff expression seemed to hint at recognition. It was hard to tell.

He took her hand. It was limp and dry. "What kind of place is this?" he yelled. 'What's wrong with her?"

"Experiments. They do experiments," one of the attendants said. She backed away from him.

"Oh, my God, my God," he said. "Let me take her." He tried to reach his hands under the sheet. The body was impossibly light. Gina screamed. He put her down gently.

"Don't lift her." The metallic contralto came from a large squat woman with a white smock and a stethoscope around her neck. "Who are you? What do you do here?" she asked in bad Italian.

"I—this is my wife!" Niccolò shouted. "Help me."

From far off someone said, "She won't help you. She's the one who did it."

"I did nothing," said the woman with the stethoscope. "The Germans did it. I only obey, you know that. If I don't take from her the organs, they take from me the organs. Or from you."

Help me, God, thought Niccolò. I don't understand any of this. The patient on the bed is Gina and not Gina. They have taken pieces of her away. No human could do that. But I see humans before me.

"If I stay with her she will recover." Niccolò sat in a white chair next to the bed and held his wife's hand. He could not bear to look at her, but he could not bring himself to look away. The seconds froze. Moans came from another woman on another bed. For the first time, Niccolò realized that there were other victims here, six women, as pale as Gina, in similar cots.

"What have they done to her?" he demanded.

One of the old women spoke of medical experiments, but he could not follow her rapid French. Something about an operation, about chemicals. At any time any one of the witnesses could have left and gone for a guard, or even for another prisoner. None of them moved, not even the woman with the stethoscope. He grabbed her and heard Gina scream. It was the piercing sound of an animal, a keening that seemed to reach for some inaudible note, then ceased as suddenly as it had begun.

Niccolò turned to look back at the bed. Gina had fallen out of it. She lay in a rigid, twisted form on the floor. The gown could not cover her thin legs. He went to her, but the woman with the stethoscope arrived first. Together they put her on the bed. The stethoscope was applied to Gina's neck. The woman opened Gina's eyes. They showed only white.

"A miracle she lasted this long," the woman said.

Without hesitation Niccolò put his hands on her thick throat.

"Where is the baby?" he wailed. His dark eyes glistened. "Where is he?"

"Please—I did not kill the boy."

"Where is he?"

The woman gestured to the window. "There . . . out there."

One more place to go, one more goal. He had come this far. . . . Niccolò released his hold and went to the window. He saw guards and beyond them the doors of five black ovens. Chimneys rose and trickles of black smoke corkscrewed their way to the sky.

He understood everything now. He looked past the chimneys at the dull sun. It was at its midway point. Noon. Poland's winter. 1944. He was to remember it as his last sane moment.

10

Carl Berlin: New York, 1944

HE PULLED OUT the file on sabotage, labeled MOSELLE AND RHINE WINES, and looked through it, translating the code as he went. Carl had always minimized the whole notion of German agents in the United States, but every time he checked the incidents he had to admit that the Old Man might have something.

The very first page told of a spy with the vaudeville name of Ignatz T. Griebl, a voluptuary, a physician, and a spy who had delivered to the Abwehr blueprints of pursuit planes built at the Seversky plant in Farmingdale, Long Island, the specifications of three destroyers and a Navy scout bomber. Now he was reported back in Vienna, practicing medicine. There was Herman Lang, once inspector at 80 Lafayette Street in Manhattan, where they were producing the Norden bombsight, plans of which were handed over to the Luftwaffe so that Lang might see his fatherland grow strong again. And William Sebold, code name Tramp, who had run a spy network until he went over to the FBI; and Simon Emil Kodel, who worked quietly in New York as an invisible man, a motion picture projectionist at the Lyric Theatre, shipping informative pieces of newsreels, inspecting arsenals as an open-faced tourist. Kodel's most trusted employee was his daughter Marie, 542 West 112 Street, who liked to rub elbows and matching accessories with sailors at the waterfront bars. Late in the evening, when she pretended to be vague and tipsy, the boys would talk; and one English sailor, Duncan Scott-Ford, spilled details that enabled Emil to write his "Report on the Conduct of Enemy Ships in Convoy at Sea in the Atlantic, Based on Conversations with British Seamen." Scott-Ford had been intrigued by espionage, and he had sold out to the Reich. But he had been careless and the Brits had caught up with him. He was hanged on November 3, 1942, and now Emil and Marie were in hiding somewhere. Sometimes you could hear Hitler laughing, the Old Man said. Or maybe it was just the wind—wind from Washington, propaganda, a line sent out to keep Stateside agents happy, make them feel that what they were doing was important. Instead of pushing papers around, like a garbage man the day after a parade.

Rathenau was nowhere to be found. Gone on vacation, his landlady said. No forwarding address. Up north somewhere. Which could be Cape Cod, Maine, Canada, or Harlem. Carl would have to wait; after all, he told himself, it's what I do best.

He was about to leave his office when the teletype began its familiar rhythms. This was only Tuesday, so it could not be the standard end of week summaries from Lisbon. He glanced at the incoming message idly. It meandered a bit about supplies and the movements of two agents from Washington to London, and there was something about inspection of stations later in the month. The item that caught his attention was almost thrown away by the sender: *Ruth Silver arrives New York from Toronto Friday 24.*

For over six months he had not seen her name on a dispatch. But for every one of those days he had thought of her, wondered where she was, what kinds of danger she had seen and experienced. It had begun long ago with a shared cup of coffee in Washington when she had briefed him

about Palestine. The whole notion of the Middle East, of
Balfour declarations and mandates, sounded like idiocy to
him. He was raised an assimilationist and even the present
European history had not changed his mind. His family had
always considered Theodore Herzl a nut, a dandy, an
egomaniac obsessed with the idea of a homeland no matter
where; once the man had even advocated Uganda. Clearly
the whole notion of Zionism was unworthy of a thinking
Jew. Ruth's family thought otherwise—and that was why
they were alive today. Mama and Papa Silver had sold their
clothing business in Alsace, and with their daughters they
had followed a wonder rabbi to Jaffa. The rest of the family
were now in concentration camps or dead; nobody knew,
nobody heard. The sisters grew healthy and tan. They
farmed, they served in volunteer armies, they grew their
own oranges, they made the desert bloom. All except Ruth.
The most restless of the children was not content to stay in
Palestine. Someone had enlisted her in British Intelligence.
From there she had gone to Canada, and then to the United
States, translating reports and advising troops who were to
parachute into France. She was a woman of quick, canny
judgments, and when Carl made his move she considered
him closely under the low light of the restaurant. She was
wearing a big hat, he remembered, and when she lowered
her face for a moment he could see nothing but straw. When
she raised it her eyes shone and her wide mouth smiled its
invitation. There was a marvelous fluency to her speech; its
edges seemed worn smooth by travel, and when she
walked, her narrow back added to the fluency: she did not
move like an American. By the third week they were
unburdening themselves of their histories and making little
confessions. Both of them dropped their guards; but Carl's
dropped a bit lower. He disliked it when she mentioned old
lovers; he dreamed about her hair; he smelled her in his
sleep. When she left him he was devastated. Love is like the
measles, he had read somewhere: the older we get the
harder it goes with us. But advice and example were no
consolation.

She had gone back to Europe because he was here, she

told him, because she had been tempted to stay in America, to indulge herself, to lose sight of her mission. Once she started on her work there was no self; she was always consumed by tomorrow, like a figure out of Chekhov. She even looked like one of the three sisters, her lips trembling with some message she could never quite articulate. All she could say was, "I have to go. Don't come any nearer. You've come too close too often." One morning when he called her there was no answer, and two days later there was a cable from Lisbon: she was on a new assignment. Presumably the Old Man had helped her get away. Sometimes there was an address; Carl had sent a few letters and never received an answer. It had taken him months to get over Ruth. He suspected that during those months he was the talk of the department. There had been a number of hints from headquarters—"Perhaps you should go to a new office for a couple of weeks"—but Carl had stayed at his post. He recovered, resolved that no one would get past his guard again.

Ruth Silver arrives New York from Toronto Friday 24. He detached the message and put it in his pocket. He had methodically destroyed memories of her, blackening or overexposing all the mental snapshots—there were no real ones. So he was astonished to learn how many conversations and erotic pictures were still stored in his skull.

There was no call from her on the weekend, and none the following week. Carl had no idea where Ruth was or what she was doing; she might have come and gone without his knowledge. Yet nine days later, when the phone rang exactly at eleven-thirty P.M., Carl, who was no believer in portents or extrasensory perceptions, was certain that she was on the other end.

"Hello, Ruth," he said.

"Carl? How did you—"

"Call it instinct."

"Better than intelligence, I hear."

"Where are you?"

"At Hotel B."

"I'd like to see you."

"Yes."

He took this for reciprocity.

"Now?" he asked, and when she repeated the word he locked up and went downstairs and found a cab and appeared at Seventy-fifth and Madison before the clock could strike midnight.

The old residence hotel was filled with superannuated refugees. The youngest person in the lobby was a lady of about seventy and the gossip was all in Yiddish or Hungarian. The concierge, another old lady with white hair dyed a bizarre greenish-yellow, looked up at him.

"Gentleman?"

"I want to visit a friend. Room 802."

"Ah." The concierge gave him a lewd grin. He smiled at the Old Man's genius for finding unlikely bases. There were other such rooms in advertising agencies and old age homes and backstage at a theater on Forty-fifth Street.

"Who is calling?" she asked.

"Mr. Robert Browning." A private joke, but a useful one. Carl and Ruth once keyed a whole series of messages to *The Ring and the Book*.

A button was pushed and the visitor announced on an intercom. Carl was shown into a wheezy elevator and taken upstairs. Ruth stood at the open door. She was thinner than before; her legs seemed longer and the blouse not quite as full. The long Modigliani face allowed itself a small grin.

"Room service?" she asked.

"You ordered an agent."

"Straight up, no chaser."

They went inside and she closed the door. Carl looked out the window. Below, in the dark foot and vehicle traffic moved somnolently.

He went to Ruth. She let him kiss her, but only for a moment.

"Carl, don't."

"Sweetheart, you were the one who called me."

"I know. I wanted to see you, I really did. I just—"

"You just what?"

"I don't know. It got too complicated last time. You have work to do. So do I."

"My work is about as important as making posters that say, 'Loose Lips Sink Ships.'"

They sat on the couch. He tried to keep his hands off her. What he saw stirred images he thought were cold. Too many nights, he reflected, too many hopes deferred.

"You've been back a long time," Carl reminded her. "Why didn't you call before this?"

"I was being debriefed." She avoided his eyes. "And then I . . . received a new assignment."

"Oh? Overseas again?"

"No. Here."

He waited for her to continue. She was obviously embarrassed about something.

"It's the Butcher business." Ruth began to walk around nervously, peering out the window as if she half-expected storm troops below. "The Old Man told me everything."

"He doesn't know everything."

"Well, he told his version of what happened. He put me on the case. For a while."

"For a while? Until when? Until you get killed? He knows the Butcher hates women. He's using you as bait is all."

"Carl, stop it. I told him I couldn't do it alone. He offered to put Van Vliet on with me. I asked for you instead."

"What did he say?"

"Well, he didn't say no."

So. The Old Man was willing to postpone the execution of Rathenau. The German would just have to wait a while to be killed, while Ruth Silver and Carl Berlin had their little adventure together. Cute.

"I might remind you," Ruth said, "that there are more people in the Marais who would slit your gizzard for a *sou* then you can find in this whole city. And here I am, without a single scar. Except where they took my appendix out when I was eight."

"Let me see," Carl demanded.

"You've already seen."

"I forgot. I have a poor memory for scars."

"I don't."

Carl shrugged. Useless to pursue that line. He stopped talking and let Ruth outline her plan. As he listened, it seemed naive: headquarters had given her some new, experimental camera that could take pictures in dim light. She would sit in a cafeteria and shoot long distance at all the people who exited from the dining room of the Blue Parrot Club, a favorite of German-Americans.

The film would be processed downtown, and then agents would examine the faces, hoping that someone new would show up, someone who might lead them to the Butcher. The simple expedient of killing someone and flushing the krauts out of the furniture seemed so much more effective to Carl. Unless, of course, the Butcher had already gone back to Germany. That seemed unlikely; there were enough psychopaths in the Fatherland already without adding an American nut. If he was American. If. Maybe. Perhaps. So many contingencies, Carl thought. He let Ruth do the planning. Maybe she would bring him luck.

On the way to Yorkville Ruth spotted Cary Grant on Fifth Avenue, sauntering and laughing with what looked like a starlet. She had crooked seams on her stockings and she linked arms with a fat man who might have been a producer or an agent. As they walked, Carl wondered about war and actors: what happened to stars in a conquered country? Were they taken over like radio stations, made to hawk the words of the conqueror? Or were they regarded as enemies of the state, tried and shot like generals?

They stopped at a newsstand. Carl passed up the *Journal American*, *The Sun* and the *World Telegram* and read the headline in *Variety*. STUDIOS SHELVE WAR STORIES AS THEY SHOW 49% BOX OFFICE DECLINE. "I'm tired of them too," he said to Ruth, but all the way up Fifth he imagined New York City under occupation, American kids hiding in shadows and selling food, dogs, sisters, themselves, anything; people dragged out and shot on the steps of brownstones, museums looted and taken over by general staffs; this place, he supposed as he passed it, the white, palatial Temple

Emanu-el, desecrated, made into a chamber of horrors, where the screams would issue at night and break through the sounds of marching and guttural orders and occasional torchlight parades.

You heard a lot these days about the softness of Americans: the signs read IN CASE OF AIR RAID, WALK, DO NOT RUN, as if to remind the folks at home that there was no reason for discomfort, just a few loud noises is all, no blood, no screams, no ambulances and litterbearers picking up the wounded or pieces of the wounded. It occurred to Carl that critics like General Patton had it all wrong. Americans were not soft. These exuberant people, with their confident, innocent airs and their ever-ready ration cards, were simply sleepwalkers. Even their songs were dreams: "My Dreams Are Getting Better All the Time," "I'll Buy That Dream," "I Had the Craziest Dream." They had never been overrun; no one had ever knocked on their doors at night. Policemen were only people who gave directions and now and then handed out a ticket. Unless you were colored, and even colored people had the aura of dreamers, in love with their President. The Americans were like the Jews of Vienna, circa 1930. Unbelievers in evil. Somnambulists.

They parted at Seventy-third Street. Alone, Carl stopped himself from thinking about the war. For half an hour he concentrated instead on sexual memories and expectations, like a man building a fire against the darkness and the cries of animals.

When he arrived at the agreed address, he looked across the street at the French restaurant with its handful of outdoor tables, Paris style. Ruth was already there. Sitting alone, looking at a copy of *Collier's*. Maybe she was reading it, certainly her attention was on the page. She never looked up. Yet Carl had the feeling that she knew exactly where he was, and who was in the Blue Parrot. Her face was tilted down, but he could see enough of it, and all that it was possible to see of her long legs.

Maybe Ruth was right. It would be easy, too easy, to lose himself in her again, to shuck the demands of a war in

which he could make very little difference, to break free
from all the intelligence work that covered him with dust
and obligations.

He sauntered into the barroom of the Blue Parrot. It was
crowded and smoky, full of middle-aged people beyond
draft age, with two tables of smooth-faced soldiers sipping
their beer. The bartender was a fat man whose hair was
parted in the middle, twenties-style. He looked like H. L.
Mencken, but he spoke with a German accent.

"Zese are awful times," he was saying to someone at the
bar. "If people know you're German zey automatically sink
Nazi. Why do they sink I left Germany? Because of ze
National Socialists. My father vas a professional soldier. To
him Hitler vas a dwarf."

He talked about the decline of beer and about the St.
Louis Browns. There was a one-armed player on the team
named Pete Gray. The idea of a one-armed player amused
him. He showed his listeners how the player caught the ball
in his glove, then tossed the ball up in the air, tucked the
glove under his stump, caught the ball again with his left
hand and pegged it home. The bartender's accent was
pronounced, but he liked to use the jargon of the baseball
announcers: "Zis guy vas a liddle shrimp," he recalled, "a
sauspaw, but even so he hit a couple of four-masters in
Beantown last year."

There was only one woman in the bar, as sallow and
knobbly as the man who sat beside her at a small table,
arguing loudly about money. "It's the yids," he said. "They
started the war and now they're getting rich on it. And good
men can't make a buck." His wife told him to shut up, that
he was making her sick with his talk about work, that
anybody with half a brain and one good eye could get a
good job somewhere. "Get out of here and get me some
money too," she sang, in an off-key imitation of Ella
Fitzgerald. Every time he opened his mouth after that she
sang. Eventually, when the bar got crowded and attention
was turned away, he hit her. She bit her lip and her eyes
filled up, but she refused to cry.

Another shiny evening in the career of a United States

Government operative, Carl observed: romance, intrigue, the battle for men's minds. Listening to two mynah birds in a cage called marriage, abusing each other in some tenth-rate bar. Attention, men: Join the club. Become a counterintelligence agent. Eavesdrop on your fellow creatures. Learn about depravity in your spare time. Only a few points off your IQ brings you financial security and peace of mind. You need not leave your regular job. Our employees know about this ad.

But he stayed on, becoming, in time, part of the background. When instinct told him to make his move, Carl rose and went in the direction of the men's room, then veered off to the right, toward the kitchen. The cook was fussing with a steaming pot. Carl opened the rear door quietly and stepped outside. He could see into the lighted window of the Blue Parrot's back room. At a bare wooden table someone was speaking in German. Carl could just make out the tops of heads. He leaned against the wall, in the shadows. It was not a comfortable place. There was nowhere to sit down except on garbage cans covered with black grease. He leaned on his cane and wished that he could edge closer. He heard outside sounds, music from a radio playing "Milkman Keep Those Bottles Quiet." The Andrew Sisters sang "Been workin' on the swing shift all night, Turning out my quota all right" before the listener swiveled his radio dial to a news broadcast and dimmed the volume. All that Carl could make out was something about rationing stamps: coffee coupon number 24 had expired. It was time for tire inspection for owners of A cards. A small breeze blew scraps of paper and grit in his face. He felt grains in his mouth and spit them out like a smoker ridding himself of tobacco bits. A phone rang in the back room. A man answered it. He said something to the others and they rose, almost as if they were responding to a command. Doubtless Carl had been spotted and they were getting ready to scatter. Fine. Ruth and her camera were ready. The group did not panic. Behind the window they gathered some belongings and exited one at a time. Carl stayed out back watching, trying to make out faces. The light was insufficient.

"Zis is not ze front door."

It was the bartender who had talked about four-masters.

"I felt a little funny." Carl looked at the big man framed in the doorway. "I went outside for air."

"Air is chust as available outside ze front door."

"Well, this seemed to be the nearest exit. I was coming out of the bathroom—"

"Ze chon also has a window open." He seemed to like the word. "Ze chon is for customers. Ze back door is for employees only."

There was a sign to that effect over the door, and when Carl stepped back inside, he was shown it. He apologized profusely. To show that he meant no harm he went back to the bar and ordered another beer and left a dollar tip. When he left the place he expected to be followed, so he got in a cab and took it two blocks south, got out at a light and hid in the shadows of an art gallery on Madison Avenue. When he was certain that no one was tailing him, he walked back to the Blue Parrot. Across the street, people lingered at the outdoor tables, but Ruth was not among them. Perhaps she had decided to take a walk or go to ze chon. He sat down and waited five minutes. When she did not appear, Carl began to feel restive: this was not what they had planned. Ruth was supposed to wait here for him and together they would drop off the file.

A waiter with an air of good breeding and hard luck came to his table.

"Good evening."

"My date was supposed to meet me here," Carl said. "A tall young woman in a green dress with a blue scarf and blue beads. Medium-length ash-blond hair. You couldn't miss her."

"No indeed, sir—one couldn't miss her. She was here at this very table."

"And?"

"She left, sir. I had the impression she was late for something."

"Anyone with her?"

The waiter hesitated: a matter of delicacy, his manner said.

"Please," Carl insisted. "It's important."

"Well, sir. There was a gentleman at another table. Shortly after she left, he followed her."

"Did he catch up?"

The waiter tried to remember: "Not that I saw, sir. A large man, not at all her sort, one would have thought."

Carl closed his eyes and tried to black out the restaurant, the night, the message so clearly evident. Ruth Silver—shrewd, experienced, heads-up Ruth—had been delivered into the hands of the Butcher.

11

Niccolò Levi: Poland, 1944

CHILDREN FELL FROM the ark and drowned in the covenant, more children than there were cities, more names than there were numbers, more sorrows than there were synagogues. Colors drained from the sky; the faces were black and white, a newsreel like a scroll. He tried to fish the young from the sea, but the water was too powerful, the wind was icy and the cries got lost in the breakers. He reached for a pair of hands and held fast to little fingers. They forced him forward and he looked down in a sea as indifferent as glass and saw the agony of his own face, then through it to the depths, past his child and his child's child. The sky was silent. He opened his own mouth to curse the world and a sound like no sound he had ever heard issued like brass and cracked the clouds and psalms rained down like sparks and the sea gave up its souls and he pulled them from the water two at a time.

Whatever they injected in his arm made his body immobile, but it did nothing to his eyes. The bed was by the window, and he was free to look out and see the square sporadically filled with soldiers and prisoners. Whenever an inspection was due in the hospital room where he was being held, the doctor—the one who had done those things to Gina—came to Niccolò and injected him again. She never said more than, "Don't move. This is necessary." He almost always found his temperature suddenly rising and his face flushing. He passed out afterward, although he continued to hear the sound of boots and shouts. He was too exhausted to feel anything. There were times when he even forgot Gina. Then all of it would come back without warning and ignite his mind. He cried out. He called for the child; he saw the boy as an adolescent and as an adult. He saw Gina whole again. He saw himself acting on the stage in some sort of farce lit by candlelight, and one of the candles fell over and set fire to the curtain and the whole theater burned down and then the statue of Christ. He remembered that some of what he was seeing had really happened and then he awoke and knew that much worse had occurred.

Conscious, he looked helplessly out the window and saw children marched to the chambers and dashed against bricks and trees, sometimes Jews, sometimes gypsies, dark children with beautiful eyes, and he watched a man thrown alive into the ovens. He saw a man taking a child into the chamber and he saw a woman throw her baby away from her when she went in and a German killing the child with a stone.

He thought of how he used to laugh at Mussolini and how Hitler seemed to be Chaplin and how impossible it was to take him seriously. Only a German could take Hitler seriously and give him power, and then Hitler became Chaplin and danced with Neville Chamberlain and Mussolini around a burning Christ.

Through dreams and days, one image and one sound kept at him: the train. He saw it arrive on narrow tracks, spilling people from cattle cars. Soldiers would slide the doors shut again and the black engine with its black smoke would pull out of the camp to pick up more human fuel. In his inflamed mind he asked a question of the world: why did the trains keep coming? Planes were bombing Naples and there were rumors even in the hospital of English bombers over Germany. But no planes ever flew over Himmeldorf. Why were there no bombs? Why did neither the English nor the Americans come with their terrible weapons to kill this place, to destroy them all, the prisoners, Niccolò among them, but also the gas chambers, the Germans, the whipping stools, the mounds of human hair and artificial limbs and prayer shawls and gold teeth and rings?

No answer came, either in his visions or in his waking hours.

On the ninth day of his confinement he heard a familiar voice. Gina's, he thought at first. Then he knew it was not hers. It was not a woman's voice at all. It came from a physician moving toward him with a white smock and a steel knife. When the doctor got very close he bent toward Niccolò and he said, "We will have you out this evening."

It was the Professor. Niccolò tried to tell him what happened. His cracked lips moved and sound came out, but it was incoherent. Even Niccolò knew that what he said made no sense. Sounds were all he could utter; the harsh ululation of an animal. The Professor did all the talking. Niccolò was alive only because of the woman doctor, he said. She had protected him from the guards. "For experiments," she had explained. She had filled him full of drugs and kept him safe.

A flash of sanity and decency; or perhaps mere guilt. She had told the authorities that Niccolò was in the throes of typhus and for more than a week they had been afraid to touch him. Now he was due to be taken out and shot and thrown into the fires. Shot, if he was lucky. Otherwise, burned alive.

So the Professor and Lerma were going to get him tonight, not only from this hospital barracks, but from Himmeldorf itself. Niccolò listened without moving. He no longer cared about anything. Let them kill him and burn him. He would be with Gina. Their ashes would become part of the weather; a reproach to God.

"We will leave in the dark," the Professor said. "It is arranged. No truck will carry us out. They are all searched.

The only way out is the way in. The train. No guard could be bribed. But the engineer is a civilian, a Pole. A Catholic. He has seen too much. He vomits every day, the way the chimney vomits smoke. He has a place, a box under the coal. More than one person can fit. It was to be you and your—" Here the Professor trailed off. He straightened up. "You and I will stay together."

Together? People were only together in death, Niccolò argued. Only a low moan came out; he was still under the influence of the drug. But it was wearing off. Ideas were returning. Sometimes history gained velocity, he thought, and then people died young. Parents buried their children. Brides were slaughtered in their beds, young men were emptied of their souls before they ever had a chance to fall in love. War speeded things up and yet some men liked war. They lived on it, the way circus performers ate fire.

Maybe the Americans were like that. And the English. They could end the killing, but they didn't. They could bomb the camp, destroy the railroad tracks. But no. No bombs ever fell on Himmeldorf.

It was a puzzle that occupied him as he lay there, able, finally, to move his fingers, then his arms and legs. When it grew dark he swung himself to the side of the bed and rose. There was no pain, only a little wooziness that vanished as he dressed.

All the time he knew he was being watched by the Professor and by other eyes he had not seen before. New arrivals. People to be experimented on. He looked for the woman doctor, but she was nowhere around. He thought he might quietly pretend to be weak and dizzy if she were near, and when she came to him, he could press his hands on her throat and push her windpipe and close it forever. He began to sob uncontrollably.

"The doctor is taken care of," the Professor said. He added no details. Niccolò cried until there were no more tears in his body. In an hour, when the purity of the dark was broken only by a few floodlights, and the locomotive engine could be heard slowly building up steam, a voice from outside said "Now" in German.

Unsteadily Niccolò followed the Professor out of the room along the corridor and outside, sliding his back against the cold brick wall. The guards were being changed quietly, with a minimum of terse commands. The air had an iron chill, but there were occasional remissions when the wind paused. When the gusts resumed the steps went faster. The new guard slapped his hands together for warmth. The prisoners could see him walking away. He would continue for thirty yards, until he reached a pool of illumination coming from a cluster of light bulbs, then he would walk back toward the infirmary. He had another five yards to go and the wind picked up again and whistled in Niccolò's ears, as it must have in the guard's. When the Professor pulled at Niccolò's sleeve and pushed him forward, and they ran to a shed in the darkest part of the quadrangle, the guard did not turn. By the time the soldier reached the lights again, the prisoners were crouched at the side of the shed, breathing silently through their mouths. The Professor took off his laboratory coat. Underneath was a German soldier's uniform. He whispered: "After tonight we will no longer talk about myths. We will *be* myths."

He reached under the building, where a group of whitewashed rocks had recently been rolled. Niccolò had seen prisoners put them there yesterday, or the day before, at one of the hours when he could see without comprehending. Under the largest of stones the Professor found what he was looking for, another uniform: a drab brown shirt and oversized trousers. "They will have to do," he said, and Niccolò changed in the dark. He scarcely felt the temperature.

Because Niccolò no longer cared, he felt indestructible. For an instant he thought he could walk unmolested through this concentration camp, cutting the barbed wire and letting the prisoners loose. Then he shivered and knew that with one wrong word he would bleed to death where he crouched.

When the Professor beckoned him, Niccolò followed. Again, he had the sensation of watching himself as he ran between buildings and ducked into crevices and night-colored shelters. The prisoners took almost an hour to reach a place where they could see the locomotive shining under lights, warming up, almost ready to go. A military stationmaster held a chart and checked off whatever freight it was carrying, while soldiers examined the cars and the undercarriages. The engineer had his back to them. There would be only a minute to reach the train; less than that if the soldiers stayed until it pulled out. Niccolò and the Professor could not run without being seen and questioned and shot. Their only hope was to approach the train boldly, like soldiers, after the real soldiers had withdrawn.

They waited, cowering, shivering. The guards were in no hurry. Niccolò wanted to go out and show himself, to draw their fire. Any fear he felt was a habit, a leftover from the old days. But so was prudence, and the wish to testify. If somehow they could cross borders, get away to Switzerland and inform the world of what was going on here, the crystals of poison on the floor, the babies, the funeral pyres . . . Impossible. Still, one must try. Every day this train brought more to die.

He looked again. The soldiers were marching away briskly and steam left their mouths in great gusts. They looked like little locomotives echoing the large one. Its wheels moved very slowly as the engineer stuck his pale head out of the window and looked backward. There was an open space of about fifteen meters between the train and Niccolò and the Professor. When he heard the word "Now!" Niccolò ran across the space and followed the Professor to the other side of the locomotive, the side away from the barracks windows. The engineer had unhooked the door. The Professor swung it open and he and Niccolò dived in and lay on the floor, the noise of their movements lost in the engine's howl.

Niccolò expected the train to stop or be stopped. He cared and he was indifferent; he was harrowed and he felt exhilarated; all the contradictions lived in him as the cars picked up speed. He knew he was no longer rational. It was as if someone had boarded him the way he had boarded the train. The dead, maybe; all the souls who had perished at

Himmeldorf. His family, running his blood, pushing his sinews. His thoughts were no longer his own. They bounced in his skull and inflamed him. He heard their voices singing in the rails. The Professor was talking now, speaking at full volume for the first time in months, but the voice he heard was Gina's: "Remember, remember. Never forget and never forgive."

After two kilometers the Professor spoke in Polish to the engineer. Niccolò understood nothing, only that they would soon have to leave. The train slowed down. "The terminal is not far," the Professor explained. "We must leap off."

The night air was clear. The prisoners could feel it in their lungs as they came to the engine's open door, looking for all the world like a tired, bone-thin German soldier and his equally fatigued superior officer.

"Now!" the Professor said, and jumped. Niccolò followed him. He heard something behind him, something leaping off the train. In the vague glow of the train lights passing, he thought he saw another soldier. After all this, could it be a trap, he wondered, a warning to other escapees? Would he and the Professor be hauled back to camp and hanged as object lessons? He remembered the three nooses dangling from wooden gibbets near the entrance of the camp. And the sign in German: ARBEIT MACHT FREI. Ah no, he knew now, they had it wrong: death makes free. You die and there is no more prison. You become—who was it? The Professor told him once. Erebus. The god of vengeance.

Ahead of him he could see the Professor lying flat against the grassy slope. Ten meters away was the other soldier. Niccolò felt the ground for any sort of weapon. A rock was within reach. It weighed about as much as a grenade. When the soldier came close he would throw it. He could see the vague outline of the man against the scattering of stars. The German was coming closer, moving over the grass quietly, with exaggerated gestures, like a villain in a silent film. Niccolò's hand tightened on the rock. In another second he would throw it.

"Are you hurt?" came the soldier's voice.

Niccolò dropped the rock. It was Lerma. He had forgotten about her, and there she was in another uniform, her hair pushed up under the cap. She was as angular as a heron. But she was alive and she was out. Lerma hugged her friends and they huddled on the grass for warmth and for some sense of assurance that it had all really happened, that they had truly escaped from Himmeldorf.

"We have to rely now on the Poles," the Professor said. "We're dead without them. And maybe with them. But we must trust. We have no choice. In five minutes a cart will come by. It is our deliverance."

How much it delivered, even the Professor could not have predicted. It came clopping up, pulled by two dray horses; the most unprepossessing chariot in history, he said. The three buried themselves under the load of hay as the old farmer and his sons looked the other way and drove on. When they had gone a good distance, Niccolò heard a train moving over the tracks and saw searchlights beamed from the cars. The Germans were looking for the escapees, shouting indistinctly. They had killed so many, and they would torture and destroy so many more with their gas chambers and crematoria, what difference would three less victims mean? Niccolò wondered. If I were still sane, I would know the answer.

At noon the cart drew up at a small farmhouse near the outskirts of Cracow. No one spoke. The Professor was gestured inside by an old man. The others followed him. There was wine on the table, and black bread. Niccolò and Lerma and the Professor ate in silence and then they were led into another room where a small fireplace burned scraps of bark. Niccolò had not eaten in too long, and he knew that he would either have to sleep or be sick. He stretched out on the floor in his uniform, with a shoe under his head, and was unconscious within a minute. The others passed out shortly afterward. None of them had the energy to dream.

When Niccolò awoke it was still dark. But it was a different night. He had slept fourteen hours. He felt ravenous and filthy. The clothes stuck to his skin and the wool smelled sour. The others had risen and washed and

changed into peasant clothing, rough blue skirt and blouse
for Lerma, brown overalls and gray shirt for the Professor.
There was a basin of warm water for Niccolò and a square
piece of linen to wash with, and a straight razor and soap
made of lard and wood ash. Bathing seemed a remission
from some creeping and fatal disease. He washed for as
long as he could and then changed into a rough shirt and
patched trousers. The Professor took the German uniforms
and fed them slowly into the fire.

"The farmers have gone." He stirred the coals, making
certain that every thread was burned beyond recognition.
"Deliberately. We will be free to talk for a while. Unless
there is a raid. Sometimes the Germans come unan-
nounced."

Niccolò looked at him with wonder. "How did all this
happen? How did we get free? The uniforms, the wagon—"

"There are still Christians in Poland. Of course, the gold
did not hurt."

"What gold?"

"You know what gold."

"Not my—but I was the only one who knew!"

"What one can hide, another can find, Niccolò."

Lerma turned to him. "One of the Nazis found it," she
said. "Months ago. He was taking it away when we
discovered him. He offered to share it with us. How do you
like that? Share it. Well, he's sharing something else with
the Jews now: earth."

So not even the gold remained. Gone; everything gone.
Niccolò turned to them but he could not say a word. He
could not even cry.

"Nicco, Nicco," Lerma said. "Without the gold we
would not be saved."

"Saved? Cowering in a farmhouse is saved? And even if
we get free—"

"If we get free," the Professor said, and his eyes
glittered in the candlelight, "if we get free we become
symbols for the fallen. Myths."

The Professor kept talking, but Niccolò scarcely heard
him. He saw himself moving away from this burned earth,

this piece of Polish hell, to awaken the world. He would resound in the squares of Britain, on the streets of America, where happy, unfeeling people would stop doing what they were doing. They would not be able to sleep anymore, or eat, or even make love. They would turn in their beds and put their fingers in their ears, but still Niccolò's voice would come through, amplified by the terrible cries of the dead. He *would* become a myth. But how? How could he draw the attention of the world, of the leaders, of Churchill or Stalin or Roosevelt to the death camps? How could he make them care when they did not come near the camp, when the railroad tracks remained shiny and the roadbeds sturdy enough to bring in thousands to be murdered or made the victims of Nazi doctors?

There was only one way.

He told his friends. He expected them to say he was crazy; after all, he *was* crazy, he knew that. But maybe they were, too. Lerma's eyes were large and shiny, like those of a predatory bird. "What if Mussolini had been assassinated early?" she asked. "Better still, Hitler? Maybe a whole war could have been stopped."

The Professor disagreed. Where one Hitler had fallen another would have risen. "A different style, perhaps. Less ranting, but still a German in Germany, the cancer of Europe. Besides, you are speaking of evil men. But you want to kill good men."

"Churchill is not a good man. Roosevelt is not a good man." Lerma began to shout and the Professor gestured with his fingers so that she would speak in a softer tone. You never knew where the wind would take your words.

She talked on: The leaders, the Americans, the Englishmen, were indifferent to suffering. The headline printed in the partisan wall-newspapers and whispered by the prisoners: RESCUE THROUGH VICTORY. What did that mean? It meant waiting for children to die is all. It meant that the Allies did not care about victims.

Perhaps, the Professor countered, perhaps the leaders, the good men, did not know what was happening in the death camps. But his tone betrayed him. Impossible not to know; the Germans had announced their intentions about the Jews long ago. They had murdered them on the streets. There were pictures . . .

"Yes, but who could know about Auschwitz and Himmeldorf? Who would believe the gas chambers?"

"They know, they know," Lerma insisted. "We were not the first to escape. Two men got out, you know their names, Professor. You told me yourself. Got out and went to Switzerland."

"Well, yes, so they say, but—"

"No 'buts.' Evil feeds on indifference. Niccolò is right."

Niccolò *is right*. But what am I right about? Niccolò wondered. We are speaking of killing. But isn't the taking of any human life wrong? Not always. Kill one man and save millions . . . Awaken the world . . . *Kill Churchill or kill Roosevelt*.

He started to speak loudly, to push his tangled thoughts out into the room. Lerma was nodding, giving him support. The Professor's arguments grew less vehement. He lost ground each minute. Several times he attempted to interrupt Niccolò, then Lerma. They would not be outshouted. The Professor held up his hand as Niccolò was speaking: something was moving around outside. At this, the debaters quieted. They sat as silently as they had in the camp, waiting. Nothing happened.

"Perhaps I was wrong," the Professor whispered. "But you cannot be too careful." He went to the window with the candlelight at his back. A perfect silhouette, Niccolò realized a second later, when the bullets shattered the glass and doubled the Professor over. He was so thin that there was not much to kill. His body sounded like falling books as it hit the floor.

Lerma extinguished the candles and hissed in the dark, "This way!" Niccolò followed without thinking. She handed him a cold black pistol. As the two German soldiers plunged through the door he pulled the trigger without aiming. There were shouts of anguish and the men fell. Lerma kept firing until the Germans were torn by bullets. She waited for more soldiers or additional noise outside.

There was none. After five minutes Lerma groped in the dark, found a match, and lit a small candle. She felt the Professor's throat. There was no pulse. She and Niccolò gathered the soldiers' weapons and money and went outside. Lerma kept looking around to find her bearings. She pointed south. "Italy," was all she said.

Later, as they walked over fields she prated about her home, about how, by now, the Americans would have overrun the country and returned it to the partisans. Niccolò kept clutching his pistol, saying nothing, thinking everything. He hated the loud stage guns and he hated this thing he held in his hand, this German device made to kill enemies of the Reich.

And yet . . . and yet. Just as a shot in the theater startled everyone's attention and made them stare at the next scene, so this Luger could be used to awaken the world. How simple it was to shoot; how simple it would be to pull the trigger again, in the theater of the world. If the target were big enough.

12

Carl Berlin: New York, 1944

HE CALLED Captain Rosen and they waited together until the report came in. Body, unidentified female, blonde, about twenty-seven, found four A.M. on Third Avenue under the tracks of the El, at Ninety-fourth Street, not far from Yorkville. The siren wailed all the way to the site, but Carl heard nothing except the remembered conversation of Ruth and the sounds of the people talking behind the Blue Parrot. Surely the Butcher was one of them.

Carl saw five policemen and a photographer squeezing off flash bulb pictures with a Speed Graphic. The press had not yet arrived.

He walked to the body. It lay in a twisted mass on the street, the narrow ankles and calves flashing out from the torn green skirt. Her arms were so thin, Carl observed; thinner than he could recall. Ruth must have missed a lot of meals. We never spoke about hunger. He bent over the body. He reached for her hair when Captain Rose put his hand on Carl's shoulder and handed him the police report. Later, the murder was not difficult to reconstruct:

The group had left the Blue Parrot singly. For Ruth it was

only a question of which one to follow. She chose the woman, for two reasons. First, no one would be suspicious of a lady following a lady. Second, the target was built along the lines of the classic *Hausfrau*: a generous bosom, thick waist, large legs. She would not be agile. If she ran she could be caught.

But the subject simply walked south for block after block. If she suspected something, she gave no notice. There was no stopping to powder her nose and look backward in the mirror, no hesitating at store windows that might give back a reflection of pursuers. She just put one foot in front of another and marched deliberately downtown.

Not until the Fifties did it occur to Ruth that it was all too easy, that she herself might have been followed. She caught some movement in a doorway and edged closer to the parked cars lining the curb on the northbound side of Fifth Avenue. There was a halfhearted blackout, and an air raid warden in a white metal hat with a triangle on it was crossing the street, looking up at the lamp as if he expected to hear the sirens any minute. Ruth smiled at this innocence, this pale copy of a real war.

While she was smiling the air raid warden came near, matched her genuine grin with his glazed one, tipped his funny hat, and hit her with it.

The blow was so quick that Ruth was unable to defend herself. It glanced off her shoulder without much pain, but it threw her off balance. The car door was open and the hands that pulled her in seemed supernaturally quick. She wanted to shout or to scream, but she also wanted to stay where she was, in this large black Hudson, watching the faces, listening to the voices.

Her sounds were muffled by a thick coat thrown over her head. She could scarcely breathe. Her hands, then her ankles, were seized by other, stronger hands, and wrapped with rubber surgical tubing. It was done quickly and poorly. The circulation in her fingers and feet was almost cut off. She felt her hands grow icy. She could see nothing. The car had been pointed downtown, and from what Ruth could tell it continued that way for a few hundred feet to pick up the woman she was following. At least four other people rode in the car, all speaking German. A few words filtered through the coat: a man, older than the rest by the sound of him, was telling the others not to talk so much. There was some chatter about a meeting. The rest was garbled. The car continued downtown, and made a right turn. They were heading west. To New Jersey, Ruth surmised; there were farms in New Jersey and it would be possible to keep an arsenal in a barn. Maybe even an airplane. . . .

But the Hudson pulled to a halt after a series of stops and starts, presumably for traffic. It backed up and then drove in an irregular pattern. Voices echoed. They had entered a building redolent of machine oil and exhaust fumes. As the Germans piled out, Ruth could make out another word: Butcher. The Butcher would know how to handle her, someone said. All four doors slammed. She was alone in the car. One of the rear windows was rolled down and she could still distinguish voices bouncing around the stone walls. The older man told the others something in a sharp voice, a lot of *"Ihr müsst"*—you must—orders of some kind. Another car started up, followed by the sound of doors slamming. It drove off. There was absolute silence for a moment, then far off came the sound of traffic and a lonely horn, different from that of an automobile. Ruth had trouble identifying it; the coat muffled everything. It might have come from a large truck. Or a boat. Yes, she was certain now that it was a boat, that they were close to the waterfront, somewhere west of Eleventh Avenue.

"So. You are comfortable?" It was the older man's voice, modulated and derisive. The words were spoken with a great deal of refinement. "I know that it is difficult to breathe. We had no choice. We did not expect you."

Ruth said nothing. She moved her fingers. There seemed to be a little warmth coming to them, a sign that the tubing was working loose. For the first time since her capture Ruth was able to rub her hands together. She heard his steps outside on the concrete, slow and delicate—he had small feet. When he was close to the car he said, "The Butcher will know what to do."

The steps went away. But still the man was in the garage somewhere. She heard him clear his throat and then she heard the ring of a nickel in a telephone and a number of clicks. There was a flow of German, none of it audible.

He was giving the Butcher the address. While he talked, Ruth worked on her hands. It required more effort than she seemed able to summon. Her heartbeat reached a panic rate, and she had to lie still, convincing herself to calm down, to relax within the tension, like a prisoner in solitary confinement. There were worse places to be, she told herself. If you were in Europe you would be in a concentration camp, and if you were in a camp you would be in a chamber, dying. You would be in hell instead of one of its suburbs. She tried again. A hand was almost loose. Ruth lost track of time. There were no sounds. The older man seemed to have gone; the Butcher had not arrived. One or two minutes more and she could get her fingers free. Then she could work on her ankles.

She wondered how far the Butcher had to come to get here, and whether he would drive or take a subway, or whether he was close enough to walk. She knew his history; she knew that no one is named the Butcher without reason. Ruth shivered under the heat. She had almost worked her fingers loose when she heard the heavy steps.

They stopped and the older man said something inaudible by way of greeting. A heavier voice said, *"Guten Abend."* The light steps worked their way out into the night. Whatever was to happen, the old man wanted no part of it. The Butcher cleared his throat and spat. He came toward the car slowly. He seemed to drag a little and his steps were the steps of a heavy, ungainly man. The voice and tread laid to rest any idle notion that the Butcher was a woman. Unless she was one of those Valkyries in trousers you used to see in Hamburg bars before the war. The steps were only a few yards away from the Hudson now.

Ruth's hands were free. She reached down for her ankles. Her fingers searched blindly for the ends of the tubing. As she found one knot, the car door swung open. The Butcher shouted or growled. The sound was inhuman. Still wrapped in the coat, blinded by cloth, Ruth threw herself at the other door and found the handle. She pushed down on it and the door swung open. She threw herself outside, still clawing at the tubing at her feet. She could see nothing; she was wrapped in darkness, and this was in another darkness of the garage, and that was itself sealed by the darkness of the city. She fell down as she rolled toward the garage door; she knew that it lay somewhere to the rear of the car. The Butcher yelled again and then pushed something that creaked loudly. Oh, God, she thought, he's closing the overhead door. She heard it fall like a guillotine in slow motion. She hurled herself toward the sound, half falling, half limping, with the hysteria of a blind animal. Ruth felt the top of the door strike her head as she went forward. The force knocked her down and she rolled forward over and over on the hard dirty cement. She heard the door slam down behind her. She rose and tried to undo the cloth around her head and that was when she fell into the arms of two bewildered Scottish sailors, fresh off H.M.S. *Mountbatten*.

The rest Carl and Ruth had to piece together later, after the sailors had brought her to the 38th Precinct station on Forty-fifth Street.

"After you escaped, the Butcher attacked the first blonde he saw," Carl surmised. "The first with the green dress that everybody's wearing this year."

"*If* the Butcher saw anything," Captain Rosen said. "These nuts, they see what the movie in their head shows them. We had a man, twenty years old—last week he raped an eighty-year-old woman. What do you think he saw? Who the hell knows—but not an old lady." He shook his head. "This guy, maybe he thought it was you, maybe he hates green dresses—I don't know."

"Who was the murdered woman?" Ruth asked.

The captain shook his head. "A hooker. No ID yet. But

what other woman would be out on Eleventh Avenue at this hour. Probably working the sailors."

"At least we know who the older man was," Carl said.

"Who?"

"Martin Gower, obviously."

"And the Butcher?"

Carl shrugged.

"I can't really swear who the old man was. We have nothing," Ruth said, "except the location of the garage."

The captain broke in. "Worthless. Just a loading dock for trucks, owned by the American Ship Company. Totally legit. Hasn't been used in six months. Somebody stole the key. They never replaced the lock."

The three looked at each other with blank, hopeless gazes.

Then Carl sat back and smiled mirthlessly. "Welcome," he said, "to the all-powerful International Jewish Conspiracy."

13

Niccolò Levi:
Czechoslovakia, 1944

HE COULD never understand why it was called the underground. Except in the beginning he had never been in basements. The rest of the time he and Lerma had waited on the top floors of old farmhouses or in trucks and trains. Now he sat with her in a silo, peering out through a crack, watching the rainwater soak into the stubble of old corn.

It was their twenty-second shelter in two months. Almost all of Poland and Czechoslovakia was farmland, as the partisans pointed out, and the Germans spent most of their time in the cities. At the first opportunity, Niccolò and Lerma were put on a milk truck specially fitted for the hiding of refugees. The carrier was designed to hold 500 liters. It had a false end, near the cab, in which two adults or five small children could hide. The truck was often accompanied by unsuspecting German soldiers who stood on the running board or sat next to the driver, or even rode directly over the concealed cargo. The milk was commandeered by the Germans; Eastern Europe was the teats, an Austrian sergeant had put it, and the Reich was the calf.

Meat, grain, milk—all went west and the farm children had hollow bellies and mouths that watered and then went dry. The Poles and Czechs had little use for Italians and none at all for Jews. But there were always a few, a trusted handful, who hated Germans even more.

They kept Niccolò and Lerma moving southeast into Slovakia, to bunkers, toolsheds, holes in the walls of depleted granaries. There were rumors of the annihilation of the Warsaw ghetto, of the roundup of Jews everywhere in Europe. An underground newspaper said that the delegate of the International Red Cross had come with funds from America attempting to rescue the Jewish children of Slovakia. He had been turned aside. A shelter for such children, the Germans said, could turn into a "center of resistance." There was constant talk of the American beachhead attacks. The names Anzio and Monte Cassino were mentioned by peasants who had never heard of them before, never spoken of anything in Italy except Naples, because of the seaport and the postcards; and Rome, because of Pope Pius XII. Things must have been going badly for the Germans; they had dropped leaflets printed in English—an attempt to persuade American soldiers to surrender by sending them demoralizing messages. These papers had been passed hand to hand from Italy and one of the Czech farmers had one, creased and folded and dirty from too much handling, but still intact. It had a picture of a fat man reading a newspaper in bed, chewing a cigar. Next to him a pretty girl lay weeping, her slip pulled down below her breasts. She was showing a lot of thigh and the legend above her was in a simple script that Niccolò could translate: "Poor little Joan! She is still thinking of Bob. . . ."

The text described a New Yorker who was drafted, leaving his girl friend back in the States to work for the fat man, Sam Levy. The American soldier was obviously meant to feel a powerful longing for his girl, but he was also meant to hate Levy, the Jew. Niccolò wondered what an American soldier might think of the message, and what his girl might think of it, and whether there were any Sam

Levys taking advantage in America where everyone was safe and warm, and what President Roosevelt and his generals would feel about the leaflet. Maybe they liked the idea of the paper because it would make the soldiers angry and fight harder. But after the war, what would happen in the United States? Would the soldiers come home ready to go to war against the Jews? The question tugged at him for days, but the picture of the half-naked girl bothered him more.

As long as there had been a chance of Gina's survival, Niccolò f. ' 'ɔ more below his abdomen than a piece of old rope. After his wife's death, and the knowledge of the child's end, there was shock, and then the strangeness of mind and the exhaustion of escape. Today the exposed breasts of the girl stirred Niccolò and he began to regard Lerma as a woman instead of merely a comrade in arms, a fellow sufferer without gender.

He noticed the touches on his arm when she talked and the occasional gaze that stayed too long. But during the first weeks of flight she might have been talking to the stones. Now he listened to her melody as well as her words.

"There was a time," he began one afternoon, "a long time when I thought I would never again look at another woman. Gina—" That was as far as he got.

Lerma put her fingers on his lips. They were unexpectedly warm and her mouth was warmer still. Her face was flushed and felt hot on his cheeks and then on his chest. "This is insane," she said. "I'm too old for you—I don't even like making love—I never did . . ." But the next hour gave the lie to all she said and most of what he believed.

He had forgotten that nudity could be a reward; in the camps it was a punishment. The erotic came to him with the force of memory and dissolved all of his concerns. Afterward she cried, for no reason she could tell him; he fell asleep with his head on her belly and dreamed of summer.

In the dream a breeze came up and froze him. He awoke cold and alone and dressed with his teeth chattering. Lerma was below, talking hurriedly to some partisans. Niccolò went downstairs to find a stolid man with a pitchfork, speaking Italian with an Austrian accent:

"From here on, you travel during the day. The Germans are out in full force now, especially at night. They shoot to kill anything that moves after curfew." He looked at Niccolò. "You want to get back home, to Italy. With good fortune, maybe you can. Without luck—" He moved his hands in an empty gesture. "The Americans are halfway up the boot. Maybe more. The war will be more ferocious. If you ask me, you're running the wrong way."

"You are not Italian," Lerma said.

The farmer sighed loudly. "Well, it's your lives. You must leave within the hour. A patrol comes by soon. And of course you cannot go dressed like that. Any man who looks in the least young is stopped and interrogated. They tell me you were an actor, a master of disguise."

"I can put on costumes, yes. But a master—"

"You had better be good. They will be looking you up and down, the Germans."

"The thing to do," said Lerma, "is find something that will make them accept you without question. If you answer with that Italian accent, we're finished."

Niccolò went over the roles he had played: fat old Falstaff, the ancient courtiers in mustaches and beards, the priest who had fooled the Germans in Rome, the Nazi soldier.

To all of these the farmer shook his head. "They suspect everyone. They stop me, a big gray-haired farmer. Why should they believe you?"

"What should I be, then?" Niccolò asked. "An animal? Once I played the front end of a horse." He walked around the room in silence. "All right," he concluded. "I'll fool them all. I'll play a woman—and not just a woman but a fat woman. And not just a fat woman but a sick, a diseased, old, fat woman."

Lerma was wary of his sudden enthusiasm. "We're not looking for applause. We're walk-ons, you and I. Bit players. That's all we ever will be."

No, not I, Niccolò thought. Before I die, I will be

noticed. I will be a lead. Not the kind I wanted to be once. But a lead nonetheless. A great assassin. Perhaps the greatest. My reviews will be in the headlines.

He crammed his shirt with discarded hair and fur and rags, shreds too worn to use even for patches. There was not much surplus on the farms anymore. His lean frame was padded out with more clothing and with animal skins. Niccolò had always been a director's joy; he learned quickly. He walked like an old man at first, but Lerma corrected him and thereafter his imitation was flawless. Lerma herself was dressed as an old farm woman, her hair streaked with chalk and her eyes disguised behind the spectacles of a war widow whose husband had been killed in a bombing raid two weeks before. When the light was just over the treetops, the farmer pointed south and gave them a destination, the town of Zistersdorf, and sent them on their way.

Zistersdorf was eight kilometers from the farmhouse. Not a great distance ordinarily, but today it was a voyage to the sun. The Germans were everywhere. Soldiers dotted the landscape and lined the roads. Columns of infantry and open trucks were transporting troops east and west. There were even some tanks wandering the low snow-covered hills. Occasionally the soldiers looked at the two old ladies moving with great deliberation, picking up an occasional seed or branch, scrounging for firewood or some pitiful scrap to eat.

Niccolò felt a strange renewal. It was the business of sleeping with Lerma, he supposed. Then he realized that it was not Lerma at all; it was the play in which he was acting. All these costumes, all this pretense—it was a star turn in some drama whose outcome was as unknown to the actors as it was to the audience. The play was incredible in parts, and too loud, and the cast was inexperienced and kept making mistakes, blowing their lines, exiting in the wrong direction, ad-libbing passages that the playwright had never written. But it was theatrical, and Niccolò Levi had a major role. Previously a farmer, a Nazi, a clergyman. Today a farm woman. Tomorrow, who knew? A black paratrooper, maybe: he had seen one once on the front page of *Il Giornale*. Or a Chinese—there was one who had a restaurant in Florence. He could mimic the oriental gestures even now. Or a blond sailor, a Scandinavian . . .

He was absorbed in his own musings, but not so absorbed that he forgot to walk like a fat old woman helping her gaunt friend. The act caused them to progress with painful deliberation. Niccolò and Lerma stayed in the fields for two hours without ever losing sight of troops. No one stopped them. They seldom spoke; there was no telling how far sound could carry, with its giveaway Italian accents. The wind did strange things with the human voice; sometimes you could hear a sergeant give orders in German almost a kilometer away.

They were undisturbed until Czerny. The road was clear and the latest company of infantrymen was moving out of sight, into a pine grove near the horizon. Niccolò knew that they were less than five kilometers from the Austrian border, if borders meant anything anymore. He was not tired, and Lerma still walked, under her artificial limp, with determination and energy. They heard a voice: *"Halt! Stehenbleiben!"* behind them and they turned. A smiling lieutenant stood leaning against a tree, negligently examining a pistol. He did not aim it, he simply motioned for the peasants to approach. As far as Niccolò could tell, the man was alone, catching up with the troops who had just pushed on.

"Old woman!" the German said. They stopped. "Come here. Where are you waddling?"

"Take a chance," Niccolò whispered to Lerma.

"If you please," she answered the lieutenant in his language, "we are going home."

He approached them.

"You are Italian?"

"We were. Before the war."

"Italy is a long way off."

"Please God, we will go there again some day."

"And if it does not please Him?" He was only a step away.

Lerma shrugged. The German looked at her, then at her body. He smiled. He looked at Niccolò with a withering grin. The lieutenant moved as if to turn away. Then he whirled on them. He reached out to Niccolò and took hold of his shoulder.

"Well, well. Thin bones for such a fat old cow." Niccolò could smell liquor on his breath. So it was going to be like this; the sober SS men would pass him by and some drunken soldier would catch him. The lieutenant said "cow" again under his breath, then took hold of the fat lady's breast, or what was supposed to be her breast. The cloth bosom collapsed under his hand. "I knew it," he said, waving his gun unsteadily at Niccolò. "What would a farm woman be doing with so much powder on her face?"

Oh, God, Niccolò thought, now I will have to kill him.

The soldier glared at him with large, astonished open blue eyes. His mouth started to say something but speech died in his throat. The pistol dropped from his hand and he fell forward. Astonished, Niccolò stepped away. The soldier had forgotten Lerma. She stood over the bleeding man with a large bread knife in her hand. With calm efficiency Lerma bent over and took the pistol and unbuckled the cartridge belt.

Niccolò stared down at him. The man was still breathing. Blood seeped through his tunic. It seemed to stain Niccolò's vision. For a moment he was uncertain of the hour or the place.

ché s' approchia la riviera del sangue, in la qual bolle qual che per violenza in altrui noccia.

The river of blood draws nigh in which everyone boils who by violence injures others.

"Do you think he would hesitate one moment over you?" Lerma snapped. Niccolò made no answer; he was wondering again: if I act like an animal, what separates me from the Germans? A dangerous idea, he knew. Start thinking that way and he would never kill at all, never seek vengeance, never arouse this dormant world. There was neither time nor space for sentiment. He looked away and all was right again; they were on their way. Lerma had managed to tuck the belt and pistol under her skirts.

Women knew how to live in such clothing, Niccolò thought. He felt hopeless in his costume. It would only be a short while before the soldiers missed their company commander and came back for him. When they found him, alive or dead, they would begin searching. Everyone would be stopped. Perhaps a trooper would remember the two women. Niccolò turned to Lerma as they scurried through a birch copse. The trees were bare; there was no place to hide or to change their costumes. She knew what he was thinking. "Yes," she said, "we must stop somewhere and change."

"To what this time? Stones?" Niccolò looked at her eyes and wondered if she was as possessed as he was.

"Nicco." She looked around. Her eyes settled on a distant group of outbuildings. "We have no time. We have to separate. You know it. So do I."

"And if only one of us makes it? Then what?"

"What you can do, I can do," she said. "I believe what you believe."

"You would kill?"

"You just saw me."

"A German soldier is not the same as an American leader."

"Niccolò Levi, you and all the dead will have to trust me. As I must trust you."

She kissed him. He could feel her body through all the garments, but there was nothing erotic about their embrace. From a distance, Niccolò thought, if anyone could see them it must seem the parting of two old sisters instead of a murderess and her accomplice planning bigger deaths.

"Where will you go?" Niccolò looked around, wondering where he himself would flee. It hardly mattered; away from here is all he wanted, south, through Austria somehow, to Italy.

"Maybe someone in those houses will know. We have to take a chance."

"Listen, Lerma—"

"No, Nicco, you listen to me."

Her suggestion had the unassailable logic of madness. Niccolò watched until she was halfway to her destination, then retraced his steps to the lieutenant. The German had stopped breathing but his body was still warm. Rapidly, as if it had been rehearsed in some other life, Niccolò exchanged the old woman's clothes for the dead man's. The tunic was blood soaked, but that, too, was part of the new plan. Niccolò would limp along like a wounded soldier. He tied a rag about his throat; if anyone stopped him he would pretend to be shell-shocked and speechless. He dragged the officer's body to the copse and covered it as best he could with branches and leaves. Maybe its discovery would be put off by another ten minutes. He would need them.

He went off again, this time in a slightly different direction. He could no longer see the houses where Lerma had headed. He came to a wide, unpaved road. Tanks had been over it; their tracks had bitten deep into the soil. Ahead, there were black dots. Horses pulling something. In back of him he could see more dots. He would have to get off the road immediately. He stood at the side, near an outcropping of black rock, watching the cart approach. If driven by farmers, it could prove his salvation. But as it came closer he could see that it was not a cart. There were German letters on the front: KRANKENWAGEN. Ambulance. Very well then, he would be the wounded officer. He stepped into the road. The horses halted. An old peasant was driving and he dismounted. No one came out of the ambulance. "Can you walk, Lieutenant?" he asked in German.

Niccolò nodded.

The driver went to the back of the old wagon and opened its doors. He motioned Niccolò in. A lantern provided some weak illumination. The doors slammed behind him. At first he thought the ambulance was empty, but in the rear, sitting on a makeshift cot, a youth, sixteen or seventeen, looked at him and held a rifle at Niccolò's heart. "Put your hands on your head," he said. "Don't give me any excuse to shoot you, German."

This madhouse of a world, Niccolò reflected. Wearing a Nazi disguise, where do I wind up? In the hands of partisans. In Italian he tried to explain what had happened. The boy understood, but he was unconvinced.

"The last one I had in here. Yesterday." He shifted his feet, but the barrel remained pointed at Niccolò. "He said he was forced into the Army. He said he was really a Communist, a student of literature. I had him empty his pockets. Inside were five gold teeth. I think they were the teeth of Communists. He was still protesting when I shot him."

He ordered Niccolò to empty his tunic pockets. It was the first time Niccolò had even looked in them. A wallet came out; it had pictures of a young, dark-haired woman. Thank God, he thought, there were no children. He could not remember whether the lieutenant had worn a wedding ring. The trouser pockets were empty except for a comb and a few coins.

"No gold?" The boy bared his teeth. "Very good." He took hold of the wallet and leafed through it.

"Look," Niccolò said, "I am not a German. I am an Italian."

"The Italians are brothers of the Germans."

"No. Only the Fascisti, not the other Italians. And certainly not the Jews."

The boy looked at him. "A Jew! You? How can a Jew survive in this land?" He laughed dryly.

Niccolò looked at the rifle and he talked. He spoke rapidly about Himmeldorf, but he could not speak about his family. He could not evoke them even if it meant his life. He mentioned the Professor and Lerma and some of the costume changes and as he rambled he heard his own voice harsh in his own ears. The boy seemed to be listening closely and Niccolò wondered whether he should go for the rifle and what would happen if it went off. The horse snorted and the ambulance shuddered to a stop. He heard orders in German and some shouts from a distance. Some one was fussing with the lock.

"Lie over here," the boy ordered, "with your back to the door."

Niccolò assumed the position of a grievously wounded soldier. The doors opened and shadows crossed the light. Men were bringing in someone, a soldier hurt in a skirmish with peasants. He had lost blood. There was plasma, but no time, voices said. The captain must be taken immediately to the field hospital. It was a long way. They must leave now. No one would be able to accompany the ambulance. The boy and the driver must do it themselves.

"Looks as though you have to take care of two men," someone said. It sounded authoritarian, but with Germans you never knew. It could be a general or a private. "The lieutenant—"

"Very badly wounded," the boy reported. "I have done what I could. If he pulls through it will be a miracle."

"Then we will order a miracle. Move on."

The doors shut violently and the ambulance lurched forward.

The boy lit another lantern, set up the can of plasma, and inserted the needle in his unconscious patient.

"If you wanted to kill me, why are you saving him?" Niccolò wondered aloud.

The boy had no answer. He made a meaningless motion that reminded Niccolò of the Romans. "He may be useful." The boy adjusted the lamp. They rode on in silence.

"You believe me, then," Niccolò said finally.

"You, too, may be useful."

Distant bombs began to rattle the walls of the ambulance. The sound of strafing came near and faded in the engine growl of a plane.

Half-awake, Niccolò progressed from fear to indifference to confidence. He knew that from the outside his prison was a first aid truck. It could move with relative safety. Of course, there was always the danger of inspection or attack. But it was not a prime target. It could plod like a turtle over this land, with a hard wooden carapace to protect it from the world. Niccolò hardly noticed when the boy fussed with a jar and shifted his position. The next move was wholly unexpected: he thrust a cloth in Niccolò's face. The odor was reminiscent of a hospital. There was not much strength in Niccolò's arms; by the time he recognized the aroma of chloroform he was under its control. Yet even then he felt no panic. They would not drug me if they meant to kill me, he concluded. To someone, I am worth more alive than dead.

He had no idea how long he was under. He was dimly aware that the ambulance had become motorized; he heard the engine knocking and growling and he could feel the hills. Niccolò shook himself into full consciousness. He felt pain from his stomach, hunger without appetite, and he watched the boy carefully. Other soldiers had been taken on. There were four Germans lying on makeshift cots.

The boy came closer. Niccolò wished that he had taken the pistol. "I know you were telling me the truth," the boy whispered. "When you were unconscious I went through your papers. I was going to kill you quietly and dump you on the road. When I took hold of your arm the sleeve ripped and I saw the tattooed number. Then I knew."

"And now what?" Niccolò sat up and rubbed his eyes. The place still stank of chloroform.

"We are in the south. We have taken on men and unloaded others, saved a few, killed a few. Sometimes the officers have papers on them. My father still drives, I still run this hospital on wheels."

"Let me go," Niccolò pleaded. "Now that you know what I am, release me."

"Release you? Here?" The boy gave a lighthouse smile. "This is a battlefield we're heading for. It would be like releasing you in a fire."

"I have escaped worse fires."

"We will release you at the proper time."

"And when will that be?"

"Eventually. Eat something. It will help to pass the time. Unless you want to sleep some more."

Niccolò accepted the dry bread and chocolate. The feast

took almost an hour to consume. He drank slowly from a jug of water and listened to the explosions. One was close enough to shake the earth beneath them and the ambulance stopped for a moment. The boy knocked on the back of the truck and a reassuring knock came from the driver.

"Go on, Papa!" he shouted. The boy's mouth was open as the bomb tore up the road and spilled the ambulance on its side. The afternoon air was cold and it seared Niccolò's lungs as his face hit the dirt. It was several minutes before he realized that the ambulance had hit a mine, that the blast had thrown the wounded man far from the place of impact, and that the red in the grass was the blood of the boy.

It was dusk. Men were speaking in a tongue he could not make out. Something slurred and difficult. A large soldier, unshaven and carrying an automatic rifle, spat out his words: "Get up, all of you!" In the fresh night air, Niccolò realized that he was surrounded by a small hostile group. An occasional cigarette illuminated three or four faces. All of the soldiers were in strange uniforms, and all of them were heavily armed. The wind cleared Niccolò's head. He recognized the language they were whispering in now. He started to laugh idiotically even when he was asked questions, until a captain slapped him, hard, across the mouth. Even that failed to darken his spirit; the officer was yelling at him in German: high-school German with a heavy American accent.

14

FDR: Washington, 1944

NO MATTER HOW self-important its popinjay of a leader, no matter how ham-handed and hair-oiled his agents, the Bureau never failed. It was absurd, Roosevelt thought, to worry about domestic crises when the FBI was around. Nothing was too minute for them to uncover, and their files were the stuff of history. He had always liked reading history; as a boy he had absorbed the stories of the distant Roosevelt, Teddy, in the White House, hunting, winning the Nobel Prize. Now Franklin Roosevelt knew that one day he would enter the history books as a leader, as *the* leader of the war years. This stuff, of course, would be left out. Nobody would be interested in Lucy. Certainly no one would read an FBI file about some hysteria in Madison Square Garden. It was strictly Eyes Only stuff. Besides, nobody would ever believe it.

This fellow Ben Hecht, for instance. A Hollywood writer was all he was; a hack. Well, maybe something more. The entire Roosevelt family had applauded *The Front Page*. Still, the playwright was hardly a knowledgeable historian or military expert. All that qualified him to criticize the administration was the fact that he was a Jew. And not much of a Jew at that, if the file was correct. Nonobservant. American-born. A loudmouth, a nut. He had organized a meeting in New York at the Ninety-fourth Street house of George S. Kaufman. Its purpose: to raise money for the Jews of Europe—and also to discredit the Roosevelt administration. And Churchill. And Stalin. Hecht had spoken for a long time about the mass murders, the death camps. He demanded that the ports of Palestine be opened—a fine thing that would be, Roosevelt muttered, with King Ibn Saud standing there, humiliated, the one dependable ally America had in the Middle East.

Publicize the atrocities in Europe, Hecht insisted, place ads in the paper, go on the radio, pressure the leaders to do something. It was the voice of a fanatic, said the report, and the audience gave it the response it deserved. When Hecht finished his diatribe, half a dozen of the guests rose and filed out silently. Edna Ferber, the novelist, shouted, "Who is paying you to do this wretched propaganda? Mr. Hitler? Or is it Mr. Goebbels?" Beatrice Kaufman, George's wife, told Hecht, "I'm sorry it turned out like this. But I didn't expect anything much different. You asked them to throw away the most valuable thing they own—the fact that they are Americans."

Nevertheless, Hecht persisted. Fanatics are always stubborn. He ran ads in the *Times* that enraged Stephen Wise. One of the pieces included a poem:

> Hang and burn, but be quiet, Jews,
> The world is busy with other news.

Infuriating. Sophomoric. And there were plans to stage a pageant: We Will Never Die. It would take place in Madison Square Garden and very likely it would raise the money Hecht had failed to win at Kaufman's. It was also certain to embarrass the administration and emphasize the sufferings of the Jews in Europe. Always as if no one else were suffering. What about the French? What about the Chinese? What about our own boys at Anzio and Midway?

True, no one herded them into gas chambers and cremators, but there were other ways to die.

Here was another report: the President and Stalin and Churchill had signed the Moscow Declaration of 1943. "Germans who take part in the wholesale shooting of Italian officers or in the execution of French, Dutch, Belgian or Norwegian hostages or of Cretan peasants, or who have shared in slaughters inflicted on the people of Poland in the territories of the Soviet Union which are now being swept clear of the enemy, will know that they will be brought back to the scene of their crimes and judged on the spot by the peoples they have outraged."

And this forthright statement, this hard line had been criticized by Hecht for not mentioning the word Jews anywhere in the Declaration. Didn't they know, these Hebrew lobbyists, how delicate things were? How rigid Britain was about keeping Palestine free of troublemakers? How Stalin felt about the Jews?

Couldn't anyone understand anything? Roosevelt tried not to think about Goldman again; it had been years since he had even mentioned Goldman. But the President realized, sitting there on this headachy morning with the sun hurting the backs of his eyes, and the metal weighing on the sixty-two-year-old legs, and the notion of another campaign crowding the mind, that he had never forgiven the man. Goldman, that bastard who had been a great financial backer of the Roosevelt campaign for governor in New York so long ago; Goldman, who had pulled out and into the Republican camp only a month before the elections. In the face of Hecht's plans, it was hard not to think of Goldman as a Jew—or of the Jews as Goldmans.

And now Hecht was working on Tom Dewey, Republican governor of New York, trying to get him to issue a proclamation declaring the day of Hecht's pageant as a New York State Day of Official Mourning, in memory of the massacred Jews of Europe. And on top of that was the transcript of a tapped telephone call from Hecht to Bernard Baruch. The redoubtable Barney, millionaire Democrat, had confided to Hecht: "I have had a two-hour talk with

President Roosevelt about the Jews and the Jewish problem. I have spoken also to Governor Dewey on the same subject. I can only tell you as a result of these talks that, despite my having been a lifelong Democrat, I would rather trust my American Jewishness in Mr. Dewey's hands than in Mr. Roosevelt's."

All this in an election year. If it ever got out. . . . Roosevelt held his head in his hands. After a while he straightened up. All right, if three letters on a piece of paper made all that difference he would supply them. But God help the man who pressured him for any more. He took up his old gold fountain pen and began jotting on the yellow notepad: "In one of the blackest crimes of all history— begun by the Nazis in the day of peace and multiplied by them a hundred times in time of war—the wholesale systematic murder of the Jews of Europe goes on unabated every hour. . . ."

It would run in the newspapers not only here but abroad. Let Tom Dewey make his declarations; let Ben Hecht have his show. What was needed from the White House was not action but words. There was never any lack of words in Washington.

DOCUMENT   FOR THE PRESIDENT   EYES ONLY

RECEIVED ALARMING REPORT THAT IN FUEHRER'S HEAD-QUARTERS PLAN DISCUSSED AND UNDER CONSIDERATION ACCORDING TO WHICH ALL JEWS IN COUNTRIES OCCUPIED OR CONTROLLED GERMANY NUMBERING 3½ MILLIONS SHOULD AFTER DEPORTATION AND CONCENTRATION IN EAST BE EXTERMINATED AT ONE BLOW TO RESOLVE ONCE FOR ALL THE JEWISH QUESTION IN EUROPE STOP THE ACTION REPORTED PLANNED FOR AUTUMN METHODS UNDER DISCUSSION INCLUDING PRUSSIC ACID . . . IN-

FORMANT STATED TO HAVE CLOSE CONNECTIONS WITH HIGHEST GERMAN AUTHORITIES AND HIS REPORTS GENERALLY SPEAKING RELIABLE. . . .

DR. R. REIGNER
REPRESENTATIVE WORLD JEWISH CONGRESS
SWITZERLAND JULY 1942

CABLE SENT TO DEPARTMENT OF STATE. AMBASSADOR LELAND HARRISON NOTES ABOVE CABLE IS BASED ON A "WILD RUMOR INSPIRED BY JEWISH FEARS."

15

Carl Berlin: New York, 1944

CAPTAIN ROSEN left them with the standard admonition not to leave town. Ruth and Carl left the station and walked for about an hour in silence. When she began to talk it was in manic bursts, followed by dejection. She was certain to have another mission soon, how could she promise not to leave town? Besides, what was the use of staying here? She was in more danger in New York than where the war was, 5,000 miles distant. In Europe she had been shot at, pursued by the SS, but never tied up like a calf, blindfolded, helpless. No, this had to happen in America.

They walked around the peripheries of Central Park. The air was clear and it brought some color to their faces. Ruth cried easily and she let Carl hold her, but when he tried to kiss the tears, she backed off.

"I don't want to feel this way," she said. "I don't want to feel any way at all. I want to be numb."

"If you were numb you wouldn't be Ruth," he told her.

"I was afraid. For the first time in years I was terrorized."

"It's a normal thing, fear."

"Not for me, Carl. For what I do, fear is a luxury. No room in the budget."

"Stay with me," he said. "I'll take care of you."

"No. That would only be encouraging the fear. When you live with someone, you set down roots. And it hurts too much when you pull them up."

Carl didn't argue. He knew she was right. There was a generation in Europe, and even here, that would always be afraid of any sign of permanence. Marriage, a child, a home, even a collection of books could be taken away. A knock on the door and you would have to run. You would not allow yourself to get attached to possessions or people because there would come a night when you would pack quickly and be gone. Roots would catch at your feet, force you to fall, make you afraid. Was it Hitler who did it? he wondered. Or was it the general vileness of the times, when even the friendly countries, the Allies, stank of hypocrisy and decay. The Moscow Conference last fall, for instance: Roosevelt, Stalin, Churchill sounding their customary harrumphs about Nazi victims, citing even Cretan peasants. But not Jews, never Jews. Except, of course, in an election year. We would hear about the Jews this year.

He stopped himself. For one thing, his stomach was too tight; more important, there was Ruth. He could not let her slip into despondency. He took her to downtown along Broadway and they went to the first movie house they saw.

The picture was *Thunder Rock*, a British import, something obviously concocted to keep up the spirits of the home folk. Carl put his arm around Ruth's shoulder and she neither refused his attention nor welcomed it. Her eyes never looked away from the screen. Michael Redgrave played a man, disgusted with modern life, who becomes a lighthouse keeper. Soon, the ghosts of passengers of a nineteenth-century shipwreck began to materialize through the walls, arguing with him, convincing him to descend from his eyrie and return to real life on the mainland. By the time Redgrave was ready to come down and fight for Britain, Carl had put on his coat. But even after they got to their feet and headed up the aisle, Ruth kept looking back for one last glimpse of the film. Her eyes shone.

He wanted to take her somewhere for a meal or a drink, but now Ruth only wanted to talk. Something in the film started her. "A metaphor for madness," she called it. She had known plenty of people who had gone into lighthouses at the beginning of the war. They were still in them when the Nazis came, and they kept babbling to ghosts even when they were led away. To them the voices of the dead were more real than the commands in the street.

She began to shiver again. Carl insisted on feeding her. She kept shaking her head and refusing all the way to his apartment. Her eyes kept staring ahead as if she were still watching the film. He poured out a scotch and soda and made one for himself and called Charlie's and told them to send up a bunch of ham and cheese sandwiches.

"What kind of bread?" Charlie asked.

"Rye."

"What kind of rye? Jewish?"

"Yes, Jewish. Everything Jewish."

"Jewish ham also?"

"Yeah. And Jewish beer, Jewish cheese, Jewish lettuce."

"I hope you got enough Jewish money."

He hung up. Ordinarily Carl liked kidding around with Charlie; sometimes it was the only voice he heard all weekend, except for the denatured babble of the radio news. But just now he had no wish to talk to anyone, only to listen to Ruth. It was not until her second drink that she stopped shivering enough to resume.

"I never let myself be afraid on missions. Even the last time. I was in Denmark to take twenty girls, the oldest of them eleven years, to Sweden. More than a week I kept them well ahead of the SS. The Germans knew we were there, but they couldn't find us. Still, by the last day they were only an hour behind. We left in the morning because at night there were patrols who shot at anything and besides you couldn't see the mines in the dark. It was a tiny trawler, but very swift. We got through the German coast guard before they could react. But the Germans knew what had happened. They sent a boat to stop us. I don't know what kind; a fat sort of boat with a machine gun on the front. We were not hard to find."

Ruth sipped more slowly, and she studied the objects around the room, the bookshelves, the table, the glass in her hand. She was no longer simply an instrument of recollection.

"America, America," she said. "Even the scotch is better than you get in Scotland."

"You forget, I'm in the liquor business."

"Yes, and I'm a translator for the Bolivian Government. If you don't believe me, look at my passport. Have you ever seen a Bolivian passport?"

"No."

"It's green. Like money. And it comes with one condition. After you buy it, you sign a paper agreeing never to set foot in the country."

She sat back and the memory rose again.

"We picked up all the speed we could. The girls huddled below. Some of them started crying for the mothers who were dead and gone. I never said anything to them, just showed them a stern face with an occasional smile to let them know everything was all right. Being shot at was just one more pebble in the shoe, I wanted to think. We had already hidden out in houses and barns and sheds. It was almost like a game to them. The German boat was not gaining on us, but I saw some sailors jumping on the deck, cheering. I looked over the side and saw what might have been a great white winding snake made of bubbles. It passed underneath us, and I realized what it was. A torpedo. The Germans had loosed a torpedo at our ship because we were carrying children! Children!"

She shook her head. "The first two missed us. The third did not. I made the girls cling to pieces of wood. A Swedish cutter picked us up an hour later. Twelve out of twenty. We looked until night but never found the other eight."

Carl came and sat by her on the long black leather couch. "Ruth, what you have to remember is the twelve you saved, not the ones you didn't."

"What I remember is never being afraid, not once. Not even in the cold water. I was not afraid of bullets, torpedoes, the Gestapo, anything. But here I still tremble."

"Ruth," he said again, "stay."

She shook her head and he held it in his hands and then kissed her face and her mouth. He moved his hands to her long waist, then slowly up to her rib cage. The heels of his hands met her breasts. He hesitated a long time. She put her hands on his neck and loosened the top buttons of his shirt and ran her fingers around his back.

It was an old gesture, with a hundred echoes.

"The hell with roots," he told her. "We'll make do with leaves and seeds."

There was a knock on the door; a boy was there with the sandwiches and beer. Carl tipped him too much and left the food on top of his large Brunswick record player.

It was still there, untouched, when the two of them rose from bed, starving, at sunrise. They had fallen asleep and awakened and made love again, and then slept fitfully. Carl had enjoyed a rare dreamless night, but something chased Ruth in her sleep and she was glad to be awakened.

"Beer for breakfast." She opened the bottles.

"Liquid bread," Carl said.

They took the food back to bed with them and set up a spread and for the first time since Carl had seen her, Ruth laughed as she tied a pillowcase around her throat for a napkin, just as the phone rang with a message that Carl was to go to the office immediately. There was no explanation.

He shrugged, got dressed and shaved, kissing her as he made swoops into the bedroom. He left her laughing and playing his old scratchy records. The music of her voice and of Puccini mixed in his mind until he reached headquarters. He was only half surprised to find the Old Man sitting in a chair, frowning.

"Sorry to rouse you out," he said. "But I don't like to chastise employees too late in the day. I haven't the energy after lunch. Too much wine, I expect."

Typical, Carl thought. "Too much wine, I expect." The man has been dining out with too many British Intelligence officers. Next thing you know, he'll start taking the lift and putting his luggage in the boot.

The Old Man looked discomfited. "This business with the Butcher," he said. "Sit down. We are far from pleased at the way things have gone."

"If it means anything, I'm not pleased either," Carl offered.

"It *doesn't* mean anything. They know we're after them, and they know they got the wrong woman, and they know who you are."

"Maybe," Carl agreed. "But nobody's made a play for me yet. Why don't we just send out an all-bureaus roundup? Kind of a big, sweeping—"

"It can hardly be a secret to anyone that there will be an invasion of Europe this summer." The Old Man took a lot of time lighting his pipe. Carl was certain that he carried it largely for effect. When the right people were looking he liked to rub the briar against his nose to bring out the grain.

Carl tried again: "All the more reason to round up the Germans now, before—"

"All the more reason to let them alone. We've cracked their code. But we have no assurance they haven't cracked ours. If they know about invasion plans, sooner or later something will go out on their wires. They'll start something here—bombing a harbor, sabotaging a factory or a railroad. Something to keep our attention diverted. Right now, they're alerted, frightened all over again. We have to give them more time to come out of the woodwork."

"Including the Butcher."

"Yes, including the Butcher. Although he's very likely a psychopath. People like that don't take orders well. They may kill him. We wouldn't like that, but it can't be helped."

No, Carl reflected, you wouldn't like that. Much better to have a few more poor whores murdered until it was convenient to haul in the bastard, to the accompaniment of flashbulbs and full coverage: POLICE DRAGNET PAYS OFF— BUTCHER CONFESSES AFTER GRILLING.

"I take it you're unhappy," Carl said. "Why don't you replace me?"

"Send you overseas, is that it? Into the briar patch."

"Well . . ."

"More valuable where you are. The Germans know you—*Nummer Vier.* No, you'll stay here and draw them out. Despite this unpleasantness, *nothing has changed.* Clear?"

"Clear."

The Old Man got up. "Oh, and about the woman. She's a very good agent, one of the best. But, like you, she has other—interests. She told you about Denmark."

"No, sir."

"Don't be a fool. We know she did. We've had a microphone in your place from the beginning."

"All right, yes, she told me about Denmark."

"Very admirable, leading the children out. What she failed to add is that she should have been in Italy. We had a plane waiting, several stations on the underground were detained. She showed up two weeks late. A bad business. We sent her here to chasten her for a while. Fat lot of good that did."

"She's tired," Carl said. "She's seen too much, been too many places."

"We've all seen too much."

"I haven't."

"You will." The Old Man showed him out.

When Carl came back to his apartment, Ruth was in the bathtub. At another time he would have wheedled until she opened the door. He would have taken off her bathrobe and sloshed back into the tub with her and tried to make them both forget what they did to make a living, if you could call this living. Instead he shouted a greeting, waited for her reply, and walked slowly around the living room looking for the device the Old Man had planted. It was in none of the expected places: the frame around the Chagall, the molding, the top of the venetian blinds. He found it in the base of a large wooden table lamp, painted brown and recessed in the walnut. The other microphone was in the bedroom, deep in the windowframe. It, too, had been placed with great efficiency. Carl found his small electric fan and set it beside the living room lamp. He turned it to On, aimed it directly at the microphone, then adhesive-taped a piece of paper to the fan screen where it flapped against the blades.

"What's that racket?" Ruth called from the bathroom.

Without replying, Carl went to the bedroom and turned his radio to the broadcast of Young Widder Brown. He raised the volume and set it on the sill where it yelled into the microphone. Satisfied, Carl tiptoed to the bathroom door and inquired gently:

"How do you get contacted for your next assignment?"

"Here, you mean?" she asked. Her voice seemed husky and still full of sleep. "In New York?"

"Yes. Do you get mail?"

"No. I sit at a table in a restaurant and an old lady comes by. It's always the same old lady. Only I think she's not old. Her hands are white: no age spots. I suppose I should tell her about the makeup. Next time—if there's a next time."

"There will be."

"How do you know?"

Carl did not answer the question. "When do you go to the restaurant?"

"Every Thursday when I'm in town. Except sometimes I don't go."

"Thursday is tomorrow. Go."

"You think she'll be there? Carl? . . . *Carl?*"

He walked back to the bedroom. He could hear Ruth splashing in the tub, humming something. He closed the bedroom door and lay down and inspected the ceiling. The Old Man would be sure to give the white-handed lady a message for Ruth. Don't leave town, the police had told her—but she would be gone within a week. The office had written the rules and Carl knew them. Fraternizing with the enemy is not what bothered them; it was fraternizing with your friends. Carl had broken the rules and now they would break him. Or they would try. His fault for having emotions. For being lonely. For screwing up. For endangering Ruth and himself, and, by implication, the office. For trying, at this late date, to discover if he was still capable of love. The word had no place in counterintelligence; it was like drawing with pastels on aluminum.

The Old Man had not mentioned Rathenau. Carl supposed the order to kill him was still in effect: *Despite the unpleasantness, nothing has changed.* He rose and opened the drawer with his pistol in it. He handled it for a minute, getting the feel of it again, watching it in the sunlight. He would wait until Ruth left him; then he would be grateful to have something to do with his hands.

16

FDR: New York, 1944

LIGHT SHATTERED into color and the faces of children were gone. In their places were indistinct blurs. Even the cheers dissolved into a low moan. It was the weather. He was sure it was the weather and not some internal problem. He should never have gone out in this freezing rain. His Navy cape was wet and Eleanor kept giving him looks that seemed an amalgam of reproach and concern. The dark gray Packard entered from left field and moved slowly toward second base. The applause bounced and then echoed. Mike Reilly, the Secret Service chief, snapped the President's braces in position. Roosevelt could feel his hair soaked to his scalp. The water washed his face and made it impossible to read through his glasses. He wiped them and glanced at his notes. The hell with the notes. He could do this with memory and a smile.

"I have never been to Ebbets Field before." The words caromed back from the stands. "But I have rooted for the Dodgers." The cheers and whistles drowned him out. He waited until they died. "And I hope to come back here some day and see them play. But the chief reason I am here today

141

is to pay a little tribute to my old friend Senator Bob Wagner. . . ."

The hell it is. I'm here to show you that an old man is not an old man. That the governor of New York is no more vigorous than your President. That if a fourth term is unheard of, these are unheard-of times. But Lordy, I am tired today. Can anybody see it? Surely not from this distance. . . .

The rain seemed to seep through his pores to his soul. His mind felt liquefied. There was so much still to do. The day passed mechanically, but the rain and cold followed the motorcade. The New York papers made him look confident, triumphant in the foul weather. All except the *Daily News*. They had come up with a Speed Graphic shot that made him look like something from Madame Tussaud's: thin and bent and troubled. Well, why not? They were backing the Republicans.

He pushed on. Through Queens, across the bridge to the Bronx, down through Harlem, the cheers undiminished in the streets, to Eleanor's apartment on Fifth Avenue. The place was crammed with Secret Service men and officials, but he could shut his eyes for a while, relax on the pillows and think about the Waldorf speech. Odd, he reflected, Eleanor has had this apartment for so many years. And yet this is the first time I have ever visited it. Marriage. Who was it said marriage was a mysterious state in which everybody in it longed to get out, and everybody outside it yearned to enter. Montaigne? Mencken? He no longer knew. His mind had trouble retaining information. He wondered if the others noticed his hands trembling, or his difficulty with certain words. He preferred not to think about deterioration. The war had produced miracle drugs. Scientists would produce one to retard aging. They probably had it already. He must speak to Admiral McIntyre. Churchill had some doctor working on it; so did Somerset Maugham. Something to do with glandular transplants. He would ask Winston when they next met. Stalin would be there. Maybe the Russians had some drug. Vodka, probably. He smiled

barracks. Strangely, until now Niccolò had not been physically ill, except for some coughing at night. There must be a reason why I am alive and all the others dead, he thought. And he remembered the reason.

"Conscious," he heard someone say in English. He looked up and saw the olive-drab underside of a tent roof. Around him young men, some of them younger than he was, hovered. One of them smiled.

"You spikka da Inglis?"

Niccolò tried to remember some English. On their London visit he and Gina had a joke—a phrase they used to repeat. It sounded operatic to the Italian ear. Something about the king: "I must abandon the throne for the woman I love." He tried to speak the phrase with as little accent as possible. The heavy, wide-faced doctor above him smiled.

"You know where you are?"

"In America."

"Not quite." He told Niccolò about the American advance, the explosion, the field hospital. Niccolò realized that there were other men in other beds, some of them receiving blood from red inverted jars with tubes that led down to their arms.

"What is wrong with me?" Niccolò asked.

"Contusions. You know what that is?"

"No."

"Bruises. Hard knocks. Shock. Nothing broken. You'll be up soon. I'm Major Evans. This is Corporal Gissen. He'll take your name and details." The major walked down to the next bed. A nervous, prematurely bald young soldier sat down in a canvas chair and introduced himself. He had a clipboard and asked a series of questions: Name, rank, serial number, outfit, last military station. Profession before military service. The corporal had a great deal of difficulty accepting the replies. When Niccolò told him about the escape from the camp, the corporal asked him to wait. A few minutes later another man came in. He was older and badly shaven and obviously fatigued. His name was Captain Genarro, Military Intelligence. Bilingual. He began to interrogate Niccolò in Italian. Genarro's American accent overlay a Milanese dialect. He asked questions about partisans and German troop movements. Niccolò's replies were slow and deliberate and accurate until Genarro inquired about Himmeldorf. Niccolò sat up. His eyes glittered.

"What's the point in talking? Whatever I tell you will go into the dustbin. You will never bomb Himmeldorf, not even the rail lines! President Roosevelt and Winston Churchill don't care if we all burn!" The tears stayed in his eyes. They changed the way his voice articulated his feelings, but Niccolò refused to cry, not now, not ever. It was too late to mourn, and too early.

Captain Genarro let him calm down and then asked irrelevant questions about the probability of floods. Niccolò knew that the Americans had all the information they needed about such things. He had seen their observation planes many times, circling high over his head. These were inquiries meant to disarm him so that he would be thrown off guard. But he was not so easily distracted; when the inquiries were repeated about the camps, Niccolò said that he could not remember, that it was long ago. For three days the captain returned, always in late morning, always with interrogations about how Niccolò was feeling: "Any pains in the head? Any twinges? You look better, do you feel better? Do you speak any other languages? Ah, French. Would you like to speak French? No? Did you understand any German when you overheard it? Did they speak German to you in the camps? Tell me about the camps."

At that point Niccolò would become vague, answering with great weariness. Gradually the captain would begin to talk. It was as Niccolò suspected. Others had escaped from Himmeldorf. Today people—ordinary people—knew what was happening there, even about the gas. This war was worse than the Great War everyone had read about in school. And yet in World War II gas had not been used against the enemy, even by Hitler. Only against the Jews. What could be done? How could the world be made to see?

The captain shook his head. "They'll know soon enough." Bedside manner, Niccolò thought. The patient was being dismissed as one more victim of shell shock. "Damaged goods," he heard the captain say, when he thought Niccolò was out of earshot. What happened to damaged goods Niccolò had no way of knowing. They would probably put him in some mental hospital around here. Well, let them. Niccolò had escaped from more forbidding places.

But escape never became necessary. Five days after he had awakened in the field hospital, when he had regained his balance, upset when the explosion did some minor damage to his inner ear, and when the bruises on his shoulder healed, he was put on an airplane. An hour later he was in another place, something they called a depot. The American soldiers fingerprinted him and took his name again, and gave him metal tags with his name on them, and a beaded metal chain to hold them around his neck. The chain left a series of black marks against his skin, but he was grateful. For the first time in he could not remember how long, his skin was clean enough to see dirt on it. When he examined his tags and looked at his gray uniform, Niccolò learned his new category: POW, prisoner of war. He was not put with the other prisoners, old soldiers and misfits who had surrendered in Calabria. Instead he was assigned some light kitchen duties, in the company of American soldiers being punished for minor violations. One of them had gone AWOL he said. Niccolò had no idea what the word meant. Another had hit a corporal for slurring Texas. Another had been mildly insubordinate, something about following a lieutenant's orders too slowly. None had seen combat; all of them were large and stupid and moved like bears. Niccolò liked them because they talked so slowly there was no chance in misunderstanding. He did as he was told, peeling carrots and potatoes, washing dishes, sweeping up. The kitchen was hot and the food was plentiful. No one minded if he opened a can of peanuts or helped himself to an extra egg. At first he ate too much and he felt sharp pains below his stomach. But by the third day he was eating like any other soldier or prisoner of war. He was

content to stay where he was until strength returned to his
mind and arms and back.

On Saturday night, as the ponderous rumble of battle
sounded from a great distance, everyone in the depot, even
the prisoners, was allowed to attend a USO performance.
The soldiers had been promised Bob Hope, but the
comedian was elsewhere. Instead, a man named Jackie
Styles came out and told jokes in such rapid succession that
Niccolò could not follow any of them.

Styles was accompanied by five pretty girls, four of them
so blond that their hair, caught in the gas-powered floodlights, hurt the eyes. They sang a medley of tunes Niccolò
did not recognize, and even when the platform shook as a
bomber took off they continued to show great ivory smiles
as if the noise, too, was part of the act. There was also a
juggler, a tall man with lank dark hair and a sad expression
who could cascade eight balls and whistle and balance a
broom on his nose. The soldiers were impatient with him;
they whistled for the girls. But Niccolò wanted to watch the
Amazing Ruggiero some more; he recognized the juggler.
They had once been in a show together, a benefit for orphans
somewhere. Naples, it was. There were always a lot of
orphans in Naples.

When the recorded music stopped playing and the women
took their final bows, Niccolò called to Ruggiero. He spoke
in Italian: "You remember? Niccolò Levi?" He shouted
over the noise of applauding GIs. "You came on just before
me. I did a scene from *Six Characters*. We shared a dressing
room. We and the Jumping Fontanas. All nine of them."

The long face responded with a sharp grin. "Yes! The
only thing they jumped was the soprano. Who I always
thought was a transvestite."

"She was. But so were the Fontanas."

An old joke, a standard exchange of Italian performers.
The Amazing Ruggiero whispered to the captain of military
police. Word was passed down, someone gestured to
Niccolò, and in a few minutes he was free to be in the
company of his old colleague. They talked about Rome and
Niccolò found himself laughing. He was introduced to the

women; he expected to find them disappointing, flawed the way beautiful actresses were when you looked at them in a room instead of across a proscenium. But all of them were dazzling. Their American skin looked edible, and their teeth were white and strong enough to pull nails out of a board. Niccolò could not take his eyes off their breasts; even the slightest girl jiggled when she shook hands with him. A captain with horn-rimmed glasses and a dark expression kept staring at him from a distance. Finally he came over and introduced himself.

"Bogen, USO. I know you," he said.

Niccolò shook his head. He was certain he had never seen the man before.

"I saw you in *The Windmill*. Your first picture. And again in London. I know your work. You were good. You were really good."

Bogen started talking fast, half to Niccolò, half to a major. He stopped looking at Niccolò and spoke exclusively to other officers. The Amazing Ruggiero began boasting about his accomplishments in the States. "Imagine me," he said, "on the same program with Abbott and Costello. At the World's Fair." Niccolò had heard of the fair in New York, but Abbott and Costello had no meaning. He assumed that Costello was Italian. "I also was at the Paramount," Ruggiero burbled on. "I was in Cleveland, Atlanta, St. Louis, Chicago. And wherever I go—"

"Applause?" Niccolò offered.

"Roaches." Ruggiero scratched himself. "Every room, roaches. Jugglers never go first class. I'm studying to be a comedian. They make much better money, stay in hotels with insecticide. How do you like this: A man stopped me on the street. 'Sir, I haven't had a bite in weeks.' So I bit him." Ruggiero shrugged. "It's much funnier in English." He told the joke in English. Niccolò forced a smile. Ruggiero continued, "Maybe it's funnier in Italian." He told the joke again in Italian and followed it with three anecdotes about his mother-in-law and one about a dog who looked at a parking meter and said, "What do you know? Pay toilets." But Niccolò had never seen a parking meter or a pay toilet, and, besides, Ruggiero was talking too fast and with no sense of comic timing. All the same, Niccolò wished he could have forced a laugh: Ruggiero looked so bereft. "So," the juggler said when he had completed his routine, "what's going to be? Back to Rome?"

"I don't know."

"I think the major would like you to come with us."

"Where?"

"To America, maybe. Last time we took back two children."

Niccolò shook his head. "I'm a prisoner of war. Prisoners of war don't go to America. Displaced people don't go to America. Jews don't go to America."

"Don't start feeling sorry for yourself. It's against the law in America."

Ruggiero went on prattling, but his words were lost. The lights shook and dimmed. There was a bombing raid in the vicinity. The soldiers and prisoners were herded back to their places. Niccolò shook hands with the juggler, but before he could say goodbye, Captain Bogen came up to him again. "Come with me," he said, and waved off an MP when he approached. Niccolò followed the captain through the dark to a large tent. There were emergency lights inside, and a small black folding table with papers on it. A gray-haired colonel, obviously exhausted, squinted at some papers, then at the USO captain and then at Niccolò. He motioned him to a canvas chair.

"Levi," he said, "they tell me you speak English."

"One or two words, sir."

"You were in prison camp in Poland?"

"I was."

"What the hell are you doing here?"

"I don't know, sir. I just—I came where the war took me."

"Either you're the biggest goddamn liar we ever interrogated or the luckiest man in Italy."

"I assure you, sir, I am neither."

The colonel shuffled the papers again. "Yeah," was all

the Salvation Army, as was the bamboo cane, and because he paid for a whole bottle the huge bartender, inescapably called Tiny, let him alone. Everyone else was drinking beer. Rathenau sat near the front with three plump men and a thin one. Tiny put down a large pitcher of Ballantine Ale and a bunch of glasses and said something that engendered an explosion of laughter. He went away and Carl called headquarters and waited ten minutes before limping to the table.

"Herr Rathenau?" he said. He removed his dark glasses. He could see clearly now; the thin man recognized him: Carl could tell from the sudden expression of concern. Rathenau looked up, puzzled. The thin man reached in his coat and Carl shot him and Rathenau in a matter of three seconds. The thin man screamed and held his shoulder. Blood seeped around his fingers. Rathenau was shot in the chest. It was doubtful if he felt anything, Carl thought. The thin man's black pistol clattered on the dirty floor. He gazed at Carl with disbelief. Carl shot Rathenau again and stayed one more moment so that his face registered with all the men at the table. He turned slowly and walked out. The Chevrolet coupé was waiting for him. He did not recognize the driver, but the man knew his job. He whisked Carl to Eleventh Avenue, took the .32 caliber pistol, parked in a gas station and motioned him to a polished old blue Cadillac. The Old Man was in the back seat. Another driver, a black man with a chauffeur's cap, took them downtown to Wall Street. No one stopped them, no one gave them more than a perfunctory glance. Everyone was more interested in the car than in its occupants. Carl recited the events of the afternoon and the Old Man nodded.

"You will go back to what you were doing," he ordered. "Be visible. Don't change your habits. Get out here and take the subway home. Walk slowly."

"I have to walk slowly," Carl said. "The limp is real."

The Old Man remained unruffled. One might almost have thought him bored. "Goodbye," he said. "I'll be in touch."

Carl obeyed his instructions. He went home on the noisy

F train and turned on the radio. The murder was not reported until the eight o'clock news. As he suspected, the police had the wrong description: he was said to have worn a black suit—in fact it was dark gray—and they called him ten years older than his actual age. He was supposed to have run from the scene. The cane had been judged a prop. The bartender said the murderer was a regular who kept to himself and spoke with a German accent. A nice touch, Carl thought. One he had thrown in for free. Even the Old Man would like that.

By the next morning Carl knew he was being tailed. The men who followed him were OSS regulars, retired cops the Old Man hired for low-level work: shadowing an agent, blackmail. Shleppers. They would have fooled only an innocent. They cupped their hands around cigarettes and filled up hotel lobbies, reading the same page of newspaper all day. Whether they fooled the Yorkville group was hard to say. Nothing happened for ten days. Then the Germans started using the code again. At first Carl thought it only an exhortation, calling for the doubling of efforts, informing their listeners that the Germans still held Brittany and controlled the Scheldt estuary in Holland. That the Führer was in full control, that Field Marshal von Witzleben had been put to death for his role in the aborted execution of Hitler. Wagnerian optimism; the song of the Walsungs; Frederick Barbarossa speaking in the cave. The usual garbage.

He read the coded cable and yawned at the torrent of self-delusion until he saw the name Vier. Four. Fear. Like the old days. Vier, it read, had "solved" the Baker. He assumed that the Baker was Rathenau. Solved was their word for killed. Like the final solution. Very neat. Very German.

19

Niccolò Levi: Hollywood, 1945

A FEW WEEKS before, he had seen an American film about a little girl who lived in a place of sepia. In a dream she visited a world of color, with magicians and incantations and songs. Niccolò knew how she must have felt. Not long ago he was certain that he would never again be warm, never again know what it was like to walk up to a store and actually buy a loaf of bread or sit undisturbed at a café and drink a cup of capuccino. He thought that he would never again see a city with streets unpocked by bullets and jackboots or people whose faces did not display the mask of the oppressor or the furtive air of hunted animals. And here it all was, music on the radio, sunshine on the streets of New York, and stores with goods that overflowed their counters; food everywhere, even in machines, banks on every corner, silver ringing in pockets.

For the first week the Army officers set him up on the fifth floor of the Hotel Taft and asked him questions every morning. In the afternoons they bought him a hot lunch and then asked him more about Rome, and about troop movements, and about Himmeldorf. "Remember," they kept demanding, as if he had been responsible for the Germans. "Remember."

Yes, he said to himself, I will remember. I will remember the "village of heaven" and the long lines of Jews, and my dead wife and baby, the Professor coughing up blood and the sound of the dogs barking in the night, and the guttural laughter and stink of Germans in the Eternal City and the high indifferent American planes.

In the end, he gave them what they wanted, invented troop movements and estimates of army strengths, and they let him go. The people from the USO appeared at his hotel room one morning and an official took him out to the airport. He was packed on a silver transport along with some enlisted men heading west. They were all young and cropped like sheep, and they laughed for the first part of the trip, then grew silent and nauseated as the plane bounced in and out of air pockets.

Niccolò tried to keep the plane aloft by thinking it upward, wishing it lighter than air and stronger than the war. But he soon grew used to the turbulence and to the roar of four motors. He knew that no simple man-made work of aluminum and wires and gasoline could do him in; not after all he had been through, not after all that remained to be done.

He asked for a paper and read the war news: General de Gaulle had begun a visit to the United States and Canada. In a night raid, RAF bombers had dropped 2500 tons of bombs on Caen. In Italy, the 86th Division occupied Volterra and the heights north and east of town. Niccolò remembered those heights and the red clay roofs that slanted north, crouched against the wind, and how on the free night the townspeople would come and applaud and ask for the author, even though the author was Pirandello, dead for two years—but didn't he hear that in Calabria in the twenties they had once asked for Plautus to take a bow?

There was an item in the paper about a British film retitled *At Dawn We Die*. In England the film had been called *Tomorrow We Live*. In three words Niccolò realized, you had the whole war. Americans thought of foreigners perishing nobly for a cause. In Europe, life was your cause. You tried to make it to the next Sunday. In a concentration camp you tried to live to the next hour. He looked at the ads for department stores: cornucopias full of warm clothing with enough jackets and sweaters on one floor to clothe all the people in the cell blocks. More than enough for—but he would not let himself think of Gina. He had learned the trick of stopping his mind the way Hindu fakirs were said to stop their hearts. He looked out the window at rivers snaking their way through dry land, safe land. The major in the next seat passed him a bottle of whiskey. He had a large swig and felt it almost immediately.

Niccolò dozed just enough to go under the sound of the propellers. He awoke to find the plane bumping its way into Los Angeles.

At the airport he went through procedures like a somnam-bulist, aided by some other majors, men who spoke very swiftly and moved like guests at a costume party at which they were required to wear military gear. None of them looked like soldiers. With good reason, he discovered. They were all movie producers with commissions. A couple of men had seen action in the Pacific Theater; at least they wore ribbons to that effect. The others smoked cigars and laughed with their mouths but not with their eyes. One who had the hardest face introduced himself as Zack Ross. He was bald and tan with fringes of ginger hair and a red mustache. Ross had a few gold teeth and a scar on his nose. When the phone rang he hesitated as if deciding whether to answer it or eat it.

While he spoke, a civilian nodded in the direction of Ross and said to Niccolò, "Looks like a cross between a rabbi and a pirate, don't he?"

Niccolò was not given a chance to reply. The man went on: "He's the only one here with balls. Zack was with Patton at Sicily. Making newsreels. The others all made training films. You know: 'Your best friend is your rifle, soldier. Sleep with it, eat with it, take it to the movies.'" He scrutinized his listener. "Hey, you understand what I'm talking about? Kapeesh?"

Niccolò nodded, although he could comprehend only a part, and that part concerned Zack Ross. The bald man had an abrasive manner; he was too used to having his own way. But somehow Niccolò trusted him. If Ross had been with General Patton, perhaps he knew something about Italians. If he was Jewish, then he would understand more.

"He was a hot producer at Warner's," the civilian said. "Now he's back, Jack Warner'll give him the sky. Zack likes you, you're in. You ought to play the nags, friend. You're one lucky refugee."

How lucky Niccolò was to find out that night. Ross drove him to a hotel somewhere in Beverly Hills and found a room with what seemed to be acres of bed and yards of towels. "Rest up. Room service'll give you whatever you want," he announced. "Just pick up the phone and ask for sandwiches in room 511. You want a girl they'll get one. Or tonight you'll pick up your own at the party. Rest, take a nap. Be ready at eight."

Niccolò was bewildered. "But I have no clothes," he protested. "And I have no English."

"Your English is fine. If it was better you wouldn't get a job in pictures. I'm going to cast you in something. I see you as a Nazi. For our audiences, one accent is as good as another. Lemme see you make a mean face. Or maybe you could play a villager. One of those guys who say, 'Follow me. They can't stop men who want to be free.' And get shot in the first reel. I'll come here with clothes at seven-thirty. You look like a 38 regular. Get some sleep."

And he was gone. Niccolò went to the bathroom and played with the dials of the shower. There were endless streams of hot water, as sharp as glass or as soft as cotton. He steamed himself and then lay across the bed naked until the water evaporated. He would remember California, he thought, as a place where towels were unnecessary. He slept intermittently, then shaved and wandered the room seeking diversion, anything to keep from thinking. The Los Angeles *Times* was on the writing table. Much of it was incomprehensible: stories of baby parades in Santa Ana and gossip of movie stars: Veronica Lake, Lana Turner, Maureen

O'Hara. Niccolò had heard about it for years; now he could see the American obsession with the female bust. It was everywhere, breasts pushing out blouses, and elevated in evening gowns, thrust coyly at photographers and straining against the restrictions of sweaters that always seemed, in the ads, two sizes too small. Borro would have loved it here, poor bastard. Was he still alive? Or had he been killed by the Fascists, the partisans, or the Americans? All of them had a motive.

At seven-thirty Ross let himself in without knocking and threw a suit and some haberdashery on the bed. "Put it on. Then we'll go to the studio party. Get you started."

He went to the radio, twirled the dial experimentally, and turned it off. "News," he said. "Gabriel Heatter. A lot he knows. Reads the stuff off a ticker. Your ribs show, you know that? They say out here you can't be too rich or too thin. But you can. We got to fatten you up if you're going to be in movies."

Even though the suit was tailored for a spare man, it hung on Niccolò like a kerchief on a stick. Ross looked at him and shook his head. "Two profiles in search of a face." He complained about Niccolò's weight all the way down Sunset Boulevard, except for the times he yelled at the occasional old Mexican who set one foot on the street as the car bore down on him. The air was sweet and undisturbed. Even the gasoline fumes had a benignity. A country at peace. War was an ocean away and nobody cared.

Ross said, "Whenever I'm in a car every pedestrian is my enemy. Whenever I'm on foot I want to blow up cars. I got unlimited gas, so if you want to see anything just yell. We can go anywhere."

Niccolò merely shrugged.

"Don't be polite. You're in America now. Plus you're in Hollywood. You won't believe what goes on in this town. I'm here nine years and I don't believe it. Ever heard of Fatty Arbuckle?"

Niccolò nodded; his father had once taken him to see four hours of Arbuckle films in Rome. He had laughed at a few of them; his father had slept through the entire program.

"Fucked a girl with a Coke bottle. Killed her. They brought in censors—tried to clean up the movies. But they couldn't do anything about the movie *makers*. Chaplin screwed everything that wasn't nailed down, Hearst probably shot a guy on a boat. There's an actress here. An alkie. Last year she's arrested, she signs the police blotter, name Frances Farmer, occupation cocksucker." Ross shook his head. "You following any of this?"

"Yes, a little."

"Then hear this. Four things ruin a man out here. Booze, pills, women, and you know what the fourth thing is?"

"No."

"Fear."

The big car swung up a wide street lined with palmetto trees. Ross rolled up his window and raised his voice. "I come from Delancey Street," he said. "I'm a pushcart Jew. To you I can say I have no more talent than the guys I grew up with, and two of them are in jail. Nevertheless, I'm a producer with a wife got three mink coats, I have a son at Dartmouth and a daughter a salutatorian in Beverly Hills High. I drew a salary while I was overseas, now I'm ready to take over the B picture productions for Fox. Why? Because I keep this clean."

He pointed to his long bent nose. "Listen, I'm human. I get blown at the studio now and then, a girl wants a part I try her out first. But I don't take dope, I don't have love affairs, and I'm not afraid. I made a living pushing a cart like my old man; I can always go back and do that. We're here. Remember. Go light on the sauce, no reefers, and don't be afraid. Come on. I'll introduce you around. You're lucky. You're single."

The house was set on an expanse of grass, illuminated by spotlights that made the lawn pale and wintry although the air seemed the temperature of blood. The lower story was built of glass bricks so thick that light could barely squeeze through. Cream-colored curtains were drawn across some of the huge picture windows, but even from the outside Niccolò could see rooms giving onto more rooms, a great expanse of white rugs and hundreds of people in loose-

fitting bright clothing. There was a lot of yellow and blue
and white. Some of the men wore pants the color of sunsets.
When he and Ross entered they heard someone playing the
piano very well and a redheaded singer with a trained voice
chanting softly, just under the percussion of conversation.

One wall was covered with mirrors: concave, flat,
convex, Florentine looking-glasses, amusement park reflec-
tors that took in people and gave back hydrocephalics and
pinheads. Niccolò remembered the observation of a rabbi
long ago: We are as glass—put a little silver on us and we
see nothing but ourselves.

The mirrors reflected fashionably haggard women, producers' wives whose faces revealed several kinds of
starvation, and men with smiling mouths and staring,
ambitious eyes, actors afraid of losing their looks or their
parts, producers radiating a peculiar uncertainty, as if at any
moment all this, even the hors d'oeuvres, might be struck so
that another, better movie with another, better cast could be
filmed on the same site.

"Same old party," Ross said. "Everybody selling,
nobody buying. Come on, I'll introduce you to a couple
people. Do you some good."

There were two aggressively tan, fit men standing near a
bookshelf speaking ironically of a colleague. "A fraud,"
one of them was saying. "He says everything twice and
they think he's great. I mean, they think he's great. And all
he does is say everything twice."

The man he was talking about, it developed, was Ernest
Hemingway. Niccolò had read the books in translation. He
had liked the Italian captain in *The Sun Also Rises: "Que
mala fortuna*. You have given more than your life," but he
was afraid to say so. He listened quietly to the critics.

Ross moved on, and began aseptically flirting with two
homely women who wore immense diamonds on their
fingers. The tan men began making a list of overrated
scenarists:

"Raymond Chandler," one said.

"William Faulkner," the other offered. "His stuff makes

less sense on the screen than it does on the page. Did you see *The Road to Glory*?" Niccolò shook his head.

"Who do you think is overrated?" he was asked.

"I don't think anyone is. You see, I—"

"What are you, a writer?"

"No. I used to be . . . an actor." He could hardly believe his words. Used to be. He was no longer an actor. Only a refugee. The men looked at him emptily and returned to their game.

"An actor?" A little man with large shiny eyes was at Niccolò's side. "Yes, Ross told me about you. Niccolò Levi. I'm a Jew myself, but I got out in time." Peter Lorre offered his hand.

He maneuvered Niccolò away from the tan men. "You know why they call them associate producers, don't you? Because nobody but a producer will associate with them. They hate us. You know the story they tell about the starlet who was so dumb she came to Hollywood and fucked an actor?"

Niccolò's face was blank.

"You can't follow me?" Lorre asked.

"I can if you talk slower."

"Yes. I'm sorry. I was the same way at first. I learned my part in *The Man Who Knew Too Much* phonetically. Syllable by syllable. I might have been speaking Hindu. You hungry?"

He maneuvered them to a tray of canapes. The variety bewildered Niccolò: rolled ham, ten different kinds of cheese, chopped liver, smoked fish, turkey. Little silver forks gleamed on the tray, surrounded by a hundred triangles of crustless white and black breads.

"Eat," said Lorre. "Don't worry. There's more. The servants live off the leftovers for weeks."

Niccolò picked at the food. He still could not bridge the cornucopia before him and the wintry deprivation he had left behind: the only ice here was in the drinks.

Lorre gestured with a piece of Munster. "Ross told us about you."

"Us?"

"The ones who really know what's going on over there."

"No . . . permit me. No one knows what's really going on over there."

"Going on over where?"

This was spoken by someone Niccolò recognized. The droll nasal delivery was familiar; so was the cigar and the bantam strut.

"My name is Emmanuel Rubenstein."

"Used to be," Lorre said. "Now Edward G. Robinson."

"What can we do?" Robinson demanded. "You need a place to stay? Cash?"

"He doesn't need a thing." Ross joined them. "He's a natural for war pictures."

Someone began telling Goldwyn jokes. "One day I wrote an ad: 'The directorial skill of Mamoulian, the radiance of Anna Sten and the genius of Goldwyn have united to make the world's greatest entertainment.' Sam tells me: *'That* is the kind of ad I like. Facts. No exaggeration.'"

A man in orange trousers recalled Goldwyn's command during *The Last Supper:* "Why only Twelve disciples? Go out and get thousands."

They talked about drunken Herman Mankiewicz, who had abruptly left his hostess's table and then returned to assure her not to worry, the white wine came up with the fish. And about his critique: "The picture was so bad they had to do retakes before they could put it on the shelf."

Then they began on Harry Cohn. "They were doing a medieval costume picture," Ross said. "Harry takes a look at the script and yells at the writers: 'What kind of hacks are you—you don't even know how people talked in the Middle Ages? You got them saying "Yes, siree." The writer says, 'That's "yes, sire," Harry.'"

Jews talking about Jews. Jews laughing at Levantine vulgarity and pretensions. Sam Spiegel billing himself as S. P. Eagle. Mankiewicz saying that Lubitsch should be billed as L. U. Bitch and Zanuck as Z. A. Nook. Goldwyn: "Tell me. How did you love the picture?" and "Let's have some new clichés." George Jessel: "My draft status is 8-T. That means I go when the Japs are in the lobby."

Below the English Niccolò could hear the singsong of Yiddish; under the tanned and flushed skins he could see the faces of immigrants. Confident, loud, they rolled over each other's conversation, shouted out the punchlines of stories before they were finished, and slew the reputations of absent associates. The women wore too much glitter and the men drank too heavily. They had the kind of ostentatious confidence born of early insecurity and sudden overpayment. Hollywood; he had heard about it for years and never believed a word. Now he knew it was all true: the bizarre houses, the vulgarity, the money, the insulation from life as ordinary people lived it. Didn't they know what was happening to their landsmen? Didn't they care? The German Jews had been confident, too. And loud. Now they were black smoke saturating the Polish air. His face was flushed. He drank from a glass Ross had put in his hand. Whiskey and soda.

"I remember a book," Niccolò began. "*Vienna Without Jews.* In the twenties it was written. It was supposed to be a comedy. See, nobody could imagine Vienna without Jews. It was a Jewish city. Like Hollywood."

Ross nodded blankly. "Yeah. Well. Listen. You gotta meet whaddyacallit, Jerry Wald. You ever see *All Through the Night?* It was about Nazis in Yorkville. Jerry made it. Good guy to know."

Ross steered him over to a man in his thirties, dressed in white linen. Wald resembled a short white cigar and he spoke nonstop. Niccolò could follow only a little: Ross was recommending him. Wald nodded.

"Listen." He took Niccolò's arm. That was what everyone said out here: Listen. And then nobody did.

"Yes, sir?"

"You think there's a picture in it? About your life?"

"I don't know how to say—"

"Maybe you could be a technical adviser or something. Ross says find something for you, I'll find something. Look at this place. It's all a set. Everything. The houses, the pools, the tennis courts, the money, the people. Every now and then I look at myself in a three-way mirror, to see if I go all the way around or it's just a front."

That Niccolò understood. Since his arrival in this mysterious loud country he had been walking around objects and people to see if they were actual. And each time he did, he felt vaguely ashamed. At this moment, with the green water winking under the lanterns nearby, he criticized himself for his doubts. These people had saved him, they had brought him to their homes. They would give him work and shelter. They knew nothing of Himmeldorf or even of Rome or Warsaw.

At the other end of the pool a girl was taking her clothes off. She had long legs and dark shoulder-length hair that caught the light. Her body was light; nothing sagged as she walked to the edge and jumped in. The sight of her flesh constricted Niccolò's throat, but the others hardly noticed. They went on singing. Wald was saying something about the girl:

"Dale, her name is. You want her? She gives good pool but you can do better."

Wald gave him a card. "We'll set up a screen test. I see you as a hostage. You know: 'For every one of us you kill, ten others will spring up. And then hundreds of thousands.' Call me in the morning."

He abandoned Niccolò in the shadows of the house near the pool. As Niccolò stared at the embossed lettering on Wald's card he remembered that he had never made a telephone call in the United States, never even written a postcard. Yet a man, a stranger, handed him what amounted to a job, a career. This is the way they got you in America; they took your mind off your aim until at last you forgot why you were here. He wrinkled the card and considered throwing it in the green water. But something stopped him; he opened the stiff paper, smoothed it out and carefully put it in his shirt pocket. He smiled at Dale; she saw him and grinned back emptily. He could make out the words of the song now. The English was strange to him, but he knew the melody. A stonemason on his street used to sing it after he came limping back from Spain. "Arise ye prisoners of starvation," they chanted. Even the girl in the pool knew the words.

20

FDR: Washington, 1945

HE COULDN'T remember. They were sitting with expectant faces, and he had to ask them what he was talking about a minute ago. He had lost the thread of thoughts today as he had lost them yesterday, and last week and the weeks before that. Congress. Something about pilotless planes.

He knew there were instances in which Dr. Admiral Ross McIntyre was right. "You may feel fine, Mr. President," he had said, "but you don't look it. Your neck is scrawny and your face is gullied by lines that have added ten years to your age." At least ten, Roosevelt conceded. "For heaven's sake get some new clothes," the admiral had advised. "That old shirt is sizes too large and the jacket hangs on your shoulders like a bag."

The President had laughed, but he knew the truth. Cigarettes tasted rotten. His hands shook. Headaches were overpowering. He was failing. The body was one thing; he was used to pain, to the inadequacy and helplessness of paralyzed legs, of a heart that had lost its power. These things happened in your sixties, especially if you had been struck down as a young man, forced to lead a life of wheelchairs and crutches. But to have the memory falter and the brain limp—neither he nor the country could face that. There were days when he thought he would die in office. One morning he had blurted out to his secretary, "If anything should happen to me while I am at sea, I want to be buried at sea. You know, it has always seemed like home to me."

He had begun to give away mementos; he had designed his own memorial, remade his will. But he did these things on the bad days. On the good days he felt the old surges. He and Lucy had their old annealing meetings and there was still a sexual renewal. If women only knew the power they had to call up youth, he thought. There should be time for Lucy now. But there wasn't. This war killed everything but love. Still, the Allies were winning. How much longer could it continue? However long, he would have to stay in harness. He would have to preside over the peace as well. Four more years the people wanted. . . .

Maybe they wouldn't want me if they knew how weak I am. What I have to face on any given day. What kind of enemy we face, backtracking, retreating, and still demanding obscenities.

From Istanbul Washington had received an offer. The Germans were again holding a sale of the world's rarest commodity: Jews. The German price for two million men, women, and children was two million cakes of soap, two hundred tons of cocoa, eight hundred tons of coffee, two hundred tons of tea and ten thousand trucks. This had later been amended; the demand for soap, tea, and coffee was dropped. Now they wanted military hardware, to be used only on the "Eastern Front." Meaning Russia. An attempt to drive a wedge between the Allies. Moscow was informed. Back came the cable from Ambassador Averell Harriman: "The Soviet does not consider it permissible or expedient to carry on any conversations whatsoever with the German Government. . . ."

God, this war! Humans for sale. Animals, the Nazis were animals. He had a growing awareness of the pleas for

European Jewry. Maybe the Zionists were right after all. A homeland somewhere. Palestine. Churchill would know what to do. He knew all about Palestine and the Arabs. The British had been there for years. How he envied the other leaders. Winston was not depleted by a long campaign for reelection. Nor Joe Stalin. Both of them seemed in for life.

"Mr. President." The face was taut. "The V-2 rockets are still falling. London, of course, and now Antwerp. The harbor is unusable."

"Is there any increased danger of the rockets reaching the United States?"

"We think not. They're still short range. Of course they could launch some from submarines. But as Admiral Leahy has informed you—"

Informed me? How? The mind spun quickly, searching for traction. Yes. He had it now.

"I know, I know. We've broken the code. We can track the subs."

But what if they change the code? What if they have an even more deadly weapon? What if they use gas? We could equip soldiers with masks. But how could we protect civilians, old people, children? Poisoned air used against civilians. No, he decided, not even the Nazis would do that.

He no longer envied Winston and Stalin. In office for life, God help them. He felt his heart twitch; pain radiated down his left arm.

"Lordy, so am I, so am I," he said to his audience. "In for life." They exchanged embarrassed glances. No one had any idea what the President was talking about.

DOCUMENT   FOR THE PRESIDENT   TOP SECRET

THE EXACT DATE WHEN HITLER DECIDED TO WIPE THE
JEWS FROM THE SURFACE OF EUROPE IN THE MOST
LITERAL SENSE OF THE WORD, NAMELY BY KILLING THEM,
IS UNKNOWN. EVACUATIONS AND DEPORTATIONS ACCOM-
PANIED BY EXECUTIONS DATE AS FAR BACK AS THE POLISH
CAMPAIGN, BUT THE ORGANIZED WHOLESALE SLAUGHTER
OF WHOLE COMMUNITIES AND TRAINLOADS OF JEWS
APPEAR TO HAVE BEEN PRACTICED.

OFFICE OF STRATEGIC SERVICES
1942

21

Carl Berlin: New York, 1945

WINTER TURNED liquid that year. It seemed to be raining everywhere. The Allied advance was slowed by rain in Italy, and in Holland the sea water mixed with the weather and forced the Canadian II Corps to retreat. Carl cursed the torrents as he limped south. "The target that walks like a man," he muttered, ducking under awnings, working his way downtown. These days all the messages came from the Western Front. The French had captured Mittelwehr, and the First Army had liberated the west bank of the Ruhr. There were all sorts of stories about the failed assassins of Hitler, summarily tried and executed.

Carl knew that he was being watched. Not trailed, not shadowed. Just picked up from time to time by telescope or binoculars. He would spot a glint from above, something barely in the range of his peripheral vision, then it would disappear. Or a curtain would be pulled back a second too late. At any time, he knew, they could have killed him, gained their revenge for the shooting of Rathenau. But no; they were saving him. For what? Capture, maybe. He would enjoy their attempts at that. If he was lucky he could

take down at least four of them. If they sent four. Then
again, why would they bother? he wondered. One kid,
aiming at the back of his head, would do. What I need, Carl
would remind himself, is a bulletproof imagination.

He kept seeing his body sprawled across innumerable
streets and parks. It would take so little to kill him. A bullet.
An automobile. Poison. And yet they waited. Maybe, he
reasoned, they know I'm being watched by other, fairly
noticeable men, men from the Office of Strategic Services,
waiting to close in on the assassins. After they've done their
job.

Nothing happened. He might have been living in a
vacuum, so regular were his days. At night he holed up in
his apartment and tried to read, or visited a bar and drank
himself into a painless state, or went to the movies, sitting
in the back row so that he could be observed. For a while he
saw a lot of Ellen, always departing a few hours before her
husband returned from Washington. Carl would leave
between four and six in the afternoon, when Curran was the
doorman. Curran was a secret boozer, although it was no
secret to the capillaries in his nose, and he always mistook
Carl for someone else. "Good night, Mr. Trook!" he would
call out. "Nice weather for ducks!" It might have been the
cane that threw Curran off, or it might be that he was only
pretending to be drunk. Doormen were the real Secret
Service of this war, Carl thought. They were the ones who
had the big confidences: the sexual ones.

He began to wonder if it was all a charade, a joke thought
up by the Old Man to drive his employee nuts. And then,
early in the New Year, after Carl had prayed emptily for
something, anything, to jar his routine, even an attempt on
his life, a sign that he had not been wholly abandoned, the
decoder clicked a message that signaled a change. For better
or worse he could not know. The bulletin was from Italy and
all it said was that Ruth Silver was coming home. *Sweet
Times* was her only message. It was not a term of affection.
"Sweet" was their private reference to Sussman.

Carl no longer made any secret of his whereabouts; he
told the doorman he would be at the movies, at the Beverly

under the Third Avenue El. It was playing *To Be or Not to Be*, a film he had seen five times. He liked Jack Benny, and he liked Lubitsch, and he liked the fun they had with Hitler and the clownish German they called Concentration Camp Erhardt. A relief from the real thing; a chance to see death in the role of a clown. As he settled back, Sussman filed in and sat softly in the row before him. The old man turned his head and whispered, using his palm as an amplifier: "On the one hand I'm anxious to talk to you."

"And on the other hand?"

"On the other hand I hate bad news. On the other hand, what other kind is there?"

"What is it, Sussman?"

"Ruth."

"What happened to her?"

"Nothing. She's all right. Let go my coat."

Sussman spoke in a sibilant whisper, so muted that Carl had to bend close and inhale the old man's odor, a combination of garlic and wet wool.

"Listen," Sussman went on, "I only know what I hear from Chicago. What I hear is, she's esked for a leave. She says she's tired."

"I can see that she would be."

"She's not. On the other hand, maybe she is. Anyhow, she has a private thing she has to do. She esked me to esk you to help."

"What is it?"

"You have to get time off. That's what I'm supposed to tell you."

"I can't ask for time off. There's a war on."

"This you don't have to tell an old Jew."

"All right, OK. I'm sorry," Carl said, but Sussman was already edging his way out. "Looks like a nice picture," the old man remarked. "On the other hand, it strains my eyes."

"Sussman," Carl whispered after him, but the bent figure was gone. Carl patted the pocket where ten thousand dollars was sealed in an envelope, the money that Sussman would ask for next Friday. Carl wanted to surprise him, send the old refugee on his mission one week early, get him out of this foul town. The movie unreeled: when Jack Benny asked a Nazi if he remembered a ham actor, the officer replied: "Certainly. What he did to Shakespeare, ve are now doink to Poland." Carl had laughed at the picture years ago; now it seemed to be played in a foreign tongue. The naiveté, the good spirit of farce was drained from the scenario. All that remained was a gothic husk. He could not watch the finish with its happy ending and its comic villain, Concentration Camp Erhardt, failing at everything, even suicide.

Carl left the theater, patted the pocket again and took a bus uptown to Eighty-sixth Street, then caught a crosstown bus through Central Park to Broadway. He stopped at the Canton Flower; Sussman would have nothing in his place to eat but stale rolls. The waiters were slow and he had nothing to read and the meal took longer than he expected. By the time Carl reached Sussman's, the sky had darkened and the sidewalks of West End Avenue were empty.

The lobby was decorated with white vases so large that children sometimes hid in them, and the doormen were dressed in uniforms that had last been cleaned and pressed before the war. The man on duty dozed in a chair in the corner. The *Daily Mirror* had fallen from his lap to the marble floor, revealing a headline about the impending liberation of Warsaw. That would make Sussman happy, Carl thought. He looked around. No one was visible. He quietly pocketed the paper and took the wheezy elevator to the eleventh floor. He rang the bell. There was no answer. Sussman had not yet arrived. Perhaps the envelope could be slipped through the mail slot. Carl bent over and opened the little metal door, and the whiff assailed his nostrils. Gas. He tried the door. It rattled but did not yield. He removed the little plastic square from his pocket and slipped it between the door and the lock. It gave way, just as they promised it would back in the Old Man's instruction course.

Sussman's apartment was dark. The living room and the bedroom were both empty. Carl ran to the meager kitchen. Sussman sat on a little three-legged stool, still in his neat brown suit. He was leaning forward, with his head almost in the oven. Carl yanked open the window and pulled Sussman away, but he knew before he felt for a pulse that the gesture was useless. He held the little body in his arms, brought it to the bedroom, then opened the windows and aired out the place. He put Sussman on the bed and tried to breathe life into him. Useless. There were bruises on the reedy throat. He had probably been dead for over an hour.

Carl knew what had happened here, knew it as if he had been an eyewitness. The Germans, Gower and Co., had murdered Sussman. It was a kind of message: we could have killed you, Vier, but we want you to squirm a while longer. So we fed another Jew to the ovens instead. One more body on its way to the Final Solution.

Carl made the requisite call to Captain Rosen and another one to the office. He left quietly, sadly, wondering about his own ability to infect anyone who touched him. He was glad now that he was working alone, gladder still that Ruth had been in Europe all this time. He hoped that her return would be brief, that whatever she had to say could be articulated in a few words, preferably on the phone so that she would not be tainted by whatever disease he was carrying.

Sussman had mentioned time off, and Carl thought of a hundred ways to ask for it, but he knew the Old Man would refuse all of them. Even a claim of ill health would not be accepted; you were in this branch of service twenty-four hours a day. For the duration. Ruth knew that; why had she made such a peculiar, impossible demand? He would have to wait for her to tell him. Ruth the adventurer; Carl the rooted. Everything backward in this stay-at-home war. He knew that Ruth would find him wherever he was. He half wanted her to make the meeting official, at headquarters, where she would be safe. She was supposed to arrive on the weekend, but he heard nothing until Tuesday morning, when his name was called out as he made his way down Fifth Avenue. Traffic moved slowly near the curb; he saw her face, a little more lined than he remembered it, and thinner, but still with its powerful vulnerability.

He got into the cab and started to tell her about Sussman, but Ruth already knew. She knew about Gower's refusal to be tempted out of hiding, about the Old Man's plans.

"I feel like a spectator of my own life," Carl complained. "You sit in Europe and you see everything. I stay here in the balcony trying to read the program in the dark."

Ruth said nothing until the cab let them off at the Washington Square arch.

"Your hours are regular as a bank clerk's, I hear." She was wearing a severe tan suit and a black cloth coat and no jewelry. Her hair was pulled back and she looked so beautiful in the gray light that it was all he could do to keep his hands still.

"I limp like a metronome," he said. "The shopkeepers set their watches by me."

"The Old Man." She shook her head. "Old-fashioned methods. Well, sometimes old-fashioned methods work."

"If you're after an old-fashioned criminal."

"Aren't you?"

"I don't know, Ruth. Sometimes I think the Nazis are something out of the caves, yelling about the Triumph of the Will. Savages with matted hair jumping around a campfire. Other times I think they're the creatures of the future. Laboratory mutants."

"Do you ever think about good Germans anymore?" she asked.

"What good Germans? Bach? Been dead two hundred years. Dürer? Hasn't picked up a paintbrush in I don't know how long. Goethe?"

"Stop it, Carl. You sound like a German talking about Jews. We can't indict a whole people."

"I can try," he replied. He was in no mood for theory. Maybe, he thought, if I had the luxury of knocking off a few of the enemy, of rescuing some of my own people, I too could afford to be generous.

They found a vacant bench in the sun. Children shouted far off, at the swings.

"Ruth, you didn't come back to talk about justice for the krauts."

"No."

She had trouble starting and she took several breaths before the story worked its way out. "I was with General

McCreery's headquarters. Near the Senio River. Flat country. Romagna. They liberated a large house near the river. Stone, very old. Picturesque, they would have called it before the war, when the British came looking for the sun."

She began to cry, for reasons that Carl could not know. He asked no questions, only held Ruth and let her continue when she was ready. He could tell by the indulgent expressions that passersby thought it was a lovers' quarrel.

"I was interpreting for the general. After the place was cleaned out and the few remaining soldiers were taken prisoner, with their hands on top of their helmets, we went in. We thought it was some kind of military intelligence center or a hospital. But no. It was what the Germans called a field whorehouse. The women in it had been captured in nearby towns or were prisoners transported from other places by troops on the move. One of them was a wasted, dying woman who had come originally from Rome. By the time of the liberation she had been beaten so many times that recovery was impossible. She was suffering from shock, disease, and God knows what else. Her story sounded implausible, even impossible, but later much of it was confirmed. I have it here." She took a folded brown paper, obviously read and reread many times, from her purse.

"'I escaped with two others,'" Ruth quoted the testimony. "'The Professor and Niccolò Levi, poor boy. The Professor I saw die. Niccolò I lost track of. Maybe he has made it across the lines. I pray so. Oh, God, how I pray so. He will avenge us all. We swore one way or another we would bring down the conscience of God, or if there is no God and no conscience, we would shriek until the attention of the world was on our people dying and burning in the furnaces. We would rouse America. We would strike down their leader. We would kill the President and sacrifice our little lives for the millions going to their deaths. They did not even bomb *near* the death camps. We will force them to awaken. Now I cannot help anymore. Gladly I would have done it, gone up to the President, all smiles with roses, I had it planned, a refugee, a heroine, and in the roses would be a thin silver knife. I would plunge it in him. But now, Niccolò alone is left. He will do it. He will kill this Roosevelt and then the world will understand.' "

"So." Ruth closed her eyes and let the tears recede. "She died. Linda Ermanelli died in my arms. But we know Niccolò did escape. We know where he is. And if what she says is true—"

"You don't believe the words of some half-crazy woman—"

"I cannot afford not to."

"Ruth, Ruth, you've been overseas too long. This is America, sweetheart. There are a thousand FBI men swarming all over Washington. Roosevelt has Secret Service men whose job it is to stop bullets with their chests. That's all they do, stand in front of the President like a shield of camel's-hair coats."

"All right. Suppose he doesn't kill him. Suppose he just shoots at him or throws a grenade or something."

Carl shook his head and attempted to answer. But Ruth went on: "Just *suppose* he does."

"Then he'll be locked up and they'll throw away the key."

"And they'll take down what he says and the next day it will be in all the newspapers and on the radio."

"The ravings of a nut."

"No. The ravings of a Jew."

There was no answer for that. Carl knew, knew better than Ruth what it was like here. He had heard, in elevators and on the street, he had seen in the ravings of the *Tablet* and the other rags, the notion that Jews had pulled America into the war in order to get rich. Every time there was a profiteering scandal, a black marketeer caught, even a cheap conman covering his face as he went into court, Carl hoped that this time he wouldn't be Jewish. He disliked Jewish names on lists, even when they were posted on the side of the angels. The protests of inequality, the fight to integrate the Major Leagues, the ads in support of the poor, the ill, the hungry, were always signed by scores of Bergs and Steins. Who knew what would happen after the war? If we could capture Hitler and put him on trial, maybe the world would believe. But to kill Roosevelt—even to *try* to kill the President—and to have a Jew do it . . . he could see the red headlines on the Hearst papers, the columnists parroting the Protocols of Zion: the International Jewish Conspiracy, the beak-nosed flock of vultures, the Judas in our midst. . . .

"Of course," Ruth said, "we don't know whether it was all in the woman's head. Maybe it was. Maybe. But suppose there is this Levi, like a long fuse waiting, burning . . ."

"Well, the first thing is to find out where the fuse is."

"That I have already done. His records are very clear. He's an actor. In Hollywood."

"Under that name?"

"Yes. I think making his first picture. He shouldn't be hard to locate. The rest . . ." She shrugged.

"You want me to go there. That's why the time off. You don't want the Old Man to know."

"Of course not. I don't want anyone to know. Can you imagine the reaction? Either they would think the two of us had lost our senses or they would begin a pogrom."

Pogrom. She still thought like a refugee, still saw Cossacks in boots, riding through the shtetl. That was not the way it would be done here. There would be no knock on the door at midnight, no concentration camp. Only a lack of trust, only an erosion of everything that had gone before. A sense that no matter how long they were here, the Jews would always be renting, never buying. Usurers. Shylocks. Wanderers. Foreigners; perpetual strangers. Surnames like Johanssen or Augustine could be native American in a generation. Three hundred years later, Rabinowitz would still sound as if it came over in steerage last week.

"All right," Carl said, "I'll do what I can. Solo."

When Ruth started to protest he added, "Difficult enough for me to give the Germans and the Service the slip. Working with you, impossible."

"But I have the contacts, the people—"

"I only need to see one person: Levi."

No matter how Ruth insisted, Carl remained intractable.

They traversed the Square, they went into a coffee shop on Waverly Place, they walked uptown and still Carl refused to travel cross-country in her company. Whatever trouble happened would happen to him alone. He began to see the trip to Hollywood as a mission, something where, for once, he could be the falcon instead of the pigeon. As foolish, as unlikely as the whole thing sounded, it was worth investigating. And if it was authentic, if Niccolò Levi *was* a potential assassin, the adventure might even have a moral purpose, something that had been lacking for more years than Carl cared to think about. Although, of course, certain problems would then intrude. . . .

"Ruth, suppose he does intend to carry out his plan?"

"Then we must stop him."

"How? Kill him? A Jew kill another Jew when we have all these nice Germans who do it for a living?"

"I don't know," Ruth answered.

She refused to look at him.

22

Niccolò Levi: Hollywood, 1945

PETER LORRE was reminiscing. "Fritz was about to make a feature, *The Vampire at Dusseldorf*," he recalled. "Suddenly the Nazis sent word: he can't do the film."

Niccolò followed the words easily. Either his English was getting better or Lorre's was deteriorating.

"So Lang spoke to the chief of propaganda. He asked him why everyone was against the Vampire, a real child murderer of the twenties. Suddenly the official gave a big grin. Everything was OK. The Nazis had misunderstood. They thought the Vampire was going to be about *them*."

"True," Lang said. "True." He shook his head. The monocle caught the light. He looked like an extra in a Rudolf Friml operetta, and his accent made Niccolò lean forward to hear him.

"I was nearly the Führer's filmmaker," Lang recalled. "Herr Goebbels gave me an audience. Hitler had seen *Metropolis*. He told his entourage: 'This man will make us *the* Nazi picture.' Wonderful, wonderful, I kept telling Goebbels. I kept looking out the window at the clock. Goebbels kept talking. The bastard talked until after two o'clock when the banks closed. 'Wonderful!' I kept saying. Any suggestion he made was a valentine. Perfect. Genius. I shook his hand and went straight home. I had five thousand marks in the house. I put them in my billfold and left for Paris that evening.''

At the studio commissary the actors seemed to regard Lang with a mixture of awe and disappointment. Things had not worked out so well for the director, Lorre whispered. Lang was too symbolic, too *German* for Hollywood. The man who had fled Germany, repelled by what it symbolized, could not shake it from his pictures. Niccolò wondered how much of Italy clung to his own work. Such work as it was. He looked around the lunchroom at the other actors and directors. It seemed to him that everyone had more to do than he did. A bit part in *Passage to Marseilles,* a picture of flashbacks within flashbacks. He had difficulty following the script, although the few speeches he had as a Devil's Island convict were easy enough. The others seemed to have a lot of fun on the set of swamps and dark corridors, but Niccolò was not included in any of the sound stage conspiracies. Lorre was giggling about the latest of his practical jokes. The star of the film watched him and smiled from time to time, but Humphrey Bogart never laughed.

Lorre continued: "You know we're not supposed to waste any celluloid. There's a war on." A broad wink accompanied the narration. "So every time Mike Curtiz wanted a take, this guy"—he indicated Bogart—"he starts telling some really stupid joke. Curtiz makes nineteen takes of the prison scene. Nothing. He starts again, and this time *I* tell a long story about a hotel in Vienna. It took Curtiz three days to find out whenever he laughed he got the scene in one take, and whenever he didn't laugh he had to shoot over and over. Two mornings later Bogey and I, hung over, start walking to the set. Mike sees us a block away and he starts giggling in advance."

The writers and actors around the table laughed and applauded. Even Bogart grinned. Niccolò faked some mirth, but he felt ambiguous about the joke, about being with actors who could be amused by so little. As he got up to leave, he saw a small, weary man at a nearby table. He had been introduced to Vladimir Sokoloff at the first rehearsal. Immediately afterward he had gone to see a Hemingway picture. The film took place in Spain, and Sokoloff played Anselmo the Gypsy. A nice part, full of sweetness and folk wisdom. Even so, when Niccolò watched Sokoloff he thought of gypsies in the camps, rounded up and dying.

Now, at the table, Niccolò was able to see the old man simply as an old man, a Russian who needed a shave, who was in the same picture with Humphrey Bogart and Peter Lorre and Claude Rains and Michele Morgan and, yes, Niccolò Levi. Still, this was no ordinary Russian; this one had known and studied with Stanislavski himself.

"Sit, sit," Sokoloff said. "Tell me more about yourself. We merely began the other day." The old man sipped his soup very slowly. In the loud, cackling commissary he alone was quiet and gentle, an old aristocrat who had unaccountably found himself dining with Tartars.

"I don't know what to say." Niccolò pulled up a hard wooden chair. "I never know what to say."

"Yes, well, you're the only young actor who admits it. The others—" Sokoloff made an empty gesture. He was used to acting in films; he could convey as much with an eyebrow as the others could by shrugging their shoulders. "You'll do well here, I think. But you have an abstracted face. You know what is abstracted?"

"Something to do with painting."

Sokoloff let it go. "You were in great trouble in Europe, they say."

"Yes . . . trouble . . ."

"So many have suffered. All these wars. I sometimes think this is the century of suffering. But then I remember. The last century was no prize. Chekhov himself wrote a line I used to say. You know *The Cherry Orchard*?"

"A little."

" 'Why are you in black?' 'I am mourning for my life.' They were mourning even then. Always people in black. Black suits, black souls."

"No, this is different now," Niccolò started to protest. "What's happening is not a play."

"I know. I know. But in old Russia the pogroms—"

"The pogroms were in another world. A few Jews—"

"A few hundred."

"But this is millions. It is"—Niccolò reached for a word—"monstrous." He looked at the old man's good face. The melancholy eyes could not accept so much evil.

"Listen, Niccolò Levi." Sokoloff drank his tea from a glass; he searched his listener's eyes. It was not hard for Niccolò to imagine him as a young man at the Moscow Art Theater listening to Konstantin Stanislavski on the actor's art. "All of us, we're emigrés, renegades. People who fled. Behind me there are the dead, too. The revolution killed my friends, my family. On the bad days, the ones you have when you first come here, you think you can scarcely go on, yes?"

Niccolò nodded.

"They go, those times. It takes a while, years maybe. But they go. And then one day you realize those dead are living through you. You must work, you must live. You are your friends, your family."

"No." The young man rose. The answer was not here, not at this table with an old Russian. Niccolò would not be some walking cemetery where the Jews of Europe were buried. "Thank you, but no," he said. "I . . . must . . ." He let the words trail off.

"You'll see," Sokoloff warned or promised; it was impossible to say which.

The set of *Passage to Marseilles* was cacophonous and Niccolò forgot himself for a while. The stars were decent to him; even Humphrey Bogart came over and spent some time. He had a package under his arm and he handed it to Niccolò with a twisted smile. It was as close as Niccolò had come to a genuine movie star, except when he passed them by in the commissary. Bogart's hair, he noticed, was thinning. A makeup man had darkened the front with short black pencil strokes. It was said that the man drank heavily, but Niccolò could not detect an aroma of liquor and there was no bleariness about the eyes. "What do you think, kid?" Bogart indicated the package. "You and I look about the same size."

Niccolò started to open the brown wrapping paper.

Bogart said, "Shirts. Ross said you could use a few. These are some old ones. I don't wear them. You might as well."

If an American liked you, they used to say in pre-war Italy, he would give you the shirt off his back. Just an expression, Niccolò once believed. Now an American had done it. A movie star.

Uncomfortably, Bogart watched Niccolò stutter his way through a sentence of gratitude. "Forget it, kid. I'm just glad somebody around here is as skinny as me."

Then he ambled away and for the rest of the week treated Niccolò as if he were the furniture, another prop hammered into place. Niccolò was exhausted by the end of each day, and he had no friends and after a drink or two with Lorre he would go home to the little bungalow Ross had found for him. By ten o'clock he would fall asleep to band music. At midnight, when the radio stations stopped broadcasting, he would awaken to the sound of static, turn off the set and sleep again until sunrise, when the light bleached his dreams and made his eyelids red. Sometimes in the shower the dreams would return to him; close-ups of people in crowd scenes. Faces of old women, of boys grown suddenly decrepit, of yelling German faces with teeth like fences and the voices of dogs. The dreams never concluded. They were replayed like continuous performances in a cheap theater with drunks and grifters in the audience.

Morning was always a blessing because it was today and Hollywood and not yesterday and Europe. He walked on the hot streets and tried to reckon the wealth of even the poorest, the most nondescript of the studio people. Beverly Hills seemed another dream, a fantasy that he would have to resist before it pulled him in. Every day it was a little harder to remember.

He avoided company until the night of Zack Ross's party. Ross had rented a peculiar house in Ocean Park along an unfashionable stretch of beach. It was a place, he liked to point out, where movies had once been made and where bodies occasionally washed up after a drowning or a murder. He had a big sign that said CHARNEL HOUSE over the door, and next to a heavy brass knocker in the shape of a penis, there was a carefully engraved legend: IT IS NO LONGER ENOUGH TO BE HUNGARIAN, YOU MUST ALSO HAVE TALENT. The interior was festooned with fish nets and shells and driftwood, painted white and gold. The side windows were in the shape of portholes and sextants, and ship's wheels decorated the walls.

Niccolò saw the familiar exothalmic eyes and walked toward Lorre, who looked up and smiled without missing a beat of his story. "A friend of mine told me that Hitchcock liked to tell jokes," he was saying to a group of women. "So when he looked my way I'd watch him very closely— you understand I didn't know a word of English—and when it looked as if he had come to a punchline I'd giggle uproariously. Hitch figured I knew the language and that's how I got to play in *The Man Who Knew Too Much*." One of the women giggled and Lorre accused her of pretending to know English.

A heavy hand took hold of Niccolò's shoulder and spun him around. Ross grinned too brightly; he was already high on his Fishhouse Punch. "You know who you should meet?" Without waiting for a reply he steered his guest to a corner. There, under a painting of a weeping clown, stood a scholarly figure, a man who might have been a rabbi or a professor except that some fleeting expression hinted at an earthier occupation. He gave the impression of physical intensity studiously kept in check. Niccolò recognized him immediately: Emile Zola—the writer who risked his career to save a Jew. "I accuse!" he had written, and forced the government to change, restored poor Dreyfus to respectability, and sent the anti-Semites down to disgrace.

"Niccolò Levi," Ross began, "this is Muni Weisenfreund. Don't look surprised. In my house, Jews can go by their right names. Everywhere else, they're goys. Remember what Harry Cohn said?"

Paul Muni nodded. "The only Jewish actors at Columbia Pictures play Indians."

Ross's words were slurred. "Jack Benny is Benny Kubelsky. June Havoc is June Hovick. Danny Kaye is David Kaminsky, Melvyn Douglas is Melvyn Hesselberg. Eddie Robinson is—"

"Zack, shut up," Muni said. "You sound like Senator Rankin. All you need is a spoonbread accent and a sheet over your head."

But Ross had already been waylaid by someone and he wandered away, babbling stage names and real ones. The actor laughed dryly. Niccolò joined him, but he was too abashed to say anything. Here was Paul Muni, who had played famous men and won an Academy Award. A Jew. This was not a man you spoke to. You listened. But all the senior actor wanted to know was how the younger one was doing. "I know about you," he said. "Zack told me. When he was sober. It's true, then? You escaped from a concentration camp?"

"Yes. Long ago." Silence. Niccolò made himself speak. "Mr. Muni?"

"Paul."

"Paul. You—you were Emile Zola."

"I *played* Emile Zola."

"You read about him?"

"Before I play a part I always read about the man. For Louis Pasteur, for example, I—"

"Zola, he really did speak up? He really did change France?"

"He changed the world."

"One man."

"One man is all it takes sometimes."

"Sometimes . . ."

"Niccolò, under that tan you look pale. Perhaps a drink?"

"Thank you, no." Niccolò looked around, wondering if he could get out without Ross noticing and taking offense. Impossible. The host was at his front door, smiling at new arrivals. A back way, maybe; Niccolò needed air. He heard his name over the noise.

"Levi? Niccolò Levi?"

She looked young in the shadowy light; as she came forward to greet him the overhead light struck her full on and lines showed in the corners of her eyes, and the strain of dieting appeared in the cords of her neck.

"Grace Curie." She offered her hand, European style.

"Like Madame Curie," her escort burbled. "Only she's not the Madame. Just one of the girls."

"Thank you, Cyril," she said. "Run along and find a young man your own age and income bracket." She turned to Niccolò. "There's an emergency exit this way. I saw you looking."

She guided him down a long, crowded hallway.

"You were a star in Europe," she began. "Before the war."

"No," Niccolò protested. "Just another actor."

"Not what I heard."

"From Ross? He doesn't know."

"He knows enough. He said you were a prisoner. He said—"

"I don't want to hear what he said."

"All right," she told him. Her voice was soft. "All right. How will you get home?" She opened a glass panel and led him onto deep grass. Insects chattered in the dark and far away a train sounded. The party might have been taking place on another planet.

"I don't know. A taxi maybe . . . I suppose I could walk."

"Where do you live?"

He told her and she laughed. Grace Curie had good teeth and a low, erotic giggle. "The cops throw people in jail for walking that far. Even the dogs ride. That silver thing you see around their necks is a driver's license."

She pointed down the driveway at her white Studebaker. "I'll take you."

He shrugged. "Very kind."

"No trouble."

She drove well and in silence for most of the trip. As they came closer to his home she said, "How does it feel to act again?"

"I don't know. Good, I guess."

"Have you made any friends?"

"Well, the people in the film. They're very good, very understanding. Even Sidney Greenstreet, you know?"

"The fat one."

"He takes time, coaches me when I'm not right."

"Yes, but have you any real friends? People you can talk to?"

"I don't want to talk to anybody. Not yet."

"Too soon after Europe and everything?"

"And everything. Yes."

When they got to the house Grace asked him: "Look, do you mind if I come in for a while? I'm suddenly very tired. My eyes hurt."

"Yes, certainly. Only I have nothing. Only some California wine."

"Wine is perfect."

They sat sipping warm burgundy that tasted like pennies and she spoke of light topics: how the weather was compared with Italy's, the silliness of the producers, the latest Goldwyn story. She sat next to him on the couch and somewhere near midnight Niccolò began to feel that he was in yet another play, talking to an actress, working through a scene with a subtext he could not quite comprehend. Zack had said all along there would be women, but Niccolò assumed that was typical American exaggeration. Yet here was Grace Curie obviously ready to stay the night, breathing close to him, doing all the tricks, loosening the top button on her blouse and smiling with wide-open lips. When she kissed him her tongue searched his mouth and her hand explored the outside of his trousers and then climbed inside with a gentle urgency. Nothing was real anymore; he took her to his bed without any coaxing, with few preliminaries. At first the lovemaking was gentle and tentative. He put his mouth on her large hard nipples and inhaled some aroma that was part sexual but principally an

attar of dahlias. She smelled expensive. Later he began to
wander over her with his mouth and tongue. He felt forces
in his body that had been dormant so long he thought they
were dead. Except for Lerma he had stayed away from
women. The great love of his early years was killed. He
thought about Gina and went on plunging into this white-
skinned moaning woman wɪ ɔ ʌook him in her hands and in
her body and then in her mouth. He pounded into her with
the insistency of a heart: he spurted until blood came.

Off the Piazza Venezia there had been an art gallery
where the owner, a thin, sallow woman with great nostrils,
oversaw her collection of primitive art. She resembled one
of her exhibits: an African witch painted white. But her
statues were the finest in the country, better than the ones in
the museums. Niccolò remembered one in particular: a New
Guinea figure of a man whose erection was enormous. It
reached to the inside of his brain. Even then, as a child,
Niccolò knew that the primitives had found the truth early
and that the Romans had lost it. Sex was another part of the
brain, something that had worked loose and floated south,
like some island whose inhabitants still had ritual connections with the mainland. It was his mind, that overheated,
pain-pierced thing that was entering her again and again.

At first Grace giggled and then she moaned, but at last
she screamed. Her face went from repose to great pleasure
to distress. She searched his face for something recogniz-
able. "For God's sake," she said, "what is it? Who is it
you're fucking?"

"What?"

"Look at me, for Chrissake. You're hurting me, you
know that?"

The flames and faces receded into pillows. He saw the
very faint metallic light of morning just before sunrise.
"I'm sorry." He rolled off her and kissed her breasts. "I'm
sorry."

"Jesus. I mean, I love humping, you know. but *Jesus*."

"I don't know what happened."

"You were a million miles away, you know that?" But
her voice lost its asperity.

"Not quite so far."

"What you must have been through. What you must have seen."

She put her arm on his shoulder. Tears ran down his eyes. It was the first time he had cried in so long he had almost forgotten how.

"Tell me," she said.

"No."

"It won't hurt you. Not now."

Perhaps out of guilt, or so long a silence, he began. He spoke of the early days in Rome and the coming of the Fascists, and then about the burning Jesus and the demand for gold and the roundup of Gina and the child and the attempts to find her. He cried again when he described the camp and finding the unhuman woman who was once Gina, and the tracks that led to the camp bringing Jews to their death every day, and how he could not spend a day without thinking of it and a night without dreaming of it, chimneys stuck in the air exhaling Jews, Jewish smoke, Jewish souls. He quoted his beloved Dante:

> *Men che dramma*
> *De sangue m' è rimaso, che no tremi;*
> *Conosco i segni dell' antica fiamma.*

> Less than a drop
> of blood remains in me that does not tremble;
> I recognize the signals of the ancient flame.

She said nothing, only listened and, after breakfast, kissed him in silence, and drove off.

Niccolò napped fitfully in the afternoon, wondering why he felt such malaise. It was only sex, after all, not love. He had betrayed no one—or so he thought until Ross called him the next morning.

"Amazing," said the familiar growl. "You're practically a war hero. It'll escalate your goddam career." Niccolò had no idea what Ross was talking about until the Los Angeles

Examiner was mentioned. Niccolò ran all the way to the newsstand and read the column on his way home.

ITALIAN ACTOR RECALLS NAZI PRISON the headline read. "Worse than any horror movie," the subhead declared. Grace Curie ran on about Niccolò and Gina Levi, the romantic Roman couple. "Something out of an opera," she wrote. She cheapened everything. Rome was depicted in the four-color prose of a travelogue featuring pines and fountains. People were dressed in costumes, not clothing, and his family was made to appear like smiling cutouts in a pop-up book. Even the Nazis were mere shadows. But the dialogue rang true: "the train tracks across Poland like lines that no one dares to erase"; "the air turned into evidence of murder." Those were his words, polished a bit, made fit for American consumption. It looked like a shameless bid for attention, for a greater role in his next picture. The column had quotes from Peter Lorre and from Michele Morgan, whom he had met only once, talking of his tragedy and his willingness to rehearse and how hard he had worked on his English. A picture accompanied the text; some studio shot in which he looked even thinner than he was now, with an artificial smile demanded by the cameraman. He threw the paper into a basket long before he got home, and although the telephone rang all day he never picked it up. He cursed Grace and he cursed the column but mostly he cursed himself.

Paparazzi. They were the same everywhere: the jackals of the press. They would ask you anything, and when you told them the most intimate details they wanted to know more; they wanted to excavate until things you had buried safely were exhumed and shown to a world that was neither shocked nor moved, only intrigued, the way they would be by a good mystery, a satisfactory plane crash. The story of the concentration camps? Fine. The murder of the innocents? Two orchestra tickets, please. Open a can of sardines in America, there would be a line waiting to get in.

The actors were suddenly solicitous; a man named John Garfield bought him a drink at the Brown Derby and stuck a fifty-dollar bill in Niccolò's shirt pocket. Garfield's closed, immigrant face had trouble finding the right expression.

"Don't believe what you see here. Do your job, save your money, go back East. I hear you used to work in the theater. So did I. You and me, we're going back there. This is no place for people with more than two dimensions."

He showed Niccolò some clips, things he had saved for his own amusement. One was an ad for a pamphlet, from *The Hollywood Reporter:* "Six Ways the World Can End." Underneath it was the legend: "23 pages of reading pleasure for the whole family." Another was from *Variety:* "No longer is it necessary to cloak the more serious thoughts and aspects behind a melodramatic yarn, or sugarcoat the messages to the public. Such terms as 'Fascists' and 'Appeasers' can be used freely." War movies were in again.

Niccolò's English was good enough; he understood all the words and most of the implications.

"Someday the theater," Niccolò said. "But here at least is work."

"In garbage."

"And there?"

"Who knows? They said you were a master of disguise. You could play anything."

Niccolò dismissed it with his hands. "A journalist says that."

"In America they believe the journalists."

Niccolò nodded. Next time he would see to it that the journalists got it right.

On the way out of the restaurant Garfield introduced Niccolò to a little bullet-headed man, a large midget named Marty Zim. The agent, like everybody else in Hollywood, it seemed, had read Grace Curie. Zim was full of greasy bonhomie, but he also appeared to be moved by the newspaper account. "My relatives also," he said cryptically, and sniffled into a large red handkerchief. "You'll let me handle you, this time next year you'll be farting through silk. There's a picture, The Mask of Whaddyacall It. They're practically cast. Demetrios. Greenstreet's already set, so is Lorre. And Cianelli. There's a couple of parts still open, I happen to know. Here." The inevitable card was presented. Niccolò discarded it but two days later Zim appeared on the set and dragged him to Jean Negulesco's office. The director tested Niccolò for the role of a Smyrna fig packer, a betrayed associate of the hero-villain, Zachary Scott. Niccolò had no way of knowing what the studio was looking for, but he was not surprised when Zim called him with the news.

"It's a small thing," the agent said. "A role you could fit in the navel of a flea and still have enough room left for a producer's heart. But it's a start. You're moving, boy-chick."

The set for *The Mask of Demetrios* proved to be just like the other. Actors walking around trying out lines, technicians setting up lights to simulate the docks of Syria, sound men whispering into microphones, perpetually dissatisfied. It was early morning and a press agent was leading a tour group around Warners' back lot. Evidently these were people from the East; they wore conservative suits and dark ties and white shirts, and they did not gawk. They were, it turned out, advertising people themselves, publicizers of inanimate products: toothpaste, breakfast food, wine, watches, come to Hollywood to examine the innards of the greatest publicity machine in the world.

Of the dozen tourists, most had the indoor pallor of executives who worked for someone else and chafed at it, too old or unfit for service, men who had stayed home and made money and felt a vague mixture of avarice and guilt. Not one of them looked comfortable and several wore dark sunglasses as if the California sun might search them out. In groups of two or three they asked questions quietly, stopping first to speak to Negulesco and then to one of the cameramen, who let them peer through his lens. One of the Easterners who affected very dark glasses was wobbly and exhaled fumes of bourbon. He made his way around the set by leaning against various objects, taking deep deliberate breaths and studying the cables that ran and looped across the floor.

He lurched toward the canvas chair where Niccolò sat studying his script.

"Sorry." The drunk steadied himself. "Liquid lunch," he explained.

Niccolò looked up, smiled indulgently, and went back to his work. The man slumped down in an empty chair. For a moment he hovered between sleep and conversation. He seemed to be looking at something over Niccolò's shoulder, something far away, in another country, in another century maybe. "Strange goddamn place," he mumbled. "At Fox they have people running around in doublets and hoop-skirts. At MGM they got pirates. Down the street cowboys are killing Apaches. Here, it's a goddamn dock in Syria. How the hell you figure out what's real at the end of the day?"

Niccolò smiled. "I'm new here. It's not so hard for me."

"Yeah? Where you from?"

"Excuse me." The actor stood up. "I have to rehearse now," he said, although the call was not for another half-hour. The drunk got to his feet laboriously. He wiped his face with a white handkerchief and removed his glasses.

"Pleased to meet you," he said thickly, and offered his hand. Niccolò thought later that the grip was surprisingly firm and that, despite the indistinct words, there was no sign of vagueness in the man's cold gray eyes. Just then, it was impossible to tell which one of them was the actor.

23

Carl Berlin and Niccolò Levi:
Hollywood, 1945

IF I HAD it to do all over again, Carl grumbled, I would have
been a baseball umpire. Or a songwriter. Something
essential to the war effort. Then they wouldn't have tapped
me. You never heard of Jocko Conlan doing intelligence
work; or Hoagy Carmichael.

The entire trip had been too easy to arrange; the Old Man
bought his story of leg pain and gave him a week off without
hesitation. A bad sign. Then the train trip had been without
incident. And then Niccolò Levi had turned out to be a shy,
stricken refugee about as dangerous as a sparrow.

For form's sake Carl tracked Levi everywhere. He tried to
engage Niccolò in conversation on the set of *The Mask of
Demetrios*. A failure. He watched him in stores and on the
streets. There was never a sign of eccentricity or impa-
tience, never any of the giveaways of fanaticism: the silent,
moving lips; the too-shiny eyes; the mix of pallor and
blushing. Now Carl tried another standard counterintelligence mode, half-ashamed of himself for its textbook
simplicity. He followed the actor's little yellow roadster to

an Italian restaurant on the Strip. After the requisite ten minutes he entered, squinting in the dim illumination. Niccolò was dining alone at a small table. A white candle shed just enough light for him to read *Variety*. Carl contrived to recognize the actor from the set and remarked on the coincidence. He stood talking to Niccolò until he was invited to sit down.

"I'll stay for just a minute." Carl pulled up a chair. He asked the waiter for a half-bottle of the only chablis on the list. "Good label, bad year," he said. "They're all bad years now, I guess." He leaned across the table, confidentially. "On me. I'll put you on the swindle sheet as a star."

"I'm not a star," Niccolò protested. "Only a bit player."

"Today a bit player. Tomorrow, who knows?"

"Yes. Tomorrow, who knows?"

Through the drinks Carl went on about Hollywood, about what an interesting job it must be to make movies, what big money there was when a character actor struck the right part. What was William Powell until *The Thin Man*? and Akim Tamiroff before *For Whom the Bell Tolls*?

That exhausted Carl's knowledge of cinema, gleaned from readings of Louella Parsons in the *Journal American*. He tried to elicit conversation, but Niccolò ate meditatively and answered questions politely but without elaboration. Even when Carl alluded to the war in Italy, the refugee only lifted his gaze from the plate and responded, "You cannot believe all that you read about me in the paper."

This time it was Carl's turn to nod without comment and to study his own plate. It was the first he had heard of the newspaper story.

Planted, no doubt, by studio publicity, and therefore available in a scrapbook at Warner Brothers' front office. When the rest of the meal proved monosyllabic, Carl excused himself and went off into the night.

The following morning a sycophant at Warner's was only too happy to help the open-faced adman from New York. He brought out the black scrapbook and proudly handed it to Carl. "Two weeks of production and we already have nine hundred inches, nationwide. Of free advertising, I mean."

"And this is all nine hundred." Carl leafed through the book.

"All but about ten inches on Zachary Scott." The willowy young man sniffed. "If that man is ten inches, I'm Errol Flynn."

The item on Niccolò was nestled between a story on Eric Ambler, whose novel was being adapted for the screen, and a long piece about the practical jokes of Greenstreet and Lorre. Carl read the column through twice and made some notes on the back of an envelope. He went for a slow drive in Beverly Hills, past the huge houses and around the sightseeing buses, where the homes of Jack Benny and the late Carole Lombard and Clark Gable were indicated by pimply high-school boys in blue uniforms with pink piping. Carl hardly noticed the bus or its cargo of gorgons with cement permanents, and their weary husbands in tow. But when the vehicle drew too close, Carl turned his head to the left. The bus almost hid a black Ford sedan. Someone on board shouted "Wait!"; Carl could hear it in the background through the open windows. The driver slammed on the brakes suddenly. The urgent cry was probably nothing more than a rider wanting to squeeze off another snapshot of Mulholland Drive; Carl never found out. For in the next instant, where the bus should have been, the Ford was unexpectedly revealed. Its driver abruptly accelerated and turned left and sped from sight before Carl could react to the blurred glimpse of the thin man he had shot along with Herr Rathenau. He thought: all this time they've had me in their sights; the rabbit who imagined himself a dog. Carl pulled to the curbside and looked at nothing and wondered what he was going to do with the rest of the day and with the rest of his life, and whether both questions amounted to the same thing. He decided that no, the Germans had no intention of killing him yet. Very likely they had followed him from New York in the belief that he was involved in some high plan. "Do *they* have the wrong number?" Carl said to the air. How they picked up his trail he could not determine.

Maybe they had a stakeout at Penn Station. Maybe the OSS was here. Maybe the Old Man was here. Maybe I ought to throw open my hotel room and send up for some ice cubes and invite them all in. A SNAFU party. Situation normal, all fucked up. But the Old Man couldn't know I was in L.A. I would have heard. Or would I? Maybe this was just what the Old Man wanted, the Germans out of the woodwork at last.

He went back to his hotel, bought a paper, and retired to his room. He tried to put through a long-distance call to Ruth in New York, but the operators told him it would be a wait of at least half an hour. When he complained, the voice on the other end reminded him there was a war on. He hesitated, recalling Sussman's Yiddish: "Who is a hero? He who suppresses a wisecrack," and was silent. While he waited he checked the paper.

In Burma the 19th Indian Division had taken the last major positions held by the Japanese in Mandalay, and Kipling's poem had been reprinted, accompanied by pictures of the British colony in Hollywood: C. Aubrey Smith, Ronald Colman, Noel Coward. The war, brought to you by 20th Century–Fox. In Los Angeles the big news was a murder, reported in scrupulous detail by five correspondents. A woman named Florence Moon, inescapably called Blue by her friends, had been found murdered in a rooming house in Watts. There were several sensational aspects to the case, all of them ideal for the Los Angeles reader bored with conventional items about the Führer and Emperor Hirohito.

The house was in the black section, but Blue Moon was white. She had been a starlet, and though Carl remembered Ben Hecht's definition of a starlet as any woman under thirty-five not actively employed in a brothel, this woman had been in two films and was to be cast in another—*The Mask of Demetrios*. A small part, almost a walk-on, her agent conceded, but still a part. She had expectations, he went on. She could have been another Gene Tierney. The same figure, the same overbite.

Even this would not have been enough to send so many

journalists in search of a story. What gripped the night editor was the manner of the murder. Florence Moon had been tortured for hours before her death. She had been tied like meat from the ceiling, upside down, for hours. Cigarette burns covered large portions of her body, notably the thighs and breasts. She had been beaten or whipped by something that left complex imprints, possibly a sashcord. There had even been some electric burns. The cause of death was strangulation. There were thumb marks around the long, narrow throat. The reporters had interviewed producers, agents, co-workers, former roommates, and Blue Moon's widowed and incoherent mother in Athens, Georgia. They had also spoken to police, who gave the customary assurances of leads and clues. An arrest was expected within forty-eight hours, Captain Henry Carras assured the public. Former boyfriends remained to be interviewed. So did a strange white man, seen driving around with a white woman, in the Negro section of town, asking for places to buy dope.

There would be no arrest within forty-eight hours; Carl was certain of that. He also knew this was a motiveless crime; there would be no real clues and no authentic leads. The twenty-six-year-old, 5′ 4″ brunette actress, Florence Moon, had been slaughtered by the Butcher. He was right here in Los Angeles; he and his friends. Carl Berlin had come west and a young woman had died because of it. One way or another, Carl thought, I am responsible. A carrier. He was still thinking about it, about all the Butcher's women, when the phone rang.

"Mr. Berlin? Collect call from Miss Ruth Silver. Will you accept charges?"

"Where are you calling from?"

"A pay booth in the Waldorf-Astoria. It's all right, Carl."

She was one of the lucky ones, Carl acknowledged; she had been to war and back many times. And she had always returned. She had even come back from the Butcher. They would have to risk the eavesdropping. He told her about Niccolò.

"There doesn't seem to be anything. Not on the surface, anyway."

"And underneath?"

"I'm not an X ray machine. I'm only a wine merchant in the wrong business."

"Carl, what's the matter? I can hear in your voice, something's not kosher."

"He's here, Ruth. The Butcher's here." He told her about the Blue Moon murder.

"You've seen the body?"

"No, I just found out about it. In the *Times*."

"The paper? You can't tell from a paper."

"I can tell."

Their voices sounded wobbly: the wires hissed.

"Come home," Ruth said. "Get out before something happens to you."

"It already did."

"Carl? You know something you're not telling me?"

"I just want to make sure Niccolò is clean before I go, is all. That's why I came three thousand miles."

"You'll call me?"

"Tomorrow morning."

She said goodbye without affection. Carl hated the episodes when she was all business; it was as if they were two sexless functionaries. Maybe that was all they would be from here on.

He forced himself to shake off the call, to go out, to think about what remained to be done. He made his way, uncertainly and in the dark, to Niccolò Levi's bungalow on Beechwood Drive. It was neat, respectable, and small, with only a few lights on in the rear. Carl rang the bell; knocks at night would not be a welcome sound to a refugee.

The actor came to the door and opened it like a man lifting off a bandage.

"Yes?" he said, and then recognized his caller. "What do you want?"

"Mr. Levi—" Carl began.

"You are not a businessman." Niccolò looked down the street and then seemed on the verge of slamming the door.

"No," Carl said quickly, "I work for the government."

"Then let me see your credentials."

Carl opened his wallet and exhibited the green cards. He knew that these would be as unconvincing as a Choctaw message on birchbark. "Look," he told Niccolò, "I'm legit. Counterintelligence we call it here. You know? Like a spy against spies. I have no time to waste. I know about the Professor and Lerma and you. I know about the plan."

He let the words hang in the air. Niccolò nodded silently.

"Come in," he said.

The furniture was teak-stained pine, the kind that decorators privately referred to as Santa Barbarian. The draperies had been chocolate once, but the sun had bleached them to a hepatic shade. The rug was copper and brown and all the accessories, the ashtrays, the coffee table on wheels, the plates, matched it.

Niccolò saw Carl taking it in. "This is none of it mine," he explained. "Belongs to a woman, a costume maker for the studio. She rents to me by the month."

Carl inspected the white wall over a fake fireplace. It displayed the customary netting. Driftwood pieces sat on the mantel. Three maps decorated the wall, two nautical, one of some land.

"It's all hers." Niccolò motioned his visitor to a white wicker chair. "She won't let me touch anything."

"Not even with a match?"

Niccolò forced an uneasy smile. "It is not very nice. But still, you know, a home. My home now. All I have."

Carl nodded and felt small and cruel. It was pointless to attack the decor. This was no foreign agent to be broken down, only a wounded traveler who had come too far too fast, a frightened man in a precarious profession.

Niccolò pleaded, "Sir, can you tell me about Lerma? Anything."

"There's nothing to tell."

"She's dead?"

"Yes. Weeks ago. The Germans got her. She escaped but she was too far gone. She lived only long enough to tell us about, you know—"

Niccolò knew. That much was obvious. He was jittery and he asked Carl if he could have a drink, as if he were already under arrest. Carl wondered if Niccolò would leave the room on the pretext of getting scotch and attempt to escape. Instead, the actor lingered, anxious to unburden himself.

"It's true," he confessed. "Yes, we had a plan. You don't know what it was like, what it's like now, if the places are still standing." He looked hard into Carl's face. "You're Jewish?"

"Yes."

"In Europe you would now be dead."

"I know."

"You don't know what it was to see the prisoners die, to hear the screams of the suffering. And never a word, never a bullet, never a bomb, never a leaflet from America. Nothing."

Carl poured drinks and sat and listened. He heard stories of Italy and the German occupation, of the thousand Roman Jews betrayed to Auschwitz after they had handed over the gold, of the incidents in the camps, the tortures and medical experiments, the burning of corpses and the turning of people into soap. He had read about all this, but Niccolò's witness was not the dry account of Eyes Only memos, or the reportage of Sussman, who had heard it third hand, smuggled from the Warsaw ghetto and set down by conscientious Swiss clerks. Several times he wanted to rise, abashed, to offer Niccolò an apology and let him go. But he stayed: Niccolò seemed to welcome the opportunity to talk to a Jew who was neither journalist nor actor.

"Yes," he admitted to Carl. "Yes. We plotted. We swore to kill the greatest figure we could find, to avenge the Jews. What Lerma said was not false. But you must realize we were crazy then. Driven mad. By sorrow, by hunger that made our minds burn, you understand?"

Carl was ashamed to sit in judgment.

Niccolò tried to find phrases adequate for his feelings. His hands moved in the air.

"We . . . knew nothing. We could see the tracks

smooth and shiny. The railroad brought people every day. Children. Old women. At night they were corpses. In the morning, smoke, ashes. The tracks were never bombed. Why?"

Carl had no answer. Niccolò did not seem to require one. His face was wet as he spoke: "Even now, not bombed, I think. We continue to die. I know, I know, Americans die too. But as soldiers. We die as cattle. Before the Germans surrender, *if* they surrender, we may all be gone. You understand why I felt what I felt? Why Lerma did? If I had seen the President then, yes, I would have killed him if I could. Even now I don't like him. I don't understand him. He smiles and smiles and still I can see in my mind those trains coming and the chimneys making the sky black. But he is the President, and the United States is my home. He is my President now."

Outside, the insects made high sounds with their wings. Carl started to speak, but Niccolò interrupted him.

"You must understand how insane I was. Truly insane. I had lost my wife. My baby. My life." He was crying now. "Excuse me," he said. "I thought I had seen the end of tears. But I can't . . . I feel . . . you must understand."

Carl thought: each job is worse than the last, each assignment more degrading until this, the bottom, manufacturing more misery for a man who thought he had got past it all. He rose.

Niccolò protested: "Please stay."

"No," Carl said. "Go to sleep. Go to work. You won't hear from us again."

Over Niccolò's protests he walked out and down the little gravel path to his car. The actor's yellow roadster looked cheerful by houselight, a mockery of what had happened inside.

That night Carl had bad dreams. He knew he would; he had spent an hour getting himself drunk in a little bar on Pico. But liquor only intensified the visions of massacre. The sounds of screams were mixed with prayer. Children were walking over a burning map. He woke up soaked in sweat and seized with an overpowering thirst. He went to the bathroom and drank too much cold water and felt nauseated. He walked around trying to shake the dream. Something else was bothering him. Something not quite physical. Something about Niccolò. Probably his terrible story. No, there was something about Niccolò himself. But what? He had been dressed in the plainest California stuff: brown slacks with white short-sleeved shirt, moccasins. The place, then. The house.

He closed his eyes against the vapid light of morning and tried to reconstruct Niccolò Levi's room with its execrable furniture and accessories. The wall with its suggestions of yachting would be as remote to an Italian as the in-jokes on the Jack Benny show: "Your money or your life." "I'm thinking, I'm thinking. . . ."

Still, maybe he liked to sail. Italians were always good sailors. Maybe he wanted to buy a boat, like Erroll Flynn. God willing, Niccolò *could* become a star; not Gable, but a character lead. Like Dane Clark, Richard Conte, John Garfield. Little men with big careers. Niccolò would have a boat and pin up his own maps of Catalina Island.

Maps.

And suddenly Carl knew. He knew why he had slept badly and what had been wrong with the place. It was not the liquor: it was the maps. Two of them were legitimate. They must have belonged to the landlady. But the third had to be Niccolò's. There was no reason for anyone in Hollywood to have a map of Warm Springs, Georgia, unless he were going there. Warm Springs was the place where polio victims went to be rehabilitated. It was the favorite retreat of the President.

Carl washed and dressed with an old efficiency he thought he had lost. On the way to Niccolò's house he kept cursing himself for being so slow, for wanting to believe the best instead of suspecting the worst. He wondered if he had overlooked anything else in his wish to see Niccolò Levi as an innocent. Yes, he concluded, there was something worse that might be under way. The Germans might know about Niccolò.

He pushed the gas pedal harder. The Germans do know.

They're not here to follow me. They're here to check on an Italian actor.

The process was easy to follow now: if Linda Ermanelli had confessed to Ruth, she had probably told as much or more to her captors. After all, the Germans had held her for months. How long could anyone keep a confidence in a Nazi prison? So the Germans had learned long ago that somewhere in America there was a potential killer, a secret weapon they could use some day. Niccolò Levi must be Ziege: the Goat. He was the reason the Germans were here.

As Carl pulled up at Niccolò's he saw that the roadster was gone. No one answered the bell. He drove to the studio: actors frequently had six A.M. calls. The board listed Niccolò's name, but one of the assistant directors was fuming. Levi was already an hour late. Only one event went Carl's way: the woman who rented the house to Niccolò was on the set. She had the consistency and strength of saddle leather, and, as Carl expected, she wore the hallowed ornaments of the Los Angeles harpy: rhinestone rings and a necklace of shells and gilt driftwood. Mrs. Vera Wills had a boy in the Coast Guard and a great respect for authority. She read Carl's government card very carefully and told him what he wanted to know: Niccolò Levi had been recommended to her by Mr. Zack Ross. Two months' rent, $240, had been paid in advance, and Mr. Levi had been a clean, neat tenant, very quiet, no complaints from the neighbors. The maps on the walls were hers and her husband's from the days when they sailed. Before the war. The boat, Xanadu, was in storage. The map of Georgia? No, there had been no map of Georgia when she visited the house last week.

The propmaster knew nothing about a map of Georgia; it had nothing to do with the movie, he said. The whole thing took place in Europe. Hadn't Carl read the book?

A makeup man shouted for Zachary Scott and Victor Francen. Carl looked at his watch. It was 7:15. Early in the morning for everybody but movie actors and people at defense plants. The middle of the night for half the world. And very, very late for Carl Berlin. Maybe too late.

He went out into the clear April day and sat in his car with his face in his hands and tried to reason the thing out.

What Ruth had suspected, what she had feared, was true. Niccolò Levi, concentration camp escapee, actor, one of the war's walking wounded, a Jew, was going to kill the President of the United States.

Levi, the paper had reported, was a "master of disguise." Even allowing for the usual Celluloid City hyperbole, that meant he could appear as anyone: an old man, a Negro, a Mexican, a postman, even a woman. He had made it to safety that way; this time he could make it to catastrophe. Carl could not tell the Old Man about it, or anyone in the organization. And if the papers got hold of the story . . .

Carl examined his chances. It would be impossible to catch Niccolò without aid. The man had a head start of at least six hours. By now he would have ditched the roadster. And then what? Trains? Hitchhiking? Was there an accomplice? Unlikely. Niccolò would be a loner, listening to voices in his head.

Carl drove around absently. He felt as if he had been anesthetized: there was nothing, absolutely nothing, he could do. He bought a paper and read some more about the Blue Moon murder. There were still no arrests, and the police were beginning to concede that the clues had gone nowhere. The suspects were all clean.

"We have hopes," Captain Carras had told the *Times*.

"You and me, Captain," Carl said. "You and me." He envied the police with their little motiveless crime.

Somewhere between Schwab's and his hotel he put his dilemma and the cops' together. He went to his room, lay on his bed, and smoked two cigarettes. He rose and walked around trying not to look at the mirror, at the drawn, hopeless face. This is the man, he acknowledged, who wanted to go to Europe and fight, who dreamed of being a tail gunner or a rifleman. And here I am, going to war against some poor civilian, a battered refugee with blood in his head. A Jew against a Jew.

Carl dialed the police. He told them that the Blue Moon

murderer was an actor named Niccolò Levi, currently
employed by Warner Brothers. The desk sergeant spoke
slowly and asked for everything twice, an old police trick.
Carl spoke tersely, gave the details he thought would arouse
some appetites at the station and hung up before the call
could be traced. He made another call to Ruth and waited
for half an hour until she could find whatever booth she used
to ring him back. The walls of the room pressed in on him
and his watch chattered rhythmically of death. By the time
New York was on the line he had imagined five possible
scenarios, each worse than the next, each bringing hell to
the New World.

He told Ruth about Niccolò's flight and about the map of
Warm Springs. He hoped she would say something mitigat-
ing. But all Ruth replied was, "Oh, God—what can we
do?"

Only two things, he told her. One had already been done.
At least the cops would put out an all-points with his
description. If Niccolò were captured he could prove his
innocence easily enough, but he would be prevented from
completing his journey. The chances were against his arrest.
There was nothing in wide-open America to keep a good
actor from slipping through the porous barriers of state
highways and bus and train terminals. Still, it was worth a
try; by now Niccolò might have grown lazy or arrogant or
careless. *Might* have. If Niccolò's route was unknown, his
destination was not a mystery. He was headed for Warm
Springs. Carl would depart immediately, if Ruth could
arrange an Army flight. There was an airfield at Fort
Benning, Georgia. From there he could get a car or
hitchhike to the resort.

Yes, and then?

Carl had no answer. He would think of something. He
would scan the faces of passersby in the town, if there was a
town. He knew nothing about Warm Springs except that it
was some sort of haven for polio patients, among them the
President.

Ruth was more confident. It was unlike her to wonder
about anything; she always looked up answers to puzzles in

the back of the book. She asked Carl to hang up and wait in
the room for a recall. Something would turn up, she said, in
a tone that had reminded him of Mr. Micawber, not the ideal
planner of clandestine missions.

The phone sat silent for too long. Carl began to wonder if
Niccolò had weapons: a rifle, maybe. Or a grenade. What
damage a grenade could do, even if it didn't hit the main
target. The blood, the headlines. A feast for the jackals of
the press, the Ku Klux Klan, the anti-Semites in the State
Department.

Ruth called back almost an hour later.

"Everything is set," she said. "Go to Fort Ord. An Army
plane will take you to Fort Benning, eight miles south of
Columbus. There will be a car waiting for you. You drive
north about fifty miles to Meriwether County. There will be
signs to Warm Springs. Find a road called Twiggs and take
it until it becomes dirt. You will see a handmade sign saying
'Silver.' It is the home of Major George Silver. A cousin.
No one will be there. The major is away. There are no
servants. I will be waiting for you."

"There's no need for you, Ruth. You don't even know
what Niccolò Levi looks like. Leave it to me."

Carl knew how absurd his reply sounded. He did not
argue with Ruth when she insisted on coming down. Plans
were already made; besides, she had once visited the
major's house. At least she knew where the dishes were.

"I don't think we'll be doing much eating in," Carl said
before signing off. Or sleeping, he thought, but did not say.
He packed and got in his car with the old feeling of rifles
trained on him from far away. Strictly a neurosis, he
decided. No one was on the street; no one was in sight. The
trip to Warm Springs might prove to be a Godsend; shake
them all off: the Germans, the Old Man, the past.

24

Niccolò Levi: Nevada, 1945

THE ENGINE SOUNDED ominous. Overheated, Niccolò guessed, and drove across the grassy shoulder to the shade of a new billboard. It advertised, in harsh colors, the merits of a sun lotion. A dog was pulling down the pants of a tan little girl, revealing very white buttocks. Anyone who drove by looked at the child, not the car. No one noticed its driver. He opened the hood and let the steam evaporate. Idly, he turned on the radio, hoping to catch some news confirming the President's whereabouts. There was only a song about a zoot suit with a reat pleat, a drape shape and a stuff cuff. America. Just when you got to understand the language they brought in new words. When you bought clothes they changed the styles. Only a nation with too much money could do such things in the middle of war. All this throw-away wealth. And the feeble signs DON'T WASTE PAPER, while billboards lined the roads. And IS THIS TRIP NECESSARY? while tourists filled the hotels. Everyone moving, no one thinking. To have a serious conversation you had to sit on a bus with a stranger and talk about God. The worst was hearing Hollywood Jews speaking of money. Whenever he tried to shift the conversation around to Europe they gave him pitying looks: Poor boy, you know he was in a concentration camp. Lost his whole family. Very sad story. Now, about your next picture, Sol . . .

The music stopped and the news came on. Good bulletins from Germany. The Third Army was advancing east, heading for the Weser River and the area of Ohrdruf. Niccolò was about to snap the radio off, to rest the battery, when he heard an item about Blue Moon. They were looking for her suspected murderer, an actor named Niccolò Levi, missing from the set of *The Mask of Demetrios*.

"Impossible!" he said aloud. A mistake. He only knew the woman from the papers: a torture killing, something reminiscent of European crimes, not American ones.

Niccolò got out of the car. He was stunned and nauseated. He lay on the grass. It was still moist. He took deep breaths and tried to calm his heart. In a while, the blood returned to his head and he knew what to do. He returned to the roadster, started the motor, and pointed the car toward a little ravine out of sight on Highway 1. He cut the engine, got out, released the emergency brake and pushed hard. The car rolled lazily downhill, bumping on rocks until it slid to a halt in a stand of high brown weeds.

Imperfect, even slovenly, but it would have to do. With luck, the vehicle would not be found for a day or so. Fortune was all he could lean on now. Niccolò walked on the grass near the road, a narrow figure in gray slacks and a short-sleeved blue shirt, carrying a large white sack, looking for all the world like another San Bernardino truck farmer. No official cars showed up between the billboard and the truck stop two miles up the road.

But there, outside the diner, a brown and white State Police Oldsmobile was parked. It was pointed west, and Niccolò assumed the worst. He looked at all five trucks waiting in the macadam lot. Four of them had California license plates. The other was from Nevada: VASQUEZ MACHINE PARTS was stenciled on its side. Niccolò kept between the truck and the road so that if the driver was near a window looking out he would not be able to see anyone approaching. Niccolò tried the truck's rear doors. They were open. He climbed in and shut the doors behind him. Pieces of tractors lay on the floor and motors were moored to poles with rope and steel chains. There would be a lot of rattling, but little hazard. Niccolò hid behind a wheel-less tractor body and made a pillow of his laundry bag. Half an hour later the driver ground the gears and started off. The rest of the journey should be so simple, Niccolò murmured. By his calculations he had 1900 miles to go.

An hour later, as the truck grunted up a hill, Niccolò thrust his hand in the bag, felt around in the costume collection until he found a chocolate bar, and ate breakfast. Afterward, he permitted himself a light sleep. It was dark in the truck, but he had thought of everything. He set up a candle, lit it, and studied a road map of the United States. If the truck was going to Nevada, it was passing through Arizona now. In all likelihood, it would not stop for a few more hours; possibly not until nightfall. The next move would be a problem. Best would be to stay south and head east. But Niccolò was a passenger; the choice of itinerary was not his; only the goal. He extinguished the candle and dozed some more.

The truck pulled off twice before arriving at its destination. It was almost midnight by Niccolò's luminous watch, and he knew the driver had stopped permanently because there were hearty sounds and the voice of a woman. When the noises faded he looked out cautiously, like an actor peering through a crack in the curtain, and stepped down. He pulled his bag with him, clicked the truck door back in place, and walked into the night.

Stars were visible by the thousands. It was possible to read by the crescent moonlight. In back of him was the farmhouse where the driver lived. Several miles up the road Niccolò saw the dim lights of another building, and, about ten miles away, another series of lights. A few cars and trucks dotted the highway. After that, nothing. He checked his compass and began walking east on the flat, arid land.

He walked until sunrise. By that time he had come to the outer reaches of a place called Roswell. Cattle country:

herds to the north and west. Sheep a few miles away, white on the soft dirt hills. The air was dry and things shimmered if he looked at them too long. Signs off the blacktop pointed to an Indian reservation. As a child, Niccolò had believed what he saw on screen: Indians wore loincloths, rode horses, killed white men with bows and arrows, drank firewater, and whooped around campfires. He had learned better when he came to the place where legends were manufactured. In Hollywood he found Indians in business suits and squaws in dresses. Some had oil money and a few acted in pictures. So there would be no necessity for him to get into costume. He would change to a work shirt and put on a gray low-brimmed hat. The rest was a matter of skin dye and a silver and turquoise lanyard around his shirt collar. He had bought it two weeks before, and while the man fussed around in a cigar box for change, Niccolò studied the way he wore his jewelry and held himself and walked. Duplicating the voice was impossible; Niccolò knew that he spoke with an Italian accent. No one in the world would mistake it for anything else. But from a distance of seven or eight feet from the cars, trudging along the highway, he could pass for an Indian walking home. Except, of course, to another Indian. He would have to trust in Providence; the President was still a long, long way away. He sat in the shade of a water tower and watched license plates for a while. Nothing farther than Texas or Oklahoma. He began to show the hitchhiker's thumb at eight o'clock. Perhaps because Niccolò was now an Indian, or because the trucks were moving at such velocity, he had to wait almost an hour before an old red van pulled up. Its side was block-lettered CURTISS CHEMICALS, and its driver looked as if he had been preserved in them. He was as bald as an onion and the same color, except for his left arm, tanned from years of leaning on an open cab window. His suspicious little eyes peered out from a cracked and age-freckled face, and he had only two teeth, both in the front, one on the upper jaw, one on the lower.

"Git in, Injun," he said. He sounded like something

from a Western. There was even a pistol resting in a holster on the dashboard. "Where you goin'?"

Niccolò pointed east. "Oklahoma." He tried to grunt in the style of the faithful Indian companion he had heard on the *Lone Ranger* program. Niccolò hoped the driver would not ask his name. He supposed that Indians had the same names as other people, but you never knew. Take Yakima Canutt, for instance, the Indian stunt man; who could make up a name like that?

"Oklahoma City?" the driver asked.

"Mmmm."

"I'll take you to Andarko. That's near Norman. You know the territory?"

"No."

"Ain't nothin' in this world as ignorant as an ignorant Injun. Lemme tell you about it." He lectured about the Sooner State and its population and its oil derricks and its past as Indian Territory. "But I guess you know about that. You know what our state flower is? Mistletoe. When I was younger, sixty even, I had mistletoe right up here in the cab. Ever' time a woman come in I kissed her. Used to lay hitchhikers during the Depression. By the hundreds. I kep' a list. Now I wouldn't even put sagebrush up there. I haven't had a woman since I was seventy-one. Don't need 'em now. Blessed relief." He started to snuffle. "Nope. I'm tellin' a lie. I miss 'em. All that perfume and them tits. Ain't nothin' in the world as appetizin' as a thin woman with big tits. I still like to look at 'em. You like tits?"

"Mmmm."

"Go ahead and sleep. Nothin' as sleepy as a sleepy Injun."

Niccolò closed his eyes. The man went on talking about women. He dwelt on various parts of their bodies and what happened to women's breasts after they had children and why he had married four times and never had any children. Through it all, Niccolò pretended to sleep, inhaling and exhaling with even, heavy breaths. When the truck pulled up, hours later, the driver said, "Goin' to take a leak and git some food. You want to come in?"

Niccolò shook his head.

"Git you somethin' to eat? Coffee?"

Again Niccolò refused. The driver shrugged and jumped down. Ostentatiously he buckled on his pistol before entering the diner. When the man was gone, Niccolò switched on the radio. It was close to two o'clock. On the hour there would be news.

The station identified itself as Texan, and the announcer had a country twang. But the news was delivered tersely and with no regionalisms. The Blue Moon murder was the third item in, just after reports about the difficult fighting on Okinawa. Niccolò Levi's car had been found. The fugitive was now referred to as a master of disguise. Someone had been reading his publicity or talking to people at the studio. Blue Moon's friends testified that she had never been seen with the suspect, never talked about him, never liked foreigners much. The police wondered what to look for. "The actor," they told reporters, "could show up as anything, a cowpuncher, a fat man, even a woman." They had a tip that he was heading east. No mention was made of Warm Springs.

Niccolò took some biscuits from his bag and munched on them slowly. He tried to imagine what had happened back in Hollywood. There was no way the police could truly link him with the murder. Whenever it took place, Niccolò was probably on the set, surrounded by scores of witnesses. So it was—what did they call it in crime pictures?—a frameup. But who would frame him? The only enemies he had were Germans. Except for Carl Berlin. The pursuer. The suspicious Intelligence man, the German Jew pitted against a fellow Jew. In Europe, commit a million murders, slaughter women and infants, and you were put in charge of whole countries. Accuse a man of one death in America, and the police in every state were after him. A monstrous, lopsided world. He sat pondering all of it when it occurred to him that a radio might be on inside the roadside restaurant. The old driver might be listening to it now. Niccolò got down from the truck and walked to an old blue Ford coupé. It still had the keys in it. He hesitated for a moment, climbed in and started the motor quietly. He drove it west, heading back the way he came. After four miles he abandoned it near a farm, took off his make-up, and changed into dirty overalls. He crossed the road and thumbed his way aboard an open pickup truck full of lettuce. The driver was fat and sleepy and made no conversation. Niccolò lowered himself in the seat and watched. In a few minutes a police car passed them going east. Twenty minutes later it sped down the road in the opposite direction. Chances are the car had been found, Niccolò reflected. Pointing back to L.A. in which case they would start looking for him back in West Texas or even in Arizona or California. Also, they would be looking for an Indian. The Master of Disguise was now a dirt farmer with gray temples.

The lettuce truck drove without incident for six hours. When Niccolò climbed down he was just outside Oklahoma City. The North River was quiet and clear; Niccolò washed in it, then doubled back and watched the truck driver enter an isolated telephone booth fifty feet from a closed Esso station. The man talked so softly that Niccolò had to get quite close before he could hear any words. He smiled to himself when he caught the drift of conversation: something harmless. The voice kept speaking about an animal. "The goat is one third of the way home," it said. Niccolò moved on. He had better things to do than eavesdrop on a farmer who wanted to talk about livestock.

25

Carl Berlin:
Warm Springs, 1945

THE HOUSE WAS on five acres, and in this case the term landscape artist was justified. Tall poplars and larches ringed the structure, and on the vast, manicured lawn stood a copper beech older than the nation. The clapboard home itself was painted white throughout, and ancestral paintings lined the halls of the stairs and decorated the living room.

Music for a Chopin mazurka lay open at the Baldwin grand piano, and the library held three thousand leather-bound volumes of history and folklore.

"I knew you were well connected," Carl said, "but I didn't know you knew Rhett Butler personally."

"Just good friends," Ruth replied. "Actually, this particular Silver family are the black sheep. One of them financed the Civil War. Part of the International Jewish Confederacy."

They sat in the living room sipping iced tea and attempting to plan the day. They knew whom they were after; certainly they had arrived ahead of the assassin. All that remained was to find the face. All. Carl smiled bitterly.

Our clever artist has cleverly concealed two rabbits, the circus, a jack-o'-lantern, two saints, and the face of Niccolò Levi in this picture of rural Georgia. See if you can find them before the trigger is pulled. . . .

"Tell me about him again," Ruth insisted. She looked as if she had not slept in a week. Her face was bleak again. The lean, graceful body had lost too much weight too soon.

Carl went through the particulars: height, weight, position of the dark eyes, shape of the ears, tone of voice, accent.

"That's the best thing we have," he said. "He can conceal his face, he can dress as anything. But he can't *sound* like anything except an Italian."

"When do you think he'll get here?"

"I don't know. We have time."

"Time for what?" Ruth started to ask. And then she knew. "Oh, that."

"Yeah, that. I thought we might go upstairs and *that* for a while."

"There is no time."

"There always used to be."

"Not now, Carl."

"Not ever, you mean."

"I didn't say that."

"Not with lyrics. Just with music."

Even so, he knew he could approach her if he went slowly, like a predator. No sudden movements; no harsh noises. He began listing the odds against Niccolò: the State Police, the distribution of his picture to the wire services, the sensational nature of the crime for which he stood, or rather ran, accused.

"Poor man," was all Ruth said.

He mimicked her tone: " 'Poor man.' What else could I do? You want him to get a free ride to Warm Springs, all expenses paid?"

"No, of course not. Only . . . he's suffered so."

"We'll all suffer if he gets through. Those were your words."

"I know, I know."

"The damn trouble is," Carl complained, "the one who throws the bomb, the one who shoots, is never who you think it's going to be. The only man who ever fired at Roosevelt was a pathetic bricklayer. And not in New York, where there were crowds. Not in Chicago, where the President was exposed on the streets. In Miami, for God's sake. You ever hear of John Shrank? He shot Teddy Roosevelt because the ghost of McKinley told him to remove any third-termer. In Milwaukee, that was. And McKinley died when Leon Czolgosz, I can't even pronounce it, pumped two bullets into him. In Buffalo. It's never who you think, it's never where you expect. Maybe we've got it all wrong, Ruth. Maybe the map was a plant. Maybe he's on his way to Hyde Park. Roosevelt lives there, too."

"No. He's coming here. You know it and so do I." She let him put his hand on hers. He bent over and kissed her hair. The same musk, the same sexual charge. Everything had changed, and nothing. He kissed her nose, and her mouth rose to meet his. He carried her to the bedroom, doing a passable imitation of Clark Gable as he walked. She giggled a little in spite of herself. But they stopped laughing in bed. She shuddered a little and clung to him. He entered her easily; she gave herself to him with slow, enveloping movements. Nothing seemed to be held back. There was no rush, no feeling of reluctance. For almost an hour the anxious world receded; Ruth had an intelligent, curious mouth. It renewed its acquaintance with his body. She was as warm as he was; there were moments when they seemed liquids flowing into each other. But something was not quite right, he felt; something indefinable. The moans that oscillated between pain and gratification gave nothing away; neither did the fingers that dug softly into his back or the quiet sibilances in his ear.

When they lay quietly, listening to the far sounds of jays and grackles in the woods, Carl said, "Ruth, when there's no war left, come live with me."

She only lay there humming softly.

"Not a chance?" he surmised.

"The lyrics didn't say that. Or the music. Only—"

"Only you'd like to get married."

"Yes. After all this, I would. And have children. I want to have many children."

"How many?"

"I don't know. As many as I can. I believe the only way to answer death is with more life."

Carl nodded and said nothing, and wondered how he could let this woman go and what kind of father he would be. He had always been delighted that his marriage produced no children; it was an easy divorce, as divorces go. His wife had remarried and given birth to two babies and was happily stuck somewhere in a New Jersey suburb. A bourgeois nightmare, to his way of thinking. He could never let himself become one of those lemmings, a commuter: one who spends his life going to and from his wife, a man who shaves and takes a train, and then rides back to shave again. Of course, they could live in the city. Lots of families did. They could—he stopped cold. Why was he allowing himself these fantasies of fatherhood or even of marriage? It was not like him; not at all. I must have deteriorated a great deal this past year, he concluded; age is catching up. He reached for her. Without playfulness or bitterness she pulled back just out of reach and searched for her clothes. He made no further attempt. By the time Ruth came back to the room she was calm and ready to go to town. Carl dressed quietly and began talking about Niccolò again. The afternoon had a valedictory feeling. In all the times we have been together, Carl realized, Ruth has never known how to say goodbye.

26

Niccolò Levi: Arkansas, 1945

NICCOLÒ BOUGHT a little radio in Paris, Arkansas. He was now dressed as an old Belgian gardener: white hair, white mustache, dirty overalls. The woman behind the counter in the big general store suspected nothing. He pointed to the items he needed, pretending to have almost no English. Niccolò knew they would be looking for someone bilingual, someone young, or who would act young. They didn't know how good he really was, how long he had spent watching old people to see how their legs struggled with gravity, how their hands oscillated, as if they were trying to erase something in the air. He checked into the ancient Seneca Hotel, paid the six dollars in advance, and plugged in his Emerson. He heard a bulletin asking the police of five states to be on the lookout for Niccolò Levi. The description was good, and he imagined that his photograph was widely circulated. He slept lightly and kept the window wide open, in case he had to escape quickly.

No one came for him. All the same, every hour of the trip had been an echo of Europe. The police with their boots and peaked hats. The sense of pursuit, the inability to be understood in an alien land. Even when he spoke English, it seemed to come out incorrectly. Arkansas. He had called it R-Kansas, like the other state. How was he to know it was Arkan*saw*? The following morning, the men in the truck laughed at his accent and made fun of his infirmity. But they let him clamber aboard. Niccolò smiled and nodded, like a lost and helpless old grandfather. The other riders had glistening bloodshot eyes and no reason to worry about out-of-state fugitives.

Two of the younger ones announced that they were just out of jail for robbery; the older grizzled men were illiterate and dumb; they said so themselves. They teased Niccolò for his intonations again and began to talk about the niggers and how the niggers had spoiled the country and would spoil it more.

"Take a nigger today, he's marching around like he owns the country. They got a nigger general, you know that?" one of them asked.

"They got a jig congressman, next thing you know they'll have a colored senator, then a colored President."

"Hell, you got that now. He's just painted white is all."

"Shit no, he's a Yid. From Jew York."

The fattest one leaned over and blew whiskey fumes in Niccolò's face. "Where you from?"

"Italy," Niccolò said.

"Dago, huh? Otsa matta fà yew?" He did a vaudeville Italian with all the gestures. Niccolò knew it well; he had heard it on the radio and seen it once in the films, when Jack Oakie parodied Mussolini in *The Great Dictator*: Napaloni from Bacteria. Very funny, then. For a moment the man pressed closer to Niccolò and raised a fist. Then the alcohol won its battle with the body. He backed away. Niccolò did his Italian shrug and pretended to sleep, curled up in a corner of the truck, bouncing loosely with the roughness of the road. When they all piled out, he said goodbye with broad, comic gestures. He wanted them to remember him, if they recalled him through the boozy fog, as an old and pathetic figure. When he was out of their sight he ran with his satchel. He stayed with the road, moving east. After midnight, when all that stirred was an occasional owl, screeching as it lifted a rabbit triumphantly from the patches of weeds, he heard a piercing, melancholy sound and he knew where to move and what his next route would be. The whistle of the Southern Railway was less than a mile away. It was a long freight and it was still passing the grading when Niccolò ran up, out of breath, wet with sweat, remembering the iron-gray skies of Poland and the lethal cars that bore their human freight. He ran alongside an open car. Up the line he could see a man with a lantern, checking for tramps. Niccolò grabbed a door handle and swung aboard. The car stank of urine, but there seemed to be no one in it. The only objects visible in the darkened atmosphere were crates marked FRAGILE GLASS THIS END UP. He flattened out behind one of them and waited. Sooner or later, at some stop or another, a man with a lantern would enter this car. The later he comes, Niccolò thought, the closer I will be to the target. The notion comforted him and he slept peacefully on his bag of disguises.

27

Carl Berlin:
Warm Springs, 1945

THE LITTLE TOWN had a palimpsest look; one epoch overlay another. It made Carl uncomfortable. The whole South made him uneasy. White theaters and Negro theaters, white restaurants and black ones, and the sons and daughters of slaves deferential to the point of mockery, while fat white loafers spat on the street and reviled the North for giving away the country. He heard them cursing Roosevelt under their breaths, although even the worst of them knew that the President had put Warm Springs back on the map. Before the Civil War—the War between the States they called it down here—Bullochville was a famous spa: big hotel, formal gardens, stables, great sweeps of lawn, and even a racetrack. Then came ruination, high weeds, fires, and the obscurity that hung on until some smart money had interested the newly crippled Franklin Delano Roosevelt in the place and proved to him, as he was later to write, that he could improve more in three weeks in the Springs than in the three years before he saw the place.

Today its streets were self-consciously spotless and the

restaurants were full. A model farm was on display, the stables were luxuriously reinstated; there were walking courts, a chapel, a Presidential residence called the Little White House, a wishing well. Pine Mountain Valley looked as if it had been freshly designed for the painters of commercial landscapes, complete with a formal scene entitled "Cascade Falls." Tourists abounded, along with hustlers—the kind who bottled local water with Epsom salts and called it Warm Springs Crystals. Doubtless, FBI and Secret Service men were here, but Carl saw few of them. Soldiers guarded the entrance to the Roosevelt compound, and gawkers looked past their shoulders and chatted about FDR and the war.

The only accents were native American, except for Ruth's.

"He's not here yet," she said. "So far we're lucky."

"Maybe." Carl kept looking around, scrutinizing everyone. "He could be anybody until he opens his mouth. He could be right in back of us and we'd never know it."

"You'd know it. So would I."

"A sixth sense?"

"A seventh. The sixth is for knowing who's hunting *you*." Carl remembered that sense four hours later, just before dinner, when he felt some configuration was wrong. Something in the air, or the streets. He and Ruth had gone different ways, to check the restaurants and the men's and women's rooms. They found nothing out of the ordinary. It had occurred to Carl early in the day that Warm Springs attracted a great many people with similar disabilities. Men and women limped the way he did, or walked with canes, or pushed themselves around in wheelchairs. The town was, after all, a refuge for the maimed, victims of infantile paralysis. Its pace was not merely Southern-slow, it was the tempo of the disabled. It would be like this a mile back of the front lines in Europe, or in the concentration camps. Perhaps Niccolò Levi would enter this scene as a paralytic, shuffling along on braces or being wheeled. No, not wheeled. He would come alone. That much was sure. This was a man without colleagues, without help of any kind.

His intimates were dead. He would trust no one. Look for a man—or a woman—alone. With a thin face. And flat thin ears close to the head: makeup artists can change everything but the ears. Something caught Carl's peripheral vision. He looked to his left and saw a familiar back. An old man with glasses. It disappeared behind a white clapboard bank. But when Carl arrived at the spot, the man was gone. Carl knew immediately whom he had seen. Not Niccolò Levi; that would have been a benison. This was a curse. The old man was Martin Gower. The Germans had arrived.

28

Niccolò Levi: Georgia, 1945

THERE WAS JUST time enough to apply the last of the makeup before the man with the lantern arrived. He held an immense pistol. Niccolò had not expected that.

"Git up." The gun was aimed directly at Niccolò's heart. He rose, blinking, as if he had been asleep. He raised his hands.

"You speak English?" the man said. He was large and sunburned, with a white mustache stained with nicotine. The dark-blue uniform made him look even larger. There was no insignia, but Niccolò guessed he was some sort of railroad policeman assigned to keep hoboes from getting a free ride.

"You speak English?" he said again. "Speakee American?" Niccolò smiled. The disguise was working. The fittings in the cheeks, the stuff that felt and smelled like rubber cement worked into the corners of his eyes, the loose-fitting sleeves and the stiff gray hair served their purpose.

He shook his head, no, he spoke no English, and took his bag in hand. The man seized it from him roughly, felt it and

handed it back. A sack of old clothes held no interest. He
did not bother to search his prisoner. An old Chinese was
not worth shaking down.

The railroad policeman kept his pistol loosely trained on
Niccolò and sat on a box quietly, smoking a dark cigar and
puzzling something out. Niccolò had his own figuring to do.
The freight train had barreled east at high speed for most of
the night. There was no way to reckon how far it had
traveled or where they were. It was dawn, that much the
fugitive could tell from the gray light coming through the
cracks in the freight car. The light was not very different on
the last flight, across country, he reflected, but oh, the cold
and the voices of the soldiers, and I could do nothing,
nothing.

"OK, Chink," the man said. He waved his gun and
Niccolò stood up. The train, already slowing for another
steep grade, pushed on a few hundred yards and groaned to
a halt. The door of the freight car rolled open. Men gathered
outside. "Got one, Hank?" a voice asked. Another said,
"John Chinaman," and laughed. The man in blue pushed
Niccolò out. He jumped from the car with his laundry bag,
careful to land badly, like an old and bewildered figure. He
was pushed on by the group, speaking ominously among
themselves. He had no idea whether he was being taken to
jail or to a lynching. He knew that men had been hanged in
the South recently. It was said that anyone unfamiliar was a
candidate for the noose. Especially those who were not
white. The morning sun was above the level of the stores
and houses in whatever town this was in whatever state.
Niccolò strained for a glimpse of a name on a plate glass
window or a billboard to tell him.

The street was narrow and traversed by a single yellow
dog. The men behind Niccolò seemed more amused than
angry, but one of them pushed him from time to time and
made him stumble. When he did the laughter took a cruel
turn.

"You want to get some kerosene, torch the dawg?" one
of them asked. Another said, "Shee-it, no, that's Jasper's
mutt."

Niccolò wondered whether they would have ignited the

animal had it been a stray. What would they do to a stray man? He would never be able to kill them all, even if he could get the weapon unstrapped from his leg.

"Here it is," the railroad man said. The group stopped before a little store at the end of the town. The morning sun glanced off the window and hurt Niccolò's eyes, but he could read the lettering on the glass: CHENG TEH LAUNDRY. The men banged insistently at the door.

It was minutes before anyone came, and during that time Niccolò weighed the possibilities of breaking away and running through one of the side streets and toward the school signs he had seen earlier. The railroad man would not fire at him if there were children nearby. *If* this was a schoolday. Niccolò was trying to remember what day it was when the door opened a crack, and then wider. An old Chinese, a real one, peered out, disturbed and nervous. He was thinner than Niccolò, a collection of ill-sorted bones. Even here, seven thousand miles from his home, with plenty to eat, he remained concave. Veins stood out on his arms like drainpipes on an old house and he chain-smoked absently as he chattered. "What you want? I open later. Not now."

"*Re*lax, Cheng," one of the men assured him. "This here is not laundry business. This is police business."

He pushed Niccolò forward. "We found him on the train. Maybe he's a Jap, maybe not. We want to find out. Ask him where he comes from. What he was doing on the train."

Cheng Teh listened and made small sounds of assent. He chattered quickly at Niccolò, who made broad hand gestures, indicating that he wanted to speak privately. The men released their captive. He stepped forward and the old Chinese put his mouth at Niccolò's ear. "You are not Chinese?" he whispered. "Who are you? *What* are you?"

It was all up now; Niccolò's pursuers were too close and Cheng Teh had no mercy in his face.

Niccolò made a last, sad attempt. "I am a fugitive," he confided softly. "I come from a long way and everyone is after me. You are my only hope." Then, almost as an afterthought, he murmered, "I can give you money." For reasons he could define, Niccolò was ashamed of himself for saying it. The old man shook his head and turned to the men.

"His name is Taio Shen. Chinese. He comes from San Francisco. He is old and tired and he has no money. He looks for his family. They live in Georgia."

He whispered to Niccolò, "I too was a fugitive when I came. I tell them my story and it becomes yours."

The men were disappointed. They were looking forward to some amusement. Now they were stuck with a dry old victim. One of them wanted to set Niccolò's clothes on fire. Another wanted to take him to jail, but someone reminded them that it was full of drunks from Dobie Cahill's party.

One of the younger men drew a pistol. "Le's have a Chinkee Chinee Circus."

Laughter greeted his suggestion. A shot was fired at Niccolò's feet, close enough to scatter fine dust on his shoes. He knew what his audience wanted; he gave it to them. Loud yells accompanied his jumps. He leaped galvanically every time a pistol went off, and when he ran he acted like an old man straining his limbs and his heart in paroxysms of terror. He hobbled and ran and jumped and fell down and recovered himself and ran again until he heard their whoops far off. Jerkily, he disappeared into a wooded acre behind a row of stores. Then he ran, truly ran until his strength gave out. He could hear trucks on a road nearby, and when he caught his breath he looked out from a stand of poplars. An Army caravan was passing by; jeeps, two-ton trucks, cars painted khaki. Niccolò looked at the sun and at the caravan. They too were heading east. He waited until a halt was called. A driver up ahead needed water for his radiator. Lieutenants got down from their perches and gave their men a five-minute break. GIs hit the ground and stretched out on the grass and smoked cigarettes. Some of them were close enough for Niccolò to touch. Surely this has been ordained, he believed. He knew exactly what to do. With any luck at all, in a day—two at the most—the President would be dead and the world would be given the message composed so long ago by the Professor and Lerma, and Niccolò himself.

29

FDR: Warm Springs, 1945

WHAT WAS IT Huey Long used to call him? Franklin De La No. *No* to so many plans and old promises. *No* to the old friends who could no longer be afforded: Al Smith, Jim Farley, Cordell Hull. *No* to the old vice president, Henry Wallace. *No* to special interest groups now that the election was over. Thank God there would be no more of that. At last he could refuse with impunity. The war would be over soon. He would be out of office in 1949. He would recover his health. Mama had lived to the age of eighty, why not I? Still, the doctors' whispers, the fluttering heart and occasional pains in the thorax. . . . The feeling of dissolution after lunch. Only half a man now, only good in the mornings. The looking glass told of the melted flesh, the sallow face, the dwindling faculties. . . . The swimming pool was gratifying. I felt weightless this morning. Lucy is here: she lifts the shadows.

Eleanor to our own daughter: "Sex, my dear, is something that a woman must learn to endure." And yet Eleanor *knew* things. I would not be here without her, wherever "here" is. History, I suppose. The violent complications of life; Lucy, Eleanor, Franklin De La No. The day becomes opaque so early now. I can no longer feel tomorrow coming. And so much to do.

The portrait artist had arrived: Madame Elizabeth Shoumatoff. A good painter. He had paid her a lot of money to make a watercolor of him in his Navy cape. For Lucy. Worth every cent.

Only one letter needed dictation. He could see the concern on Anita Kelly's face, about his aging, his ailments. But that was why he was in Warm Springs. It had always worked before. It would work now.

To King Ibn Saud: "Your Majesty will recall on previous occasions I communicated to you the attitude of the American government toward Palestine. . . . Your Majesty will also doubtless recall that during our recent conversation I assured you that I would take no action, in my capacity as Chief of the Executive Branch of this government, which might prove hostile to the Arab people."

A reverberation. He remembered his speech to Congress: "On the problem of Arabia, I learned more about that whole problem—the Moslem problem, the Jewish problem—by talking with Ibn Saud for five minutes than I could have learned in the exchange of two- or three-dozen letters."

Of course Sam Rosenman objected, politely as always. To him Ibn Saud was a global anti-Semite. But there were bigger considerations than voting blocs, Roosevelt informed him. Besides, the election was over. There would be no more concessions. No more. Yes, the Jews had suffered, he knew that. Doubtless something would be done. The news of the concentration camps would soon be made public. Everyone would see the top secret photographs of the gas ovens and the ghastly bodies stacked in mounds. Justice would be done about it. It was a matter for the military or the United Nations. Not for him, not for him. Why can none of them understand that the presidency has its limits? He had heard from John Edgar Hoover about Ben Hecht's latest play, to be titled *Call the Next Case*. In it, Roosevelt would be "summoned before the Bar of History to state what he had done to save the Jews of Europe." The jury trying the case would consist of twelve dead Jews from the German crematoria.

Of course, the FBI could be wrong. They often were. Hoover tended to see assassins in crowds, ghosts in books, and malefactors everywhere. He must be mistaken about Hecht. The playwright was too smart to libel the most popular President in this nation's history. The report *had* to be false. Of all the people who welcomed FDR's return to office, who cheered louder than the Jews?

30

Carl Berlin:
Warm Springs, 1945

CARL HAD TO shout. He knew that his voice carried through
the wooden telephone booth, but no one in the hotel lobby
looked up. The desk clerk listened to two stout, voluble
women in short-sleeved dresses. None of them could
possibly have been Niccolò. Otherwise the room was
empty.

For ten minutes a series of voices told Carl to wait for
Captain Rosen. Every one of them asked what the call was
in reference to. Each was told "official business." Carl was
about to slam down the receiver when Rosen got on the line.
The policeman listened without comment. Carl could
imagine him yawning on the other side, or gesturing to a
fellow officer, making a circle around his ear—another nut
caller. Still, Carl had to try. "The Blue Moon murderer," he
said. "I think he might be coming my way."

"What makes you think so?"

"Privileged information."

"Uh-huh. So I tell you what I know, but you don't tell me
what you know, and you make the arrest. Nice."

"If we spot him, you can have him. We just want him stopped. We think the guy who killed the girl might be in with the Butcher."

"Way out in L.A.? I saw the story. A poor wop actor, he's the Butcher? Nuts."

"I didn't say that. He's part of something bigger—listen, I can't explain anything now. All I want to know is if there's still a forty-eight-state watch for Niccolò Levi."

"Yeah, but not a very enthusiastic one." Another voice sounded and faded. "There's already six guys confessed to the murder. Also a woman. Screwballs, probably, but it tends to take some of the zip off our fastball."

"Do you have anything, anything at all on anyone suspicious in the Southern states? Someone who might be Levi?"

"I haven't looked. We only get big stuff unless we ask for it. Levi isn't in a league with bank robbers or spies. He isn't a spy, is he?"

"He might be."

"Ah." Rosen's voice brightened. "Then if we take him, we get headlines."

"If."

"What do you want to know?"

"What I said. Anything about anyone who *could* have been Levi anywhere along the line from California to here. Figure the Southern route. I don't think he'd try the long way around."

"But he could have."

"We'll have to take that chance."

"Call you back."

"No, I'll call you. In one hour."

"Not enough time."

"In one hour."

The captain breathed hard through his nose. "In one hour."

Carl joined Ruth outside and they walked slowly up the narrow, larch-lined clay road, moving as close as they could to the Little White House. Before the three fluted columns two MPs stood at parade rest, guarding the main entrance.

Some very obvious Secret Service men walked around the building in pairs, tugging at white collars, their dark-blue suits even darker under the arms and between their shoulders. It seemed inconceivable that Niccolò Levi could get by them: they stopped every tradesman who brought ice or vegetables.

"A mosquito would need credentials to sting somebody," Carl said. "I think all Levi'll do is make a scene. *If* he gets here."

Ruth disagreed: if he gets here, it's not simply to shout slogans. He hasn't come all this way for that. This is a man who got out of a concentration camp, remember. He got away from the Germans, he can do anything.

The Germans, the Germans . . . Carl had kept them from his mind for a while. They were back and Ruth was with him and their target was twice as big. They could be anywhere, although there were no large buildings here, no place for long-range rifles. Carl put his hand against a hotel drainpipe and immediately pulled it away. The metal was as hot as a stove and the air was heavy with the aroma of pines. The day was turning into a furnace. Ruth wanted to check the streets independently, to wander through the stores once more. But Carl kept her at his side to spot the things he didn't, to keep reminding him of Niccolò Levi's capacities for hiding and changing. Or so he said. In fact, he could no longer allow her out of his sight. Where the Germans were, the Butcher was. He had almost finished her once. Carl would not give him a second chance.

For over an hour they walked slowly, examining alleys, stores, rest rooms, parked cars, and buses. They saw no indications of anything or anyone remotely like Niccolò, no sudden arrivals or departures. They walked back to the hotel and Carl called New York again. This time, Captain Rosen was a little more forthcoming.

"You want it all?" he asked.

"How much is there?"

"About twenty possibilities."

It was worse than having none. The police of Oklahoma, Arkansas, Tennessee, and Georgia had reported misde-

meanors or violent crimes committed by Negroes, farm
women, an Indian with a Doberman pinscher, and a variety
of tramps and vagrants. Nothing Rosen said seemed of
value, but Carl listened closely, hoping for some odd hint,
some fresh scent.

"Any help?" the captain asked at the end of his recital.

"I don't think so. I can't check every Negro, Indian, and
dog that comes in here."

"Why don't you have the Army do it for you?"

"There's not much Army down here."

"There's Fort Benning. Lots of boys down there itching
to be of service. Eight hundred new ones yesterday."

"How do you know that?"

"You asked for all the events on the blotter. There were
two white GIs arrested last night for rape. On their way with
798 others from Alabama to Fort Benning. Both of them
nineteen. Neither one could have been the Butcher. Sorry. I
guess none of this leads anywhere."

"You never know," Carl replied slowly. As he rang off he
was smiling for the first time in weeks.

He stood in the booth staring and wondering about his
obtuseness. He remembered a Chesterton story he had read
as a boy, a tale entitled *The Invisible Man*, about a priest
who found a criminal when no one else could. The
malefactor was an invisible man not because he was
immaterial, but because people never noticed him. He was a
mailman, a civil servant, therefore faceless, featureless,
like any man in uniform, seen too often. Ruth rapped on the
door of the booth. "Find anything?" she wanted to know.

"Everything," he told her.

31

Niccolò Levi:
Warm Springs, 1945

Surely this was what Dante meant:

> *E'n la sua volontàdè nostra pace.*
> In his will is our peace.

A CALM descended on him from the hour he joined the
soldiers. He never imagined it would be this way when he
planned the journey back in Los Angeles, dreaming on the
set, tracing maps on the kitchen table, saving money,
cleaning and oiling his pistol again and again, memorizing
the slogans he would say to the authorities after the
necessary murder. He had not wanted to depart so abruptly,
but the man, the investigator Berlin, had not allowed him
the luxury of time. A blessing, it turned out. If there was no
time to plan, there was also no time to fret, to worry about
possible catastrophes. And so the hazards were left un-
imagined; the ghosts never rose. He was here.

Niccolò had changed clothes in the woods as the soldiers
took their break, lolling and smoking at the roadside. His

uniform was from the wardrobe department, and it fitted better than a real uniform, better than the khaki shirts and trousers of the men lining the road. No one noticed the difference; he had put on the white helmet and the armband of an MP. His rank was sergeant and his carriage was erect and a bit disdainful, a characteristic of the military police he had observed in American cities. He wore dark glasses and stayed twenty yards from the soldiers. The other MPs were far up the line, looking east, down the road. When the shouted order came to get back on the olive-drab vehicles, Niccolò walked to the last open truck. It was hauling a black cannon bolted to the floorboards. He hopped aboard and stood alert, a parody of the sergeants on the carriers ahead. The caravan did not pause again until it reached the outskirts of Fort Benning. There the trucks slowed to a crawl and Niccolò jumped off and walked alongside the cannon for a hundred yards, then turned off and vanished into high shrubbery. He doubled back and walked to the town of Columbus, bought the few items he needed at a drugstore, entered a diner and washed and shaved in the men's room. He ordered a meal in terse monosyllables and when he finished he strolled to the road and held up a hand-lettered sign made with a black crayon. It said WARM SPRINGS, and a pleasant old couple picked him up within five minutes. He pointed to the bandage around his throat: a war wound; *Anzio,* he wrote on his scratchpad. The couple dutifully clucked and talked about the war and how it was nearly over. A matter of months. They wanted to take him into town, but Niccolò's notes insisted that the doctors wanted their patients to walk, to keep their hearts and lungs moving. The couple understood; they had a boy in the service themselves, a clerk typist at Fort Chaffee, Arkansas. Their simplicity was troubling: they, the Chinese who refused to betray a stranger; the producers and actors in Hollywood who were so kind. How could he reconcile them with his mission? These hosts, these generous, naive Americans—would they understand his words after he found Roosevelt with his bullets?

32

FDR: Warm Springs, 1945

A NEW BRITISH rumor: Hitler dying in a bunker. Heinrich Himmler the new Führer. Nazis surrendering to us. We are pounding Boulogne. Okinawa is almost ours. I must hang on.

Prettyman helped him dress. The President tried to read some of the Atlanta *Constitution*, but Prettyman reminded him that the woman was waiting for him. Shoumatoff. The painter.

I need my striped Harvard tie. Lucy wants me in that tie. I don't want to be painted. This grinding hurt. I would like to stay here, reading *The Punch and Judy Murders*. Carter Dickson. A good man. I can never guess who did it. The President turned to page 98, the beginning of a chapter entitled "Six Feet of Earth." This afternoon he would finish the book. If they let him alone for a minute. If he could get away.

Women. Women everywhere. Cousin Polly Delano. Margaret Suckley, another beloved cousin. Lucy. Lucy, thank God. And the damn painter. "Lift the chin," she asked. I can't. If Hitler is not dead we will put him on trial. A tribunal of all countries.

"I'm going to resign from the Presidency," he announced suddenly. He was amused at the shock on their faces, but he did not smile. The effort was too great.

"You are?" Polly searched his face for humor or irony. She found none.

"If I can get the job I'll head the United Nations."

They will save us. No more Hitlers. Have I done enough? No President can do enough. We can restrain Stalin at the United Nations. We can try the criminals. I don't care what Winston says: "A long drawn-out trial is going to provide a sounding board for Nazi propaganda." Who would be convinced by such propaganda? Winston wants to shoot the top men and tell the world they are dead: Goering, Ribbentrop, Goebbels, Himmler, Streicher. . . . But then, how are we different from the Nazis? I will not be remembered as a man who condoned murder. I—Oh Lord, these temples. The woman wants me to turn this way in the light so she can paint me. My skull holds a world of chaos, worse than the one outside.

He signed papers when they were brought in, things no longer in focus. Commodity Credit Corporation. A lie to Stalin: "Thank you for your frank explanation of the Soviet point of view. . . ." State Department prose. Unreadable. But not unsignable.

He smiled at Lucy and idly fingered some documents. He took out his wallet; stamps to give away. To whom? I had the name here somewhere. So much to remember. This thing. So long since I looked at it.

He tossed the little card in a wastebasket. The women looked at it: Franklin Delano Roosevelt's official draft card; he had carried it since 1940.

Mrs. Shoumatoff asked him to move again. She painted the maroon and black tie. He rubbed his forehead and she asked him please, Mr. President, not to do that. To keep erect. He did not listen. He pressed his left temple.

No more of this. Lucy smiling is all I want, and the Southern sun shining as it did before this war. And no enemies. And peace. The pursuit of happiness is the freedom from pain. From office. From life.

He shifted in the chair. When the women looked at him he summed up the entire year:

"I have," Roosevelt said, "a terrific headache."

33

Carl Berlin:
Warm Springs, 1945

WHITE. Chrome-white storefronts. Bleached-white side-walks. White linen suits. WHITES ONLY signs. Little White House. White helmet. White gloves. White piping.

They stood a hundred yards from the Little White House and watched the fifth military policeman walking his rounds. The other four were manifestly assigned to guard the Presidential residence. The soldiers stood as still as they could, and halted tradespeople who came near, and checked the credentials of the occasional official who arrived—Carl recognized FDR's aide William Hassett and the White House communications officer, Dewey Long. Fifty yards from them another MP walked. Dark glasses hid his eyes; the helmet obscured his face. The other guards did not give him much notice; he was away from their beat. He looked as official as they did, but even starchier and more aloof and wary. Too wary.

"You're absolutely certain?" Ruth kept scrutinizing the soldier, looking for any sign of the foreigner, the interloper.

"No, I'm not *ab*solutely certain. But he's the right

height, the right weight. Everybody looks the same in uniform, especially with a helmet and sunglasses. It makes sense."

"Go and talk to him."

"No," Carl said. They were far from the MP, and Carl gave the guards his back. He was watching it all reflected in Ruth's pocket mirror. "He'll recognize me. You go up, ask him something. Where to find a ladies' room, anything. If you hear an Italian accent, drop your pocketbook."

"And then?"

"I'll detain him."

"What does that mean, detain?"

"I won't shoot him unless I have to."

"There are four MPs right there with pistols, Carl. You'll be killed."

"But not the President."

Ruth tried to demur, but Carl walked away from her, behind the corner of a building housing the Bryan Pharmacy. He could no longer see the MP. Ruth walked on, wondering what to say, how to approach her suspect. When she drew to within ten feet the MP stiffened. This was normal, she assumed; guards were constantly on the qui vive.

A few sightseers drew near, all of advanced age. Several walked with difficulty and it took them more than a minute to move away from the area. Another minute and they were gone. Before anyone else came in view, Ruth said, "I beg your pardon."

The soldier looked at her. She could not see his eyes behind the dark spectacles.

"I wondered, is there a chance the President will come out today?"

He shrugged.

"How long are you on duty?" she persisted.

He looked at his watch and held up a finger.

"One more hour?" she asked. He nodded.

Worthless, she thought. Foolish questions, no time to think. Anything I ask can be answered with a gesture. Urgently she called, "Can you tell me the time, please?"

deliberately staying too far away for him to hold up his timepiece.

"One-thirty," was all he said.

And then she knew. Three syllables and it was all there: the intonations, the inability to say "one" without a trailing vowel; the "thirty" spoken with distortion; all of this disguised, hardly more than a hint, but sufficient to damn him. The MP was no military policeman. He was Niccolò Levi.

The pocketbook fell from her fingers and landed softly on the sidewalk. It would all come down now, she thought, but Ruth could not imagine the sudden rush of incident. Carl came toward them, limping with unbelievable speed. Niccolò turned to the moving figure and instantly recognized him. He stiffened and his hand went to the holster of his .45. The other MPs, the legitimate ones, disturbed by any sudden movements, reacted. One put his hand on his own holster.

From in back of the guards a shout sounded. The door of the Little White House swung open and someone called. The words were inaudible but the feminine voice was acutely distressed. A male voice from deep in the house was louder. Two of the four MPs turned and moved toward the house. As they drew closer, they could understand what had occurred. They began to run. The second MP flashed a sign to the others: *Move in, on the double.* The other two quickened their pace. Niccolò was left to face Carl. He turned and shouted, "Don't come closer!" For an instant Carl stopped. "What's going on in there?" he demanded.

"I don't know!" Niccolò's agitated voice was louder than he intended, but there was no one to hear it but Carl and Ruth. In the middle of the day the old people, the infirm, had retired for lunch and naps. Briefly, the trio was alone. "Go away," he said. "Let me do what I must."

He turned away from them and took a step toward the Little White House. Carl lifted his cane.

"Wait!" Carl said. "Please, Niccolò—"

"*Mi dispiace,* Nicco." Ruth tried to reach him in Italian. The words wounded Niccolò. They sounded in the strange air like an echo of Gina. He turned to Ruth and the high arc of Carl's cane landed at the base of Niccolò's neck, just below the helmet. He gave a great twitch and collapsed. Blood streamed from his nose onto the sidewalk.

Ruth ran down the street to their Chevrolet while Carl lifted Niccolò. The soldier's uniform was hot against his arms. Carl tried to make it look as if Niccolò were leaning against him, looking at the ground, but still no one seemed to be watching. The door of the Little White House opened again and there were more shouts. Voices kept sounding from inside the house. Distantly, a siren began. A man in a blue suit ran down the steps, speaking over his shoulder. Ruth brought the car to the curb and swung open the door. Carl pushed the collapsed Niccolò before him and climbed in the back seat. The door slammed shut as the Chevrolet's rear tires screamed. Carl looked through the long oval rear window at the Little White House. Whatever drama was occurring was obscured by thick exhaust and then by buildings.

"How is he?" Ruth drove slowly, within the wartime 35-mile-an-hour speed limit. The car that approached in the opposite direction was doing at least 60. It raised a trail of dust and gray fumes. When it got closer, she could see that it was a Georgia State Police car and she slowed to 30, but the men in it had no interest in traffic. They were headed for town.

"I don't know," Carl answered. "I may have killed him. There's an awful lot of blood."

"Oh, God—I didn't want it like this."

"Nobody ever wants it like this."

She looked at him in the rearview mirror. For a moment she could see winter in the gray eyes. "You always objected when I was cold and professional," she said. The words drowned in the engine noise. "But you were the iciest of us all. The Old Man should have found something better for you to do in the war." She turned on the car radio. It was worse than useless. All that was heard was a grinding sound every time the car hit a bump. Someone had broken off the aerial. She turned the volume down and they drove the rest of the way without speaking.

When the car pulled up to the house she helped Carl carry Niccolò. The body was so limp that they had to put an arm around each shoulder. Niccolò's shoes dug little trenches in the dirt as they dragged him to the steps. Carl held him as Ruth fussed with the key and opened the front door. The house felt cool; a sanctuary from the hell outside. They put Niccolò on the couch, took off his helmet and shoes, and loosened his collar. Carl put his fingers on Niccolò's throat.

"I can't feel a pulse," he said.

"Let me—" Ruth began.

"Why not let me?" the voice asked from the other end of the living room. Crouching over the prostrate soldier, they looked up at the benign and courteous face of Martin Gower. He was unarmed, but all the others with him had guns.

34

Carl Berlin:
Warm Springs, 1945

"PATIENCE IS EVERYTHING," Gower said from the kitchen.
Tiny agreed and smiled. The big bartender had been smiling
for a long time. Neither Carl nor Ruth had fought when the
cuffs were put on their wrists and ankles. Any struggle, Carl
had reasoned, and the guns would be used. Besides, the fact
that the Germans were using shackles meant that they did
not intend to kill. Indeed, Tiny was solicitous when he
attached the metal rings to Ruth; Gower had insisted on
that. He and his assistants went about their work leisurely;
time seemed of no consequence. All of them had an
abstracted air, as if they were looking for something.
Whatever it was did not appear to be tangible. The house
was in order; nothing had been overturned or violently
opened.

Irregularly, police cars whined through the distant roads,
always headed to town. But no one came near the house.
Somewhere in Warm Springs bigger crimes had evidently
occurred. That worried Carl far more than Tiny's Luger.
Tiny amused himself by cleaning his pistol, drinking beer,

and trying to throw cards into a fedora. "I once got all fifty-two," he said pleasantly after he had missed with most of the deck. He bent over, groaning, picked up the cards, and went through the process again. He did it much of the afternoon. In the next room, Gower and the others listened to the radio. From time to time they looked in, watched Tiny at play, and looked at Carl and Ruth seated uncomfortably on the floor with their arms behind them, locked to opposite legs of the heavy couch. Both prisoners knew better than to say anything; Tiny was grinning, but his eyes seemed lit with madness, and any provocation, no matter how slight, might tilt him. Just before five P.M. Gower and the other two men, neither of them as gross as Tiny or as finely detailed as Gower, entered the room.

"So you succeeded after all." Gower's manner was expansive and he was unusually animated. He walked around the room, keeping his eyes on his captives. "The President is dead."

Carl turned away: he's lying; the Germans would lie about anything.

Gower merely smiled. Tiny grinned and exited heavily. He returned with a small wooden Emerson radio. As soon as it was plugged into the wall socket Carl heard the strains of Tchaikovsky's *Andante Cantabile*. Sporadically, an announcer would break in to say: "A press association has just announced that President Roosevelt is dead. There are no further details as yet, but CBS World News will return to the air in just a few minutes with more information."

Carl clung to disbelief for a few minutes longer; it was still possible that this was yet another of Gower's little amusements. The voice came on again . . . "Mrs. Roosevelt notified her four sons . . . Harry S. Truman called to the White House in secrecy . . . emergency Cabinet meeting . . . the widow will fly to Warm Springs . . ." The dial was turned to other stations. They repeated the solemn news: "Admiral Ross McIntyre . . . Interment at Hyde Park . . . The President had gone to Warm Springs for a rest . . . Massive cerebral hemorrhage . . ."

Carl looked at Ruth. Her face was streaked, and he knew

what she was thinking: Niccolò did it. Somehow he got through.

"I was a fool, a simpleton," Gower admitted. "I had no idea what your function was. None of us did. We only knew you were Number Four. Vier. That you were important. How important we could not tell."

Carl kept his silence. He watched Ruth in his peripheral vision and hoped that she would not interrupt. He needed to know what had happened, whether he had added yet another failure to his long list.

"We followed you everywhere. But of course you know that." Gower decided to sit down. "We could have killed you at any time. We nearly did more than once. But then we thought: If we 'knock you off' "—Carl could hear the quotes in the man's careful speech—"they will send another in your place, and we will have to find out who he is, what he looks like, where he lives. Tedious. So we let you live."

"Danke," Carl muttered, audible only to Ruth.

"Then came that unfortunate business about the Butcher. You let me go. Very stupid. Or was it? I was uncertain until you killed Frederick Rathenau. Now, why would you shoot such an insignificant figure, a man of no consequence?"

The question was rhetorical. Carl continued to let Gower have the floor.

"Because you were now ready to have *us* come after *you*. You wanted us rounded up, put away. And why? I asked myself. To stop some sabotage? And then I knew. Because you were ready to make a move so important you could not afford to have anyone preoccupy you. What I did not guess was that your group was going to assassinate the President."

Sirens sounded from miles away. More cars were going to Warm Springs, more policemen to guard the body, now that it needed none.

"I should have known. Wasn't our own Führer endangered by a plot against his life? By his own general soldiers? But Hitler has escaped. Franklin Roosevelt has not. Germany has executed its criminals. America has not. So I will be the instrument of justice."

The planes of the face, the delicate bone structure, seemed to thicken a bit as the daylight faded. The late afternoon took on a gaudy, cheap aspect as Gower reached his hand to Tiny. The large man handed him his pistol. Gower fussed with a silencer, turning it clockwise onto the Luger with ostentatious care.

There were no more seconds to waste. Carl tried to engage Gower in conversation. "How did you find me?"

"Find you? You never left our sight. There was always somebody behind you, or listening to you through walls. Sometimes we paid a servant or the girl at a switchboard. Money is all it takes in America."

"You heard us talk about Warm Springs?"

"Indeed."

"Then you must know we tried to prevent a murder, not to cause one."

Gower raised his hand. "Please, Mr. Berlin. Mr. Baline. You see, I know your real, your Levantine name. We know about cover stories, lies one tells in case one is overheard."

Carl began to reply, then stopped. There was never any point in clarifying things for an enemy.

Gower finished with the pistol and blew on it. "Your associate did his job well. With our help, of course."

Carl's expression betrayed him. Gower looked down.

"Surely you didn't think a poor little Jewish actor could escape the police all by himself. We were behind him when he left Hollywood, aided him in choosing his disguises, gave him lifts on the road, distracted officers who came too close. He never knew; he was a perfect *Ziege*—an ideal goat. The same large, believing eyes. And he ended as a goat should: slaughtered."

Ruth began to cry.

Carl wished she could contain her tears; he hated to give Gower any satisfaction. "At least Niccolò never made his speech," Carl said to her. And then, half to himself: "It was a trade, that's all. His silence for ours."

"A bloody silence," Gower agreed. "We will have a lot of cleaning up to do. He is a mess of red. You people fight amongst each other like dogs. Americans always have.

Still, you do our work for us. We should be grateful. The Reich will hear of the President's death. It will make a difference."

He turned to Tiny. "I want you and the others to go outside now."

"You going to be all right?" Tiny hovered solicitously.

"Perfectly. You are to join Madame. She will tell you where to stand guard. The police will be driving by constantly. Do nothing to arouse them."

The three men assented and left the room. A screen door banged shut. The radio was barely audible. All this time it had been broadcasting under Gower's voice and under the heavy breathing and the movements of the others. Now the voice was clear enough; it was talking about the shock of the nation. Words from dignitaries were beginning to come in. The title "President Truman" sounded peculiar. There was a click. Carl looked up as Ruth gave an involuntary shout of distress. It was less a cry or a word than something emitted directly from the viscera. Gower leveled the gun. Carl instinctively tried to twist away, aware that there was no place to run, nowhere to hide. The shot was barely audible. It entered his chest several inches to the right of the heart. Bones were broken and the pain opened inward, violently. Carl retched and lost consciousness for a moment. When he opened his eyes he saw through a red filter. He squinted, pretending to be dead, but Gower no longer had any interest in him. The old German was on his knees, bent over Ruth. He had turned the music on very loud: Mozart's Requiem Mass, played in honor of the fallen leader.

Carl battled against the pain and fought to stay conscious. But his strength coursed out with the blood he saw flooding over his shirt and jacket. Gower pulled at the collar of Ruth's tan blouse. The buttons popped and the cloth ripped. The sound was louder than the Mozart. Ruth was crying, but not at what was happening to her. She was looking with a kind of furious grief at Carl. Whatever she said or cried was indistinct. Gower cut her brassiere with a kitchen knife and without hesitation took a match and set fire to the brown fragments of cloth. Ruth screamed and extinguished the flames by blowing on them. Gower grunted and cursed in German and lit another match. This time he pulled her skirt up to her thighs and lit the hem. Ruth shouted something again and this time Carl, teetering to insensibility and then back to awareness, knew what she was repeating: *"Schlächter, Schlächter,"* Butcher, Butcher. Martin Gower, the vestryman, dealer in antiques, lover of Mozart, was also the sadist, the killer of women. He was the divided soul of Germany, the refined monstrosity, the hideous exemplar of what Hitler was all about: Deutschland in love with death, murderer of any culture outside its own. The bloodstained, inhuman Germany, still killing civilians, still committing its obscene acts while Wagner was performed in its opera houses. Did they really think Roosevelt's death would change a thing, rescue them from certain annihilation? Half-naked, Ruth screamed again from behind the flames rising upward from her skirt. She bounced and twisted as Gower leaned over her with a glinting fragmented smile. No wonder he had exiled the others to the outside. Carl could not stand the agony any longer. He shouted "Butcher!" through bloody teeth. The sound gurgled in his throat.

Gower turned to the unearthly noise and heard another, louder one. He opened his unbelieving eyes wide and put his hands on his stomach. He fumbled with his gun and fired once. He wailed again and another bullet struck him in the mouth, and then there was no mouth. Niccolò stood in the doorway like an apparition, holding the MP's .45, the one the Germans had failed to confiscate. He fired twice more at the place where Gower had stood and began to sink to his knees. Carl stared until the tableau of vengeance faded from his vision.

At the sound of Niccolò's shot, firing began outside. Niccolò, barely conscious, prepared himself for one more shot. No one entered the room. He beat the flames out on Ruth's clothing, slapping at them with his hands. The effort was too much. He collapsed over her and the MP's big .45 clattered to the bare floor out of her reach.

Ruth Silver waited for the Germans to return. They would kill her now, but they would probably shoot her outright. There would not be any torture; the Butcher was dead. No one came. She writhed miserably. Maybe the guards had taken to fighting among themselves. Perhaps they had gone away, frightened by what had happened. The radio chattered about Roosevelt.

"At least I won't have to call the son of a bitch Commander in Chief any more." The Old Man stomped in, speaking rapidly to a larger man with a hunter's cap. The hunter carried a rifle with a telescopic sight. Ruth could make out other sounds outside, and she heard jeeps move across the lawn. The Old Man took in the room at a glance. He said over his shoulder, "Release Miss Silver and see to the others. And for God's sake, put your raincoat around her." Nakedness, even wounded half-nudity, embarrassed him. Death did not.

He walked to Niccolò, bent over, shook his head, rose, walked to Carl, and made a similar gesture. There was no need to bother with Gower. "If you had informed me of your whereabouts, much of this could have been avoided," he said to Ruth as she was released and covered.

Some official-looking men came in, but the Old Man dismissed them. "Stay out there until the wagon arrives."

"You knew my whereabouts." Ruth looked at him with hot eyes. "You knew it all. You had us followed from the beginning, didn't you?"

"Calm down," the Old Man said. "Just calm down."

"You had this place staked out, didn't you? You could have shot Gower at any time."

"Not at any time. We had no idea what he was going to do, or why he was here. We watched you and Berlin arrive. We waited longer, hoping for more arrivals. We heard a shot. Then we knew we could wait no longer. We opened fire on all of them. None escaped."

"There was a shot before the one you heard." Ruth motioned at Gower's body. "He had a silencer."

"Ah. I never dreamed of that."

Ruth began to weep. "You should have dreamed." She tried to go to Niccolò or to Carl, but he restrained her.

"You came to Warm Springs because they were coming here, is that it?"

"You're in Intelligence. You tell *me*."

"I'll overlook that. You've been through a great deal this evening. But any more such outbursts would be extremely ill advised. You are still in service. The war is still on."

"The war is over."

"For you, perhaps."

"For me, perhaps. For them, definitely."

"We know who the false MP was now," the Old Man informed her. "We could cover up much of this if you tell us why he was here, what he meant to you and Berlin."

"He was part of the International Jewish Conspiracy," Ruth told him between her teeth.

"We can also expose what we know," he warned.

"So can I. I can tell the world how much regard you have for human life. I can tell the world how close you are to the butchers, you who use people like laboratory animals and stand by while they kill children overseas."

"Come." He offered a hand. "We'll all feel differently in the morning."

"No." A car honked insistently from the winding road. "No," she cried again, and looked down at the bodies. "Not all."

HAIFA, 1981

THE HOT MORNING edged through cracks around the thick white shade. The boy slept on; he was used to the brilliant mornings. His grandfather, even after all these years, was not. The white-haired man had dreamed something terrible, sleeping in the chair. What was it? Vestiges of memory scattered in the light.

"The two of you looked so peaceful, I hated to wake you last night," his wife whispered at the door.

He rested his chin on the head of his Malacca cane and regarded her. His gray eyes watered a little. She had not been treated kindly by circumstance, but time had been indulgent. If her hair was no longer ash, neither was it quite gray, and she had not gained an ounce in all these years. "Everything is a little lower nowadays," she liked to say when he complimented her. But she still worked in the orange groves alongside the young Sabras; she was still proud of her long, narrow waist, and her legs.

He recalled fragments of the dream as he rose and washed and dressed for work. Persistent images; he was never quite rid of them. They returned last night because the boy had asked him about the past, and that brought back the bad years, the failed journey that was not quite a failure. The

President had died a natural death. There had been scandal, no pogrom. At the time those were not small achievements.

A car honked: the Americans had sent a chauffeur. "Let him wait," Ruth said. "Finish your breakfast."

Her husband drank his coffee and remembered more than he wanted. Such a long time past, such a different world in the days when he lay recuperating in Bethesda Hospital. The Old Man had pieced the story together. But he could do nothing. The new President, the Bomb, the end of the war, stayed his hand. In the end he agreed to let them both leave the country, on condition that they never return. An Army plane took them to her sisters' home in Jaffa. He and Ruth mourned for six months. It had taken a year before he felt human again. The sun at last did its work, and the tide and salt of the Mediterranean. Later, after the recovery, there had been work, once he learned Hebrew. That, too, had been therapeutic. Physical labor on the kibbutz. Jobs in his old specialty. He had earned a small reputation for that. Teaching at the little school, a strange experience for him, reading stories to the young. And then there were his own to read to. Ben, Ruth's favorite, killed in the Yom Kippur War. Esdras, a professor of engineering, teaching in Washington, D.C., an irony that still troubled his parents' sleep. And Sarah, the perpetual student, the specialist in ancient history. Fine: the more ancient, the better. Mother of the little sleeper, now surrounded by his toy weapons. Let him have his toys. Thank God there were real weapons only a few miles away. Hitler was dead; Eichmann had been executed right here; but there was never a shortage of those who wanted to kill Jewish children.

It would not do to think about that now, he decided. He finished dressing, kissed Ruth, and took another look at his only grandchild. The boy turned, murmured incoherently and continued his little snores. Last night he had wanted to watch his grandfather work. "I'll get up early," he promised. And here he was, at seven A.M., a bundle of pajamas. Let him sleep. There would be other times.

The grandfather kissed his wife again, entered the blue Citroen, and smiled at the chauffeur. He received a scowl in return. The driver had the glowering, combustible manner of a Manhattan cabbie. All this week the grandfather had dreaded these trips, dreaded working again with American teams of specialists. The pain of living through his old life was insupportable. He was afraid of memory, afraid of times to come.

Yet the Americans were respectful; they admired his work. They even liked his looks—God knows why. He took out a pocket mirror and scrutinized his face. A lot of changes resided there; a lot of history. He wrinkled his nose and blinked. The rest of the dream came to him then and he could not blink away the tide of grief. But when it receded, he was no longer afraid, not even of fear itself. Carefully he removed the little round pieces of plastic the director had wanted him to wear. The hell with contact lenses—he would be as God made him. It was no longer possible to appear as someone else, even in his dreams. The old business of running away was finished.

The dark, shiny eyes looked at a barbed wire construction fifty yards ahead. It was astonishing how much like Himmeldorf they had made it.

"Stop here," he ordered. "We want to get out."

He clicked the door behind him and limped toward the movie set.

"We?" the driver droned. "Who's we?"

"The dead," said Niccolò Levi. He straightened his back and walked the rest of the way.

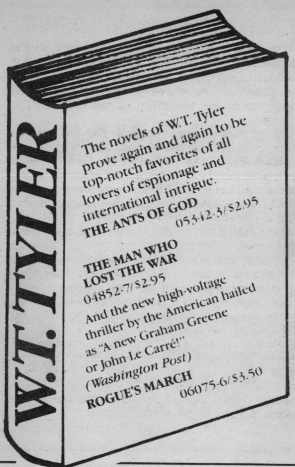